Forgotten Sin

Brian Hershey

Reader2writer Press
www.reader2writer.com

To request permissions, contact the publisher at hersheybm@reader2writer.com

Paperback: 9780578308180
Ebook: 9780578308197

Library of Congress Number: 2021948687

First paperback edition August of 2014.
Second paperback edition November of 2021.

Edited by Bart Bishop & Kayla Hardin
Cover art by Brendon Miller

Printed by Reader2writer Press in the USA.

Reader2writer Press
Cincinnati, Ohio

www.reader2writer.com

I would like to dedicate this book to my family.
-Brian Hershey

Preface

Horrific stories that begin behind the veil of shadow should be left in shadow. Many were born of darkness long ago and have continued to live, forgotten and hidden, amongst the sinister deeds of humanity. However, it is important to remember that the greatest trick the devil performed on the world was convincing humanity that he doesn't exist…

PART I

Chapter #1

Dr. Mya Bishop
Wednesday, October 28, 2009
4:15 p.m.

A monstrous wolf-like creature clamped down its fierce jaws into the midsection of a Roma woman thus ending my slide show with this horrific 18th-century engraving. The designation scrolled at the bottom read:

Presented By
Dr. Mya Bishop
Cambridge University

Every eye, except mine, in the dim lecture hall remained fixated on the morbid image. It was tough for me to view since it represented such a likeness to one of my memories. Most of the students were still writing the last of the information that I had given them while I fingered an envelope marked *Urgent* that lay atop of my notes. It was delivered to me earlier that day; though desperate to know its contents, I slipped the envelope into my open briefcase. *Now is not the time to open it,* I thought.

Before stepping from behind the podium, I adjusted my skirt and brushed the hair from my forehead. A sea of faces stretched out before me. In the time remaining of the lecture, I wanted to further explain my points about werewolves and answer any questions the students had pertaining to the slide show.

That was when I noticed him. An older gentleman wearing a grey, tweed sport coat sat on the aisle's edge about three-quarters back in the lecture hall. He had silvering hair and sat poised with his hands resting in his lap. I did not let his presence hinder my train of thought.

"We have come to believe that individuals cursed with lycanthropy, or who are considered werewolves, take on certain characteristics of wolves as humans. We think they should stand out in some fashion or another…overly hairy body parts, shape of one's teeth or something more pronounced about their overall structure. However, many of these instances can be explained away through diseases such as Porphyria and Hypertrichosis in which the afflicted develops excessive amounts of body hair on their face and torso. Unfortunately, the images seen in the slide show depict stories of many persons that were afflicted with these diseases before they were understood. These people were ridiculed and shunned from society based upon their outward appearances. Since they were not given the opportunity to be properly educated and groomed with etiquette, they were more likely to act out with more instinctual and uncivilized mannerisms."

Much of the student body in the auditorium seemed restless, but I continued lecturing. "Most of the stories pertaining to werewolves also involve a person being human first before encountering the beast. A person would then change from their normal human state to that of a wolf-like monster. Some have gone so far as to say that human genetics are more dominant and that is why the cursed individual can walk upright like a human instead of being a quadruped like a true wolf." Several hands shot into the air with the hope of offering some expertise on the matter, but I merely waved them down as I continued with my point. "Unfortunately, since the mythology behind these creatures predates Greek and Roman Mythology, mankind has come up with some creative ways of explaining away the myth, or on the other hand to even validate their own theories pertaining to the matter. Much of the truth behind these stories has been lost in interpretation. The first – "

"Excuse me, Professor Bishop," a shaggy haired young man sitting towards the middle of the auditorium interrupted.

"You're not suggesting that some people still believe in this nonsense?"

"Actually, I was going to acknowledge the fact that several sound scientific explanations have been presented and offer good rationale as to why people believed in werewolves. If I may, sir, continue?" I paused for a moment to let the weight of his interruption set in. "It is difficult to understand what lives in the far reaches of the world and walks in the shadows of nightfall, but modern science has provided us with the knowledge of diseases that were not widely understood or studied until the end of the Middle Ages. Mental illness of all kinds and the diagnosis of such disabilities is a relatively recent phenomenon. Lycanthropy, for example, can be closely compared to that of cannibalism." Several gasps, and snickers, could be heard throughout the crowd at the mention of the taboo, as if to suggest that the two shouldn't be compared. "Both lycanthropy and cannibalism share a common thread of insanity pertaining to the bloodthirsty killing that ensues. A person thought to be plagued with lycanthropy would exhibit behaviors that are similar to that of an animal, specifically a wolf, which by nature is programmed to hunt and kill. Cannibalism is the result of much the same behavior, hunting and killing."

Chatter spread across the lecture hall and several hands were again raised into the air. The man in the tweed sport coat did not move; he merely sat there with his arms crossed, smirking at the excitement. Trying not to be distracted too much by him, I pointed to another student sitting closer to the front of the auditorium. A girl with blond hair, pulled away from of her face into a ponytail, adjusted her glasses and cleared her throat before asking, "In addition to illnesses such as Porphyria and Hypertrichosis are there any other genetic diseases that can help to account for the strange behavior people exhibited when believed to be a…werewolf?"

"Absolutely," I responded quickly. "Schizophrenia was one of the most misdiagnosed diseases of the Middle Ages and the few who actually had such a condition were also not looked upon too highly from the rest of society. In fact, many were accused of having dealings with witches or shaman and were further persecuted."

"Isn't it true, that lycanthropy was born of the devil?" a student shouted from the back row of the hall.

Several heads turned, including the man in the tweed sport coat, to identify the person that threw out such a bold question. "Some Christian scholars see it that way," I said calmly. "Others say that the werewolf wasn't derived by the devil but is in fact the devil himself. Again, much of this belief stems from paranoia during the Middle Ages. Witches were thought to possess the power to transform into a wolf and roam the countryside. In American lore, the *Navajo* people believed in the Yenaldooshi, a term meaning Skinwalker, where an individual will assume the form of any animal by wearing its hide. Though this was viewed as evil, their lore gives *no* mention of a devil-like entity. The term Lycanthropy has its origin in Greek mythology as it pertains to King Lycaon being transformed into a wolf after angering Zeus, not Hades. However, the church has gone to great lengths to combat such heresies and put a stop to Pagan practices. Since witchcraft was so widely believed to be the spawn of the devil, lycanthropy was coined as the same. Especially since there are interpretations of the exorcisms performed by Jesus Christ in the New Testament being done on two individuals badly afflicted with lycanthropy. But, you would've already known that if you had read my book, which was the assigned reading for this class. I believe its chapter eight that offers my comparative analysis."

Chuckles spread throughout the auditorium. Another student, younger than his peers, cautiously raised his hand as though he wasn't sure how to ask his question, "So…with so many cultural versions, what does the old myth of the full moon have to do with werewolves? I mean…why does that cause them to change?

I paused before I answered. The older gentleman shifted in his seat, as though he too was anticipating my response. "That's a very good question, one that no one has been able to fully understand, let alone answer. The best response I can offer you now is that the wolf is an opportunistic hunter, and the full moon offers a better hunting scenario than if there were no moonlight at all. Wolves howl to locate one another. When the moon is full and they are more active, they howl more to stay in a pack. Both the hunting and howling became more of an association with the change than anything else."

The look on the student's face seemed disappointed as though he wanted more, but my answer would have to do. Time was short and I was *not* prepared to delve into my theory behind the full moon. There was no way to fully prove it, despite my numerous attempts to uncover the right information. Fortunately, another student distracted the situation before any further questions were asked about the full moon.

"Professor why is it said that silver is the preferred means of killing werewolves?" the student asked.

Though I had anticipated that this question would come up during the lecture, time constraints prevented me from answering it. Instead, I gave a half-hearted answer to end the lecture, "Much of the use of silver comes from religious beliefs, again. Silver was a pure and holy metal. Quite often crucifixes designed for exorcisms were made of silver, so naturally the metal transferred over to fend off werewolves. Some also say that it is related to the thirty pieces of silver that Judas received to betray Jesus. Unfortunately, the full answer to that question will have to wait until next time. I am afraid our time here has expired."

Most of the students in the class seemed displeased the lecture was over. A spatter of several conversations could be heard amongst them as they left the lecture hall. All were discussing possible reasons silver was used to kill werewolves. I took a moment at the podium to collect my belongings. A few students stayed behind to ask further questions. The older gentleman in the tweed sport coat made his way through several passing individuals to where I stood at the front stage.

"Well, I must say Dr. Mya Bishop, your lectures on lycanthropy are always nothing less than fascinating!" the man said as he greeted me.

"Dean William Garris, to what do I owe the pleasure? After all, you have seen these lectures several years in a row. I would think someone of your literary genius would have better things to do with his time," I responded before giving him a warm, inviting hug.

"Though a literary giant I may be, werewolves help to foster my inner child for a moment. I'm always thrilled to see how the brightest students in England interpret your thoughts on the matter." He paused for a moment, glancing at the gold charm around my neck before continuing, "Forgive me for saying this, but I'm still amazed at how much you look like your mother, Cassandra. I know it has been eleven years since her passing, but each time I see you I am reminded of her youthful appearance and her drive for literary excellence. I'm happy to see the same traits in you."

I made sure the charm was secure behind my blouse before I responded, "It is nice to see you too. Nevertheless, you still came down here for a reason, or are you just hell-bent on making me nervous while I lecture?"

"Ah Mya, you're always keen to observe the facts. Any reason to come here and engage in discourse with one of my favorite colleagues is a good enough reason. However, I merely wanted to know if you would be willing to interact with the youth of Cambridge in the 'Common Talk' we're conducting on Saturday? Most of the students are astounded by your work. Besides, whenever you speak, it seems to bring about good publicity for the university and your books."

Aware that William was trying to augment the event by getting me to discuss something more Halloween appropriate, a smirk spread across my face. I closed my briefcase, adjusted my suit coat before taking his arm with mine and walking out of the now-empty auditorium. The students that were waiting had left, but I paid them no mind. I continued to listen as William showered me with compliments; they were nice to hear.

"You already know that the talk will be held here, in this same lecture hall. Your knowledge is vast, so you won't have to do much to prepare. In fact, you could give the same lecture you just gave and maybe expand upon some points you didn't have time for today. Mildred and I would also love to have you over for dinner afterward. She's so fond of you, Mya, and given that Saturday is Halloween, I selfishly would love to hear more of your ghastly tales about werewolves and other things that go bump in the night!" William's eyes were wild with anticipation.

"William, thank you for being so thoughtful. I also adore Mildred. Your wife is the salt of the earth, but as I already told you earlier in the month, I have a prior engagement to which I must attend." William and Mildred always offered a pleasant evening of interesting conversation, but I could not afford to miss my appointment.

"Hopefully, it has nothing to do with work. You put enough into your work while you're here. Your student evaluations speak only praises for how you handle your duties, but you're still young, no older than thirty, right?"

"Now William, a lady never reveals her *true* age."

"Well, young people need to be involved with activities and other people. Furthermore, you need to get away from that stuffy old estate of yours," he declared, his tone taking on a fatherly approach.

"I greatly appreciate your concern, but I think I can manage my own personal life," I said as we stopped walking in front of the offices for Arts and Humanities. The wind had kicked up, sending a chilling sensation through my body. Sounds of the day were fading into the distance, and darkness was beginning to overtake the sky. An African man dressed in dark clothing and a Barbour coat stood on the corner across the street. His stature was strong, and he was watching both William and me.

"Forgive me, I over-stepped my bounds," my attention snapped back to William. He apparently noticed that I dodged his comments. "It's just that we loved and admired your mother so much…and it's a shame that we didn't get to be a part of your life until you came here. Not having a local family can make it difficult to have a normal life…I'm just very worried for you."

When I looked back towards the man across the street he was gone. I hugged William one last time, "You both are wonderful people and I think I should take a rain check on dinner and shoot for an appropriate time at the beginning of next month. For now, I must check on one thing in my office before I head home. Tell Mildred I said hello."

He seemed satisfied with my response and graciously nodded before turning to continue his walk along Mill Lane towards Trumpington Street. William always seemed nervous around me; it was difficult to pinpoint the reason, but I could see the worry in his face, more so than that of the caring friend. Tears welled up in my eyes as I recalled one of the last things he said to me; *A normal life…*

As the door shut behind me, a deafening silence fell over the open area of the building. *There's nothing normal about my life.* Portraits of past prominent individuals hung on both sides of the hallway, mostly former deans of the college or special contributors to the university. These pictures fit nicely with the musty smell of old books and parchments that could be found littered throughout most of the offices.

I stopped in front of William's portrait. His painted portrait looked kind and gentle. It contrasted with my saddened reflection in the glass that protected the painting. My brown hair looked black in the dimness of the hall and the auburn highlights were barely visible. If he only knew the truth, I thought as I closed my eyes momentarily before continuing further down the hall.

The sound of my heels tapping on the marble flooring echoed into the high ceilings and created an eerie atmosphere as I passed each of the now dark rooms that preceded my office. Once inside, I closed the door and turned on the banker's lamp that leaned over my workspace. Lying flat on my desk next to several hardcover books on medieval mythology was a newspaper that I had kept from a few weeks prior that had the headline:

"EXOTIC ANIMAL SPECIALIST MAKES NEW DISCOVERY IN AUSTRALIA!"

This stood out amongst several other headlines that involved the results of the football match-up between England and Germany. Robert Osborne, a prominent Member of Parliament, had clearly spent a tremendous amount of money on jargon to promote his new political campaign. Neither of which I cared about.

Before sitting down, I unhooked the charm around my neck and held it under the light over my desk. Gently, I rubbed my finger across the image of the Archangel Michael before letting it rest on the surface. *Who was that person on the street corner?* I took off my suit coat and draped it over the back of the chair and lifted my blouse from my skirt. Snapping open my briefcase, I removed the letter marked "Urgent". The yellow parchment-like envelope had been postmarked from Sydney, Australia. The idea of what this letter said had consumed my thoughts since I had received it that morning. I tore it open. It read:

> October 25, 2009
> Dear Dr. Mya Bishop,
>
> After receiving your inquiry pertaining to £25,000, it is with great enthusiasm that I shall accept your offer. My flight shall be arriving in London at approximately 4:30 p.m. on Saturday, October 31, 2009. I appreciate that you have taken care of my flight expenses and have already made arrangements for me to be transported to your estate.
>
> Sincerely,
>
> Marcus Holland
> Animal Specialist/Researcher

Chapter #2

Mya
Friday, October 30, 2009
11:05 a.m.

Incense still lingered in the air at St. Teresa's Cathedral from the 10:00 a.m. Mass as I entered. To the right side of the church was a bulky display that had several prayer candles that recessed upwards, flickering light against the dark wood walls. I dropped two pounds into the donation box before whispering a quick prayer and lighting a candle of my own. By the amount of wax that was gone from each candle, many had been burning for a long time. I wondered how many held a prayer that involved passing a final examination at the end of the semester. As I walked down the center aisle towards the front of the church, I noticed that the only people still there were those seeking confession or perhaps simply needing a momentary place to pray.

I bent one knee in genuflection and made the sign of the cross as I entered the second row to the right. The sun shined brilliantly through the stained-glass windows -- reflecting off the white marble columns and archways -- yet withholding its warmth from the mahogany pews as they still felt cold. Patiently, I waited as the last person went into the confessional only to reemerge moments later making the sign of the cross over their head and torso. Father Preston Mathew, a short, bald man filled to the brim with energy, appeared from within the confessional shortly thereafter. Standing, I meandered over towards Father Mathew who still had his head bowed in prayer as he walked.

"Father, may I speak with you for a moment?"

"Dr. Bishop, I should've guessed that you would be here today," he responded.

"Does that mean you're not pleased to see me?"

"No, that's not it at all. It's just that you come to celebrate the sacrament of reconciliation every month or so, and I'm afraid to say you've become quite predictable." He smiled and held his arms stretched open in a welcoming manner. "Please, let us talk. It has been in my prayers that God has been able to be generous in your life over the past month and that some of the ailments we discussed last time have been alleviated."

Sitting face-to-face, divided by a mesh screen so Father Mathew's face was obscured, it only took a moment once I entered the confessional before I jumped into my declaration of guilt with tear-filled eyes, "Father, forgive me for I have sinned, sinned so much that I don't know how to confess such things anymore. It's been a full month since my last confession, and I feel God hasn't answered my prayers. I feel myself growing more and more resentful towards Him because He hasn't helped me. I still feel responsible for my family's death, and I'm filled with anger."

"Mya, we've talked about this several times. I've come to know your situation well and I see that your heart is good. Let me assure you that God also sees it. Remember, God judges us by what we give to Him and all He asks for is your brokenness. This I'm sure you have already given to Him. You just have to forgive yourself and realize that what you have no control over God does not rebuke."

"It still doesn't change the fact that they are dead. All of them! It's my fault!" I snapped.

"Mya, the accident your family suffered wasn't your fault. Only God knows why their time expired when it did. Let's think about this rationally for a minute, shall we? You've been coming to me every month for a year, for confession and every month you confess the same thing about feeling guilty regarding your family's death. From what you've told me, your family members died eleven years ago and that would make you a youth when it happened. How could a young girl be responsible for the death of her entire family, especially since you mentioned that they died in an automobile accident?"

"Father, you don't understand…"

"Mya, what's really troubling you? I know that there's more to these feelings than what you're leading on. I want to help you, but I can't if I don't know what ails you."

"I need forgiveness father, that's all. Forgiveness for the horrific acts I've committed and for the uncontrollable feelings I have."

Father Mathew sighed gently, finished the sacrament, instructed me on some prayers for penitence, and ended with the sign of the cross. Before I could walk out of the confessional, Father Mathew put his hand to the mesh screen and said, "No matter what you believe, God and the church are always with you."

"Thank you, father," I said, tears blurring my vision. I stood quickly and walked out of the confessional towards the exit, pausing momentarily to dip my finger into the basin filled with holy water positioned by the ornate wooden doors. Making the sign of the cross one last time, I glanced around the church. The rich whiteness of the marble took on an iridescent look, while the massive pipe organ tucked into a nook shone down in all its ethereal brilliance. A single cross stood erect on the front of the center altar, gleaming as the sunlight radiated off the polished metallic edges.

Alas, I turned and walked from the church before any more emotions spilled out. Across the street, I rested my arms on the cold, wrought iron railing that ran along the wall parallel to Hills Road just southeast of the university. Each time I went to confession the pain inside of me grew stronger. Guilt for the deeds I had done in the past and the memories that accompanied them haunted me daily.

The ringing church bells momentarily disrupted my thoughts with its half-hour chimes and reminded me of my meeting with the animal specialist from Australia on Saturday.

I had cancelled my lectures for the afternoon, informing my department that I had taken ill. Fortunately, the teaching associates that I worked with on a regular basis knew my curriculum quite well and were willing to fill-in for me. Dean Garris would no doubt proffer a phone call to my estate, knowing full well that I was supposed to have other plans and would probably conclude the two happenstances are related. He was going to worry about my wellbeing even more and I felt dreadful about misleading him in such a way. William had always been kind to me and deserved a better explanation, but this was necessary. I had to make arrangements for the weekend and time was escaping. It was the only opportunity I had to find the answers to the questions that held the key to my future. *I'm desperate to be free from this torment.* With that thought, I turned and walked up the street towards the South Park and Ride at the Cambridge station to get my car.

Chapter #3

Father Preston Mathew's Log

Friday, October 30, 2009

Today, my thoughts have been filled by a young lady that appears to be troubled beyond any spiritual guidance that I can give her. Faithfully, or perhaps, ritually, she appears for confession every twenty-eight days. Many of my associates have told me this is simply a coincidence that she must be on a strict schedule to allow for the other responsibilities in her life. I guess I should accept this notion as true; after all she is a professor at the University of Cambridge. But the peculiar thing about this person is that she confesses the same thing each month. She is convinced that she is responsible for her family's death, specifically claiming the fault to be her own. Truly, this does not make rational sense. She has informed me that her family died in a car accident eleven years ago, which I would presume would make her a young teenager. I wonder why she was not in the car with them? Perhaps they were traveling to her when the accident occurred? This may be the source of some of her guilt.

Against my better judgment, and may God forgive me for invading the privacy of another without their permission, but I've started looking into this matter more. I wanted to know what kind of schedule she is on so that I can better service her needs. As it turns out she is a very busy lady with the university researching medieval mythology and folktales, but she is also a very well-known author on the subject and travels a great deal for book signings. However, this does not explain the exact regularity of her visits. She would still have the time to come for confession at any time, rather than every twenty-eight days. When researching the accident she mentioned, I unfortunately was unable to find anything more than a brief newspaper report pertaining to the incident along with a funeral announcement. It stated that her mother Cassandra Bishop was killed, but there was no mention of other family members. I feel that she may be harboring more details of the event and she is reluctant to tell the truth.

My other conclusion is that this poor soul is being afflicted by some mental disorder that has caused her to think that she is responsible for her family's death. Perhaps schizophrenia or some other mental disability prompts her to act in a manner that ultimately reinforces her thinking. This situation has me greatly concerned. I worry for her. I sense uneasiness within her and feel that evil forces may be at work within this servant of God. Nonetheless, I have resolved to be patient and have concluded that upon her next visit, I shall ask her if she needs to speak with a medical specialist to whom I have many references. May God help His servant before it is too late.

- Rev. Preston Mathew S.J.

Chapter #4

Animal Specialist
Marcus Holland
Saturday, October 31, 2009

The plane touched down at London Heathrow Airport with a screech and an abrupt rush of pressure as it slowed along the runway. I gripped the armrest of my seat and grunted. Usually, flying had no effect on me and I find myself to be quite comfortable, but this flight was different. It could have been that the plane was running a bit behind and after having a thirteen-hour flight my nerves were shot. Perhaps it was the fact that I was here on business that was sketchy at best. I was not sure why I was going through with this, but something peculiar, haunting even, struck me about a telegram I had received a couple of weeks earlier. Reaching into my jacket pocket, I pulled out the telegram and reread it to familiarize myself with my instructions. The letter read:

October 16, 2009

Dear Mr. Marcus Holland,

Since you have become a reputable figure in your field of research as evidenced in your recent recognition, I would like to employ your services for a few days here in England. My name is Dr. Mya Bishop, and I would like you to observe an animal which very few people in the world have seen. As a means of compensation for your travels and time away from your current research, I am prepared to offer you £25,000.

It is of great importance that you respond to this inquiry no later than the 26th of October. I have conducted research of my own but have determined that expertise such as yours may prove useful. I hope this letter finds you well and please, discretion is a must. Please respond by using the envelope provided.

Arrangements for you to be transferred to my estate in Essex County just outside of Saffron Walden will be provided upon your arrival at London Heathrow Airport. A driver will be waiting with a sign that has your name designated on it. I have also enclosed a certified check of £5,000 for traveling expenses.

Sincerely,

Dr. Mya Bishop
Professor of Medieval Literature and Folklore
University of Cambridge

I tucked the telegram back into my pocket as the plane slowly made its way to the terminal. Before confirming this engagement, I took a day to research this person. I needed to know that I was not flying all this way to listen to someone pitch a new product for my team to use in the field. Dr. Bishop, as it turned out, was also known for her research and work at the university level, yet her work was completely unrelated to mine. The picture on the back of her latest book, *Demystifying on an Old Myth: A Comparative Look at Lycanthropy*, depicted her as a young, yet studious individual dressed formally. I suspected this image was taken several years prior and was expecting to meet someone closer my age. I rationalized this was the reason she sent a telegram instead of making a phone call or sending an e-mail. Perhaps she was more traditional in her correspondence? I thought as I slid her book into my carry-on bag. Yet, with modern technology, couldn't this meeting have been done through video conferencing? Skepticism filled my insides; however, having £5,000 to cover travel expenses spoke more validity into the situation especially since one British pound sterling was worth more than one Australian dollar. Immediately, Dr. Bishop set herself apart from the would-be sale personnel that I was used to encountering. Most simply offered the exact amount for the airfare, but her offer far exceeded that.

I had no idea what kind of animal I was going to observe; therefore, I packed rather light, and managed to sneak by with just one carry-on bag. Some equipment that I had was required to be checked before boarding the plane. It didn't take long to move through customs and eventually the baggage claim. Before I knew it, I was standing outside of the airport looking for a person holding a sign with my name. The air was dense with fog and the coldness of the fast-approaching evening took little time to take hold; however, after traveling for thirteen hours on a stuffy airplane the cold was somewhat refreshing.

I waited outside for approximately ten minutes before I noticed a man dressed in a black suit, holding a sign, standing completely still. Everyone else around him was scurrying about to catch taxis or trying to meet friends or family members, yet he remained unchanged in his posture. As it turned out, the sign that he was holding read:

HOLLAND

"Excuse me, mate, but are you here to pick up someone by the name of Marcus Holland?" I finally asked.

"Yes sir, are you him?"

"Yah mate, I'm your guy!"

"Very good sir, right this way." He grabbed the equipment bag that I had brought along and moved it over to a black Mercedes Benz S 500. I followed him to the back of the car and gave him my carry-on as well. Once he secured everything in the trunk, he graciously opened the door to the back seat.

"No, I'm alright, mate. I prefer to sit in the front."

"Suit yourself, sir. I must insist we get going. Dr. Bishop was adamant that we arrive before seven o'clock; in fact, she paid extra to make it happen. Seeing that we're already running a bit behind schedule – "

"No problem mate!" I sat down in the front seat of the black Mercedes. The car was brand new and smelled as though it had just been bought off the showroom floor. The driver wasted no time pulling out and did so with a squeal of the tires. Several other cars honked their horns in protest. "Crikey mate! I think she wants me to arrive alive and in one piece!"

His only response was a very quick, monotone, "Very good sir." People dressed in warm coats walked to and fro on the streets of London some carrying bags with names I recognized like Debenhams and Harrods, whereas others clung to each other to fend off the chill of the evening. I had never been to London, but before I had a chance to enjoy the high-rise buildings, the local cuisine or even a good pub, I was carted off to the countryside of Northwest Essex County.

It was quite a bit different from that of Australia. The hills rolled over themselves and I could tell that despite the growing darkness that patches were brown, but most were lush with green. Trees had multiple colors from red and orange to different shades of yellow. Puffy dark clouds hung in the sky and reflected the remaining bits of light cast from the sun that had already set over the horizon. The driver merely faced forward barely saying a word as though he was programmed to do nothing but drive the same speed without distraction. The silence was broken when an electronic voice from the GPS system in the dashboard informed us to turn in 1.2 kilometers.

"So, you got a name or should I just call you mate?" I asked, desperate for some conversation. Though England's rural areas were pretty, I needed something further to stimulate my mind before fatigue of the trip overtook it.

"My name is Brody Michaels."

"Have you known Dr. Bishop long?"

"No, I've never met her. I don't work for her. I work for the company that she hired to take you from the airport to her estate. You see, sir, our clients simply call into our offices and make arrangements to drive to and from the airports or wherever the destination. Most of our clients are high end and don't want to be bothered by the madness of taxis and the sort."

"Got it. How much further are we from her estate?"

"Well Sir, according to the navigational system, we should be arriving at 6:47 p.m. Another ten minutes or so."

Ten minutes felt longer than it really was mainly due to the conversation dying off. As we pulled down the dirt road towards the estate, I could tell from the headlights of the car that the road had lots of overgrowth backed by a tree line on either side. The estate house itself was massive and had what appeared to be several thousand vines of ivy climbing its walls. If I had to guess, I would say the vines looked like they had taken residence on this house many years before. A few of the windows were lit, indicating that someone was in fact home. We pulled up in front of a stairway leading to giant, double-hung oak doors.

I stepped out of the vehicle and noticed instantly that the air was not quite as dense as it was in the city and smelled fresh and clean. The driver unloaded my things and carried them to the door before utilizing the oversized knocker that hung on the door to the right. Strangely, he did not wait for a reply but, instead, made his way towards me and waited expectantly for his service tip. I shook the man's hand and offered him what I thought was a fair tip in pounds before he drove off.

Still very unsure as to what I should expect, an eerie feeling came over me as though something was stalking me. I knew this feeling very well from the numerous dangerous animals I had observed and hunted in the wild. Turning to look around, all I could see was a large fountain that was not turned on and a place for a vehicle to park where an older, yet well cared for, Land Rover rested; however, my observation was interrupted by the opening of the oak doors behind me. Standing before me was not a middle-aged professor of literature but instead a strikingly beautiful lady in what I guessed to be her mid-twenties. Her hair was a deep chestnut brown with an auburn streak interwoven along her face. She was wearing a thick burgundy sweater that swooped in the front a bit and a pair of slim fitting jeans with no shoes. Though casually dressed, the woman was strangely alluring. The word *discretion* from the letter took on a different meaning, but my thoughts quickly rooted themselves back to reality as I realized she probably was *not* interested in a forty-six-year-old Aborigine, with wild looking hair and a pouchy stomach.

"Marcus Holland, I presume?" she finally asked. It was obvious that I was not expecting to see someone of her nature.

"Ah yah, that's me. Are you…Dr. Bishop?" I stumbled over my words.

"Yes, I am. I trust that you had a good trip?" Standing barefoot she opened the door wider so I could enter. "Do come in." I grabbed my things and followed her into the house where I was met with a well-tended foyer with a sitting bench and an antique coat rack. A massive marble spiral staircase extended upwards to the right. At the landing to the left was an archway to a large parlor area where two leather chairs, split by a small table rested next to a stone fireplace that had a few smoldering logs in it that crackled gently.

"Yah I did, it was long but uneventful," I said, again trying not to stumble over my words. "I'm sorry Dr. Bishop. I am acting a little strange…I was not expecting someone…well, someone so – "

"Young?" she interrupted. "Don't feel bad I get that a lot. Trust me when I say I'm older than you think. Please, sit. I wanted a chance to talk with you before we begin our work. Can I offer you a drink and a bit to eat?"

My heart sank a little at the thought of beginning tonight. Fatigue was becoming a hindrance at this point. The serene atmosphere and being offered food would not make it any better. "I'll just have a beer if you got one. Are you sure you want to begin work tonight? You may not know that when I observe animals, it usually takes many days, sometimes weeks, to accomplish this?" I draped the sport coat I was wearing over the armrest of the chair.

She turned and opened a small freezer box located in the corner of the room under the counter and pulled from it a Manns Brown Ale. I did not prefer English Ales, but given the strangeness of the situation, I was not going to complain. Besides, she went to all this trouble to get me out here with a fancy ride and the promise of more money.

"I understand Mr. Holland, and I also understand that your methods are very pragmatic, but unfortunately we have to start tonight." She walked back over and handed me the beer with a pint glass. "Are you married, Mr. Holland?"

"No, I'm not. Given the nature of my work, it doesn't lend itself to long-term relationships very well." I was still hoping that I would be able to convince her that it was in our best interest to begin fresh in the morning. "However, since you seem to understand my methods of research already, then I am assuming that you realize it may take several weeks just to track down the animal you want me to observe."

Dr. Bishop ignored my plight. "I know that you have traveled a long way and are probably very tired and skeptical as to why I brought you here, so let me begin by also letting you have this."

She leaned over her own chair and pulled an envelope from a side stand. It was rather thick and somewhat heavy as she handed it to me. I opened it and found a mass of money with varying denominations. I instantly felt livelier, and the skeptical feeling I had on the plane that had stayed with me until now simply evaporated like a small puddle in the Great Victorian Desert. I nearly spilled the beer I was holding. "Ok, now you've got my attention!"

"There is ten thousand British pounds in the envelope and after tonight is over, you'll get the remaining fifteen thousand as promised," she explained.

"You're not shit'n me with any of this are you? And you aren't trying to sell me anything either?"

"Afraid not. I really need your help, and this should prove that I'm serious. When I say we need to start tonight, understand that I wouldn't do this unless it was absolutely necessary. I would also like to apologize for the means of communication, but emails and phone calls provide too much of a trail to follow. I learned a long time ago that the less people that know about this, the better. With that in mind, I do need you to sign this form stating that what is observed within the confines of my estate remains discrete. I trust your methods, Mr. Holland. I have been keeping track of your career for a while and I've read many articles about the things you have accomplished with the Australian dingoes."

I had seen and signed many of these forms in the past for other private clients that wanted my team to test new devices on the animals we tagged in the bush. Patents were usually the reason for the form. No one wanted their device or discovery taken. The form was fairly standard in that I could face legal ramifications should I divulge the information to an outside source. Ultimately, it was the legal confines that stopped my team from testing products; however, none of the other clients ever paid as well as Dr. Bishop for something as simple as an observation. Struggling to write to sign the paper, I could only blurt out, "So, how is it that a person with your background has come in contact with an animal that has the likeness of a dingo? I mean, aren't you a Professor of Medieval Literature and an author?"

"Yes, I am. Mr. Holland, it is always difficult to explain how anybody comes to a particular situation. For example, if I turned the question around and asked you how you came to study a wild and dangerous animal such as the Australian dingo, and various other exotic creatures your country has to offer, the answer wouldn't be so clear, would it?"

"During my walkabout when I was a youth, I was attacked by dingoes. Later in life, I went to the University of Sydney to study animal science. I get your point: one thing many times leads to another without much explanation in between."

She smirked as if her point was made more so than I understood. I tried to bring the conversation back to the immediate situation, "So…so, what exactly are we dealing with here? If we must observe it tonight, I assume it must be nocturnal then?"

"You're correct. This animal is very dangerous and very rare. I specifically sought you out, for this reason. You're the best in your field at studying exotic animals; the strange ones most people don't come in contact with or even can't come in contact with on a regular basis. Your discovery with the fabled Tasmanian Tiger, the Thylacine, really caught my attention."

"That was one of our disappointments. We were really hoping to find one, but extinct they remain. We did hope though. We wanted something to study more than the bones we found. As it turns out, the carbon dating on the bones went back to the early 1940s and is still congruent with the extinction dates. Last one seen alive was in the mid-1930s. Poor guy died in a zoo."

"You were still able to follow rumors and hearsays, as you called them, and made a discovery. Tonight, I just want you to know that something just as fabled exists," she paused to look at the small clock that was positioned above the fireplace on the mantle. "Unfortunately, time is fading from us fast and the animal that we must observe is in another location of the house."

"In the house! I thought you just said that it was very dangerous! I know I haven't seen this animal yet, but it's fair to guess that it's a predator of some sort and it's in your house?"

"Yes it is, but the animal is contained…for the moment," she said in an attempt to settle my anxiety.

"Look lady, if you've got a dangerous animal in your house with the possibility of it getting loose, perhaps we should call some other – "

"No! There's no other that we can call. Just trust me," Dr. Bishop interrupted in a calm yet direct manner. "If you would please, follow me. We have to go to the lower level. It's better to see it than for me to tell you about it."

Nervous and bewildered, I set my beer on a nearby table, reached into my carry-on bag and pulled my journal before following her down a long hallway that had several antiquated portraits illuminated by lit sconces on either side. "Lower level?" I asked as we passed one darkened room after another. They appeared to be dens or libraries or other places to gather if an event called for it.

"My past family members were merchants, and the lower level of the house was where they stored most of the inventory. I inherited this house when my family was killed in an accident."

"No wild animals, I hope?" She stopped at the foot of the stairwell leading down and glared at me in the most sinister of ways, as though I had just insulted the very existence of her entire family. "I take it back. I was just kidding, given the state of things."

She said nothing more as we went further into the bowels of the house. The stairs were solid stone as were the walls that spiraled down. I felt as though we were in a castle's dungeon rather than a cellar of an old manor. A damp smell indicated that there was not much air flow, and that water was probably seeping into the lower level through some point in the foundation. I looked behind me only to see the light from the hallway being swallowed by the darkness I was descending into. A strange chill crept up my spine as I followed the silhouette of Dr. Bishop down further. It was similar to one I felt outside the manor, as though something sinister was stalking me, waiting for the right moment to strike and there was nothing I could do about it.

Upon completing our descent, the shadowy chamber opened to an area with several darkened nooks, each divided by a thick wall lit by the occasional sconce. We walked past the gloomy stalls to the back end of this level where a cage-like structure resided. Judging by the size of the bars and the manner in which they were imbedded into the ceiling, I could only assume this was where the animal should be. The structure was empty with its door wide open and instantly panic set in. "I thought you said it was contained?" I blurted out.

"Not to worry, please, just listen to me for a moment. Have a seat." Dr. Bishop pointed to a wooden chair resting against the wall. A rustic cabinet with only one drawer stood next to it. Atop the cabinet was a lamp plugged into a single outlet that was already turned on. A rocks glass, typically used for drinking whisky, rested under it. A black robe hung on one of several hooks in the wall. There was a small, square window in the room, which must have led out along the foundation. This window had metal bars stretching across it embedded into the wall and ceiling, much the way the larger cage-like structure was built. It allowed very little light to shine into the room, but a person could still see out to the night sky if they wanted.

Below the window was a metal box mounted to the wall. It hung open displaying several syringes and small vials of clear, unknown liquid. A set of large keys hung to the left of the box. Dr. Bishop walked into the massive cage and shut the door.

"What are you doing? Blimey woman, are you mad?"

She ignored my questions and proceeded to lock several oversized padlocks into place. First, she locked the ones on the side with the massive hinges, followed by the locks on the other side of the door, nine all together. "Those are the keys to these locks, hanging on the wall. In the drawer of the cabinet is a bottle of water. You will also notice that there is a tranquilizer gun on the other side of the chair. Mr. Holland…I brought you here tonight to observe an animal. More specifically, I brought you here to observe me."

Stunned by what was taking place, I could barely speak. "You're kidding, right?"

"No," she stated with her head hung low. Before I could say anything else, she removed her sweater and took off her pants. There, standing before me completely naked, she looked deep into my eyes half expecting me to understand what she was saying.

"Dr. Bishop, I'm not a psychiatrist or a medical doctor. This isn't my area of expertise!"

"Mr. Holland, this is more your expertise than you know." Her voice quivered as though she was frightened or perhaps saddened, holding back emotions beyond my understanding. The look in her eyes almost suggested an apology, as if to say sorry for bringing you here. Her body was perfectly proportioned, and her brown hair hung over her shoulders to the top of her breasts. A crude scar stretched across her right thigh as though she, too, were attacked at some point by a vicious dingo. I wondered if it was from the same animal she wanted me to observe.

She backed herself against the stone wall. Shadows fell over her face and body. The only noticeable trait was the iridescence of her emerald green eyes from behind her tousled auburn locks. "I'm a very dangerous animal, Mr. Holland. I must stay in here until it's over."

"Until what's over? What are you talking about?"

"I'm not human…I'm…a werewolf," she said as her voice wavered.

"A WHAT?!"

"A Lycanthrope, a Werewolf."

I would wager that most people would have walked out in disbelief, but the seriousness she carried in her eyes froze me in place and sent another chill down my spine. I sat down on the chair, not taking my eyes off her for an instant and half expecting to wake up from some kind of weird dream. The situation did not change, yet I was now very aware of the tranquilizer gun resting next to the chair. "Ok, let me get this straight. You flew me here all the way from Sydney, Australia…you claim to be a werewolf and you want me to do what now?"

"Around 8:30 p.m. the full moon will climb high enough to shine through that small window and when it does, I will change. I only want you to look at me tonight, and then shoot me with the tranquilizer gun. It won't hurt me, but it will cause me to fall asleep. I want you to know with your own senses what I am and believe it. I've spent too long with no one knowing what I truly am. After tonight, I hope that you will help me. If you are gone in the morning, I will understand, but please, discretion is a must."

We sat for several minutes locked in each other's gaze as I tried to let my conscious mind wrap around the idea that behind this cage was a werewolf. I was no stranger to what it was. I was simply having trouble believing that they were actually *real*; however, the fragile barrier between reality and myth was shattered the moment the moonlight from outside poured through the tiny window and caught Dr. Bishop's face. It started with a cry, as she doubled over clutching her stomach.

I jumped to my feet and rushed to the cage, fearing that she was sick or suffocating. Her head snapped upwards in my direction as her emerald eyes began glowing the same as a dingo's would if a lamp were shined in its face at night "Back away from the cage!" she shouted in a voice that was now baritone and unrecognizable from the soft one it once was.

I leapt back with a start, my stomach tightening as Dr. Bishop's face contorted and she screamed as if the pits of hell licked at her feet. I watched her alabaster skin, so flawless only a few minutes before, split and peel as her petite frame began to grow in height. Dark brown fur erupted from every part of her body as her face extended forward to form a snout bearing huge canine teeth. Her torso pulled inward to form a slim stomach region and an immense chest cavity. I backed myself as far away from the cage as I possibly could and nearly fell over the cabinet and chair against the wall. I barely noticed the sound of the rocks glass as it fell to the ground and shattered. Time stood still as all other sounds became muted.

Scrambling to catch my footing, I glanced down and quickly grabbed the tranquilizer gun. In place of the Dr. Bishop I had met a mere ninety minutes earlier stood a towering beast on its hind legs. Its lean, muscular arms steadied its torso as it lowered itself in a stance ready to pounce. My hands shook as my heart pounded against my chest. Weakness spilled into my knees, and I grew wobbly. Trembling, barely able to stand, I struggled to even look at it. The beast let out a wicked snarl and lunged towards the cage door. The locks holding the door in place clanged violently against the metal bars as the monster repeated the first lunge with a second…then a third…but the fourth failed as it fell to the ground with a thud and let out a low moan. Six tranquilizer darts stuck into the beast. I dropped the gun as dizziness forced me to slide down the wall. Shaking all over, I let my head fall into my hands.

Chapter #5

Shannon Maia Bishop
Sunday, November 1, 2009

I woke to a sense of dizziness and blurred vision. A musty smell and a cold hard floor reminded me that I was in the lower level of my estate. Dull light poured through the small window indicating that the morning was upon us, but the sun had not fully risen. Visions of the night before still lingered in my mind. The violent crashing and thrashing against the metal cage, then sleep. A sleep without dreams or feelings, peaceful yet terrifying. Terrifying with the implication that this is how I would picture an eternal rest, one where time has no meaning, and the body no longer senses change.

Sitting in a chair outside the cage was Marcus, with a half-drunk bottle of water in his left hand and a tranquilizer gun draped over his lap, gripped tightly with his right hand. He appeared to be awake but deep in thought. A journal with some markings in it lay open on the rustic cabinet that stood next to him. Broken glass littered the floor and crunched under Mr. Holland's feet as he shifted in the chair. He dropped the bottle of water and pointed the tranquilizer gun at me once he noticed that I was awake.

"There's no need for that now. It's over…for the moment." My voice was weak. Each movement was painful as I shifted to a sitting position. I was still naked. My vision was blurry. I continued to blink my eyes as I slowly began to pull the darts from my chest. One-by-one I removed each of them. The once-clotted openings began to bleed. I just let them drip. "Would you be so kind as to hand me the robe hung just over there?"

I leaned to my right and pointed to the robe hanging on the wall. Without saying a word, Marcus looked at the robe and immediately back at me. He did this a couple of times before pulling the robe from the wall and throwing it in the direction of the cage. I reached my arm through the bars to grab it. After several attempts, I managed to pull it into the cage. I slipped my arms through the armholes one after the other and wrapped the rest of it around my body. I asked, "Could you unlock the door to the cage? I…I'm glad you stayed, otherwise it would be more difficult for me to get out of here."

"I think you should stay in there for a while, until…until I've… had time to think this through."

"Mr. Holland, nothing is going to happen. I only change when the moon is out. Besides, judging by the amount of fatigue on your face, it could be some time before you're thinking straight. I suggest –"

"I suggest…that, that you just…" he cut off before finishing his sentence, fear and confusion obviously taking a toll on his ability to speak.

"Please…Mr. Holland, unlock the cage door so that we can go upstairs. You could use a brew…you look exhausted."

"No! What I am is a little freaked out at who or I mean…what you are!"

"I understand," I said in a calm voice. "Since you decided to stay the rest of the night, the remaining fifteen thousand pounds are yours. However, it's upstairs locked inside a safe. Should you want it, you are going to have to let me out of here. I promise nothing is going to happen."

He finally lowered the gun and walked over to the wall where the keys were hanging. Mr. Holland cautiously approached the cage door but did nothing until I moved back against the wall. After unlocking the oversized padlocks and letting each one fall to the floor, he backed away from the cage and pointed the gun at me again. Dizziness, no doubt from the tranquilizers but more so from my change, kept my vision cloudy. The room shifted from side to side as I staggered to the heavy gate and nudged it open. I walked past Mr. Holland and headed towards the stone stairs, using the wall as a crutch to keep from falling. I could hear Mr. Holland walking a short distance behind me. His careful steps gave him away. Assuming he still had the tranquilizer gun pointed in my direction, I did not turn around so as to not startle him again and risk being shot with another dart.

The stone steps were cold under my feet as I made my way to the upper levels. The sconces that were lit the night before had all burned down and gone out. The air was cleaner which helped to dispel my dizziness as I walked down the dimly lit hallway to my den. Within the book-covered walls, an antique wooden desk rested at the back of the room. An oil-painted portrait of my family hung directly behind the desk covering the safe that held the rest of the promised money. I fumbled with the combination a few times. Mr. Holland had also entered the room. I knew he was there, not because he made a noise but because I could smell him coming down the hallway. As he entered the room, the scent of perspiration was almost overwhelming. It had been masked a bit by the musty odor in the lower level. Turning to face him, I noticed that he had already sunk down into one of the two leather chairs in front of my desk. I handed him another envelope. "Here, take it. Fifteen thousand pounds as promised."

The fresh air had also helped Mr. Holland, for some of his weariness had begun to subside. He stared at me in awe, ignoring the envelope on the desk before saying, "What am I supposed to do?" Sooner than I could respond, he went on, "I don't even know how to help you. You're unlike anything in this world. I thought briefly while you slept that perhaps I should start with wolves or dingoes but you're not even that. Frankly speaking, I don't know where the hell to start…I don't even want to get close to you, yet at the same time I find myself compelled to stay. Your very presence worries me. I noted in my journal everything that happened last night so that I can reference it later. I'm not sure that I can even trust my senses at this point."

I sat down at my desk chair and listened for an hour as he rehashed several times every happening from the night before. The more he talked the less tired he became. I did not say a word until he asked me the most basic of questions, one in which I felt compelled to respond. "Who are you?"

It was so simple, yet so complicated at the same time. My response was just as simple yet carried a complex depth: "Shannon Maia Bishop." Closing my eyes, I shook my head a bit before continuing, "It's ironic because my first name means 'old' and 'wise'. I have also been Maia Murphy, Shanna Murphy, just recently Dr. Cassandra Bishop and currently Dr. Mya Bishop, at least by record."

"By record?" he asked.

"I have changed my name several times. I can get maybe thirty or forty years in one place before I have to move again. I always claim to be the daughter of a name I had used before, which again buys me more time. These auburn streaks in my hair are actually grey, but I dye them to make myself look different. As time goes by, I let the grey come in completely, thus making me look older. I do this so I can hide the fact that I'm not aging. The grey in my hair started to appear within the first year of becoming a werewolf. Naturally, I have to move around quite a bit."

"How old are you?"

"I was born in 1790, in this very house."

"That would make you over two hundred years old! How have you been able to stay a secret for so long given that you change every month into, well, you know?"

"It has been very difficult; I dipped down into a world that most people never see. Much of my time in the beginning was spent as a nomad traveling all over Europe. I probably spent the better half of a century moving from place to place, studying the areas, searching for clues, and learning what I could about this thing I had become. I found refuge in local Catholic churches. The nuns and priests would provide me with shelter and food. I would lie and say my name was something other than what it really was; they never really knew me at all. When I knew the full moon was coming, I would retreat to some secluded place in the mountains or deep within a forest. I'm sad to say that it…it didn't always work. Occasionally people traveling through the mountains or forest would catch a glimpse of me in werewolf form or, worse, actually get attacked by me." Tears spilled from my eyes. I lowered my head as I let the heavy words of my story fall from my lips, "A few times the travelers were just injured, but on several occasions, they didn't survive my attack. What became of the injured parties, I don't know? Unfortunately, I cannot control myself when I change. I remember everything that happens. It's hazy, but I can see what is taking place around me, but it's as though someone else is controlling me. Last night, I recall crashing into the cage door three different times. I didn't want to, but like I said I had no control over what I was doing and I'm afraid to say that if I were to have gotten out, you wouldn't be sitting before me as you are."

I paused to compose myself before continuing, "Wars made it easy to stay secret and keep the same name for a while. Every twenty years or so, some region wanted to get into a fight with another and every time that happened England was involved. With each war that passed through England's possession I would claim that my family members were killed, providing me with a reason for being alone, with no papers of recognition. After the Great World Wars had ended, I began taking up residence in places all over England becoming a different person each time I settled down into a new area. Again, my unanswered questions were my motivation to stay in an area. Each time I changed my name I had to pay hundreds and eventually thousands of dollars for criminals to forge paperwork; however, the world forgets about you and in time I made it a point not to be remembered. So, eventually I was able to come back to my birth name of Bishop. But a person can only go so long as a ghost before it starts to weigh heavily on the conscious. Oh how I longed for companionship, someone to talk to and to confide my secret. The money I inherited from family, though great at the time, eventually dried up, forcing me to take odd jobs for a while. I watched the world change around me whilst I stayed the same. These jobs kept me in contact with humanity. In the fullness of time, I attended a university to gather more information. University libraries were some of the best in the world. While at the University of Birmingham, I astounded my professors with how much I knew about medieval literature, and I quickly made my way to earning a Ph.D. in Medieval Literature and Folklore and became a professor at the University of Cambridge. I chose this university because it had one of largest libraries in the world; housing millions of books. It's the second oldest university in the English-speaking world, second only to Oxford. To disguise my obsession for research I began writing books. These books about medieval literature and folklore were great sellers in the academic world and required very few appearances, but brought in a lot of money because I could require my students to buy them." Marcus turned to look at the books displayed on the shelf.

"I have your latest one of them with me. I only skimmed it though." He rubbed his forehead. "If I would've known that you were writing from personal experience, I would've read it more closely."

I half ignored his comment. "Writing these books allowed me to disappear for a while if need be. The last time I disappeared for an extended period of time was eleven years ago. Dr. Cassandra Bishop succumbed to an untimely death, while I was supposedly studying abroad at a boarding school. I re-emerged later as her daughter Dr. Mya Bishop. I staged my own death again to disguise my age and I dyed my most recognizable trait, the infamous grey streaks to auburn. There was no actual body to bury, just a proper service. In actuality, my real mother died in 1815." Uncertainty spread across his face, but he continued to follow my story.

"During my so-called disappearance, I made my way back to this estate. I hadn't been back for almost two hundred years. No one had lived in the manor after my family's death. Too many people thought the place to be cursed. It was. Eventually the estate was turned over to the governing body of the time and it stayed abandoned because no one had claim to the deed. When I returned, I spent most of my nights sleeping curled up on the floor of my old room. Day after day I searched for memories of my past amongst the disheveled mess. In my father's den, the oil painting had fallen to the floor exposing a small hole that had been carved into the wall. Inside I found the deed to the manor that my father kept inside a small chest. No one knew it was there because of the oil painting. Being that I was the one now holding the original deed to the land, there wasn't much dispute. I merely provided the rationale that this deed was entrusted to me upon my eighteenth birthday and that it should remain amongst my bloodline. Besides, not too many people were interested in an abandoned estate that was practically unlivable. That being said, no one asked questions when I decided to refurbish the entire interior. I turned the hole in the wall into a safe and rehung the oil painting to conceal it. The cage in the lower level was built by a specialty contractor. I discovered that if I avoided the moonlight, I wouldn't change into the hideous beast you met last night; however, the darkness inside cannot be so easily contained. Gradually, it was as though my body was beginning to welcome the darkness and fought against my mind if I decided to shield myself from the moonlight. Evil such as this needs to be released, but the more I fought it the harder it became to overcome. You have to understand Mr. Holland, as terrible as it is to change into a werewolf, the power it exudes is seductive. I fear that one day the human side of me will no longer exist.

Every day I pray that God will lift this curse from me, for I feel my humanity getting weaker."

Mr. Holland hung onto my every word. It wasn't until I had finished explaining how I had made several other discoveries on my own, but had no way of truly testing them, that he asked the question I feared he was going to ask, "How did your family die?"

His question struck me like a hammer on an anvil. I paused for a moment before I answered, "It's not something I can talk about." I turned from him fighting back emotions I didn't want him to see as I reached back into the safe behind the portrait. I pulled out a tattered, leather-bound diary, brushed the dust off the cover, turned and laid it upon the desk. "Here, this should answer your question. This is my diary. I began writing in it shortly before becoming a werewolf. It holds the true memories of what happened to me and my family. Mr. Holland --"

"Marcus, we're a bit past the formal stage."

"Marcus, please don't judge me for the wrongs I've done. Like I said, I have no control during my episodes. Now that you know what I am, you know why I need your help."

Marcus picked up the diary, thumbed through a few of the pages making special note of the dates written atop each page. "Many of these entries are dated 1815…according to you…the year of your mother's actual death." He looked up at me and said, "Dr. Bishop, are you trying to say that you --"

"Mya, please call me Mya," I interrupted. "Just read it. Like I said, I can't talk about it. Now that we've talked away the morning, there's no doubt you're starving. Tonight is another full moon, but I want you to sedate me before the moon rises. I believe that this will prevent me from changing, or at least if I do change having enough tranquilizing drugs in me will allow me to stay asleep through it. Once I'm asleep, you can read the diary."

Chapter #6

Shannon Maia Bishop's Diary
Marcus

Much of the previous night was a blur. The morning had passed by quickly and rolled into the afternoon without much notice. It was tough to describe how I was feeling. Physically, my body was stiff and fatigued from the plane ride and not sleeping; however, mentally I was much worse. Everything I had witnessed defied all the logic that I have based my entire career on perfecting. I could not trust my senses, even though I came face-to-face with one of the most dangerous creatures this world had ever known. I saw it with my own eyes and heard it with my own ears. *How is it possible that a creature such as a werewolf can even exist?* I pondered this thought over and over again as I slowly sipped a bitter cup of Earl Grey tea and stared at a plate mounding with a variety of pastries. Sitting across from me was Mya Bishop who I barely knew yet knew enough to understand the dark secret that has been discretely caged inside of her for over two hundred years. I could feel her vibrant, green eyes looking over me, studying whether I was going to say anything. I would glance up on occasion and catch her avoiding my gaze, much the way a dog would if it were being told not to do something. This silent interaction continued for a great while before the sound of her soft voice spoke, "Marcus…I know that this…" she said before it was broken by a long pause. "I know this is difficult to understand and that you are probably wondering …"

"Stop," I interrupted. "Mya, you have to understand, most things I observe and study I do so in the Outback, and they usually stay in one form. I truly know nothing about what you are, so I have no plan for beginning the process of helping you."

"Perhaps after you read the diary, you'll know more of my story and a better solution may present itself."

We sat for a little while longer before I agreed to observe her for one more night. We made our way back down the stone stairs into the musty cellar of the estate. Once again, I looked at the massive cage at the end of the open area. My breath escaped my mouth and struggled to return as I was reminded of the horrifying event that took place the night before. A few moments passed before I could continue to follow Mya through the shadows of the lower level. I carried my journal and the diary she gave me in one arm while in the other I still held the tranquilizer gun. Mya had once again made her way towards the cage structure and locked herself inside. She assured me that the moon would not rise for another three hours, and that sleep was the best thing for me. As much as I hated the idea of falling asleep with a beast like her in such proximity, she was right. If I did not get any sleep for another night, my ability to perform the duties required of me would drastically diminish.

"Here," Mya stated as she stuck her arm through the metal bars. "You can sedate me now so that you can rest awhile. More tranquilizers and sedatives are in the metal box just below the window. I trust that you have had experience with sedating animals, so you should know what vial to get from the box. Remember, you need to give me enough so that I sleep through the night; and…don't worry about giving me too much. A dose that would normally kill an animal will only cause me to sleep longer. I tried to overdose one night and only managed to sleep for two days straight."

Not saying a word, I walked over to the box below the window and began eyeballing the vials of sedatives. After reading several labels, I finally came to one that read: *Telazol*. Several syringes were next to the glass container.

"I'm not going to ask how you came about getting this anesthetic. Most people have to be a registered vet or technician to get it."

Mya merely smirked as I filled one of the syringes full. I pressed the needle into the vein in the bend of her arm and, within moments, Mya began blinking her eyes rapidly as she lowered herself to the floor of the cage. I set the alarm on my wristwatch to go off in two and a half hours. I waited fifteen minutes before settling down next to the wall across from where she slept. The weight of my fatigue did not take long to force my eyes closed. Air passed slowly through my nose and echoed in my mind.

I knelt by the pile of bones…odd looking…path hazy, difficult to follow. A voice said, "Their old, too old to be new…" The bush was thick around me. I picked up the skull, examined it closely. Brushed the dirt from the eye sockets. Sharp canines, different jaw…distant howl…feeling of running…the wind passing by my ears. Green eyes cut though the darkness from behind the haze. The skull mesmerized…sockets began to glow green…

I awoke with a start and sat up quickly as the alarm on my wrist beeped wildly. I breathed long and deep as I shook off the drowsy feeling that remained from my nap. My heart beat fast; I could feel it pulsing through my neck. Mya remained in the cage. Moonlight soon poured in from the window and shone on the beautiful, youthful woman I had met the day before, resting unchanged and undisturbed from the position in which she originally lay. I noted the findings in my journal before a thought filled my head: How does someone as innocent as this become such a dark creature? I secured the tranquilizer gun across my lap and opened Mya's diary cautiously, as though the contents within held the knowledge that would change the course of my life for whatever number of years remained…

June 12. 1815

Dear Diary,

I feel most fortunate to be writing today. The air is fresh, and the grass is cool and wet under my feet. I guess it is always this way after an early summer rain. I love this time of year; it makes me feel full of life. For the longest, rain has invaded our landscape, soaking our gardens, but also making the flowers grow full and wild. It is so nice to be able to sit for a moment and take in these wonderful backdrops of nature's beauty.

Papa said that I should not fill this book full of silly things such as stories of flowers and feelings that come from the gales of wind that ~~carry scent of a nearby glade;~~ instead, according to him, books such as these should be filled with important stuff like business transactions. He is fond of showing me his musty merchant log even though it is not becoming of ladies to deal with such things. I feel that he is simply gloating that he knows how to conduct business in such an organized fashion; however, I simply cannot resist what I write. There is so much more to the world we live in than musty old ledgers and bookkeeping. Besides, I am a girl in love and a girl in love should write of beautiful things.

Speaking of love, I must take a moment to attribute this feeling today to the dashing, overly handsome suitor of mine, Brayden Murphy. I should not talk of him with such vulgarities; it is simply not lady-like. But my heart flutters when he is near, and I cannot ignore his charm. He has a mysterious yet kind way about him. His dark hair complements his facial features, makes them appear strong and structured. When we dance, I can tell that his body is as strong as his face portrays. Yet, my favorite feature still remains his warm, polite smile. Both of my sisters, Anna and Martha, though younger than I, fancy his playful side. For Brayden is not above showing a few tricks with a deck of playing cards to make them laugh or to instill a sense of wonder within them. Papa says that tricks are for jesters and street performers and that an educated man from Oxford should deal with more serious issues. He says this as he puffs his broad chest making his stature appear more robust. I tease Papa and tell him that more of his silver hair will fall out if he worries of these things. Although Papa means well, I think he secretly is hoping to have Brayden as a business partner more so than a son-in-law. Oh dear me, there I go again wishing for things that have not happened yet. Here is where I must stop for today, besides I am going riding this afternoon and I certainly cannot be atop Rupert barefoot.

Shannon Maia Bishop

June 14, 1815

Dear Diary,

    Brayden seemed rather peculiar today. He was pacing about and carried an unusual amount of distress towards discussing a private matter with Papa. I tried to say hello, but he was at a loss for words. I do pray that everything is alright. Brayden has been working so hard lately and speaking with Papa can only mean that something is not well in his business dealings. Perhaps one of the other local merchants has tried to conduct business in a manner unbecoming of that of a noble Englishman. Whatever it may be, Papa will certainly assist Brayden and make things right.

    I truly hope that I did not do something to be offensive in any manner. Mother has always taught my sisters and I to be very lady-like and proper. The thought that I may have caused

Brayden to not want to be close is quite disturbing to me.

Shannon Maia Bishop

June 15, 1815

Dear Diary,

    Today, the love of my life Brayden Murphy has asked me to marry him! I love him...and I have said YES! Oh what a thrill this is! I could not help but notice that my two sisters were less than delighted to learn of this. I feel that they too were hoping to gain his affection, more so than he was already allowing. Never the matter, youthful hearts play tricks on the mind. I, being of maturity, know that I am in love with him, and my happiness is overflowing on this day.

Shannon Maia Bishop

June 19, 1815

Dear Diary,

Four days have passed since the engagement announcement and plans for the wedding have already begun. People are running around the manor like scared mice, scrambling to accomplish the orders of Mother and Papa. Both seem to be mad! Everything is a bit of a blur, dizzying almost. Mother has already taken the measurements for the dress and Papa is currently preparing our estate for the ceremony. I have not had a spare moment to myself to even enjoy the fact that I now have a fiance. I am barely twenty five years of old and some would think of me as hag, with no other chance to marry. In fact, Brayden and I have not even decided on what day we would like to be married. To make matters worse, my beloved Brayden is away from the manor tending to business, no doubt of great importance.

I am so proud of him! His understanding of business is so important to many people, and he puts forth so much effort that both of my parents are deeply impressed with him. I...simply miss him. I miss his strong arms...the way they hold me close. I miss the way he smells and ah yes...the way we kiss. I eagerly anticipate his return tonight. Though he has only been gone for two days, it feels like oceans of time. Never before have I loved a man the way I love him. I am genuinely happy with him, and I am thrilled to spend the rest of my days beside him. Silly me, I have gotten carried away again. The air is warm tonight. I shall ride Rupert again this evening. Perhaps we will catch a glimpse of the moon tonight; last night it looked as though it was almost full, and it rose early in the evening.

Shannon Maia Bishop

June 20, 1815

Dear Diary,

The most peculiar thing happened yesterday evening. So peculiar that I feel compelled to write about it this morning. It was not but a moment or two after returning from my ride that I stabled Rupert and noticed that he seemed a bit put out. On most occasions, Rupert is very docile and is more than willing to let me brush his brown hair or pick the stones that have gotten wedged in his shoes; however, on this occasion I had to implore the help of two stable boys just to have his saddle removed. It was as though he was frightened of something.

My darling Brayden assured me at supper last night that Rupert would be fine and that his disturbance was probably caused from a sore spot on his hoof or the change in wind. Papa agreed and added that a fox may have been moving around in the moonlight and that they are very common in our parts. Mother simply concluded that Rupert is a horse and that animals such as him act unpredictably at times. I know I should feel that all is well, but I simply cannot. I have never seen him act the way he did. I shall check with the stable boys later today to see if they have discovered anything wrong with him.

Shannon Maia Bishop

June 26, 1815

Dear Diary,

I have not written in nearly a week and even the words I write now are difficult to put to paper, for I am having trouble sitting at my desk. I have rested in my bed staring at the white ceiling of my room, still recovering from a severe bite I sustained from an animal of some sort. Much of my thoughts have been muddled, for the bite has manifested into a fever. The night in question is hazy yet I can still see the horrible image of my horse, Rupert, who was viciously attacked by a beast.

I had resolved to see to my horse the evening after he seemed disturbed. Upon reaching the stable, I found it to be most unusual. The stable boys had taken leave for the evening, but the wooden doors were slung open and broken. Pulled from the hinges by which they were mounted. Fearing my horse had become frightened and run off, I rushed inside only to find blood. Massive amounts of blood covered the stable walls. At that moment the meaning of everything drained from my mind as I saw the body of my beloved horse. His head had been torn from his torso. I could not make sense of anything; all I could do was scream. I screamed out in fear. I screamed out of sadness. I screamed to bring feeling back to my numb body.

And that is when I saw it! The black fur, the teeth, the size...and those eyes. Eyes I will never forget for the rest of my days. Sinister red against the dimness of the stable. It only took a moment before it was upon me. The sheer force of the beast threw me to the ground as I released the lantern from my hand. Then came the sound of tearing flesh as the brute sunk its teeth into my right thigh. An excruciating pain shot down to my foot. I have never been so frightened in my life. Tears streamed down my face as I wailed with agony and swung my arms widely against the monster's face. It twisted its head back and forth ripping at the muscle in my leg. My arms flung backwards as the creature lifted me partially off the ground. I reached for anything to grab onto, and my fingers found the lantern I was carrying. I swung the lantern towards the thing and struck its head.

Glass shattered and oil spilled onto the beast and the floor of the stable. The creature released its jaws from my thigh as the oil burst into flames. Fire engulfed it and also caught the piles of nearby hay ablaze. Fire spread quickly through the stable as I desperately crawled towards the broken doors. The beast let out an agonizing howl before it crashed through the right side of the structure. A part of roof collapsed smothering most of the fire. Much of the stable now lay in ruins. As for the beast, it has not returned according to my father. I do not know what it was. I do not know how to describe it. It looked like a wolf but was not a wolf. It moved like a man but was not a man.

Papa claims that the fever has my mind in a twist and that it could not have been anything other than just a regular wolf. I have never known a wolf to walk upright like a man or to be that big or to attack a horse the way that it did. The day after I heard Brayden and Papa discussing what remained of the horse carcass. His front legs were both broken, and his midsection was over half eaten with nearly all his entrails missing. My poor Rupert.

Papa and Brayden have formed hunting parties to search for the monster every day since…

Shannon Maia Bishop

June 28, 1815

Dear Diary,

I write now with the thought that these may be my last words. My fever has gotten worse. It is dark in my room, and I have been asleep for two days. My dreams at night are filled with death and demons. I do not know what reality is anymore. Fear and sadness are the same now. I cannot tell if I am awake or if this is another dreadful nightmare.

Mother, in her prissy way, has not stopped her worry and my two sisters have not been able to keep from crying. My poor family. I worry for them as much as they worry for me. Papa keeps doctors waiting on me day and night. Against my protests, they had me take off the charm of the Archangel Michael from around my neck. As a good Catholic Christian, I have worn this charm since Papa put it on me at my first communion. The doctors said it was going to interfere with their care. I relinquished my keep over it with the understanding that only Brayden hold it safe. Shall I die it will be something that he can use to carry on the memory of me.

My darling Brayden has not left my bed side. He loves me so much. He sleeps in a chair as I write these words. Even as he sleeps, Brayden holds the charm safe. He said the closer the charm was to me the better off I was going to be and since he was the only one I would allow to hold it, he would remain by my side. I hope he knows how much I love him. I want him to know that my life was meaningless before him. Oh, how I pray to see the day that I am dressed in a gown of white and standing before me dressed in formal wear my beloved Brayden. My dress is so pretty. I want him to see it. I want him to see the way my hair falls behind the veil. I want him to see how beautiful I am and how beautiful I will be for him. I fear that my recovery my may never com

Chapter #7

Shannon Maia Bishop's Diary
Marcus

I glanced up from Mya's diary. Her words seem to trail off from the last entry I had read. I made note from my watch that it was 2:37 a.m. She remained unchanged. The moonlight still poured through the small window, but it no longer shone into the cage where Mya slept. Her breathing was slow and controlled while her body remained still and motionless. *She's a modern woman with a way about her that exudes intelligence and great insight into the world. The woman described in the pages of the book seems weaker than this woman, more feminine perhaps*, I thought.

My neck was stiff and fatigued while my eyes watered from the minimal amount of light I was using to read the hand-written diary. Though the lamp on the cabinet brightened the shadowy cellar, it still was not enough to sustain reading for a long while. This did not matter all that much, I was used to observing things that had the potential for killing me in Australia in far worse conditions. Usually, I enjoyed the thrill of knowing the animal well enough to outsmart it; however, this time was different. My anxiety was stronger because this animal, or thing, was equally as smart as I was, perhaps smarter and I had no method of study that I could use to my advantage. The only thing keeping me alive was that it was sedated inside a cage. I rolled my head from shoulder to shoulder, rubbed my eyes one last time and continued reading the diary, desperate for more knowledge…

July 2, 1815

Dear Diary,

    I have slept more than any normal person should. I am compelled to write today because…well, because I feel wonderful. Every breath I breathe carries a new sensation. It is like my senses have been awakened to the world for the first time. I can smell the scent of jasmine and wild herbs from my bedroom window, but the landscape holds no such growth in any of the nearby pastures. The wound on my thigh, though scarred, looks as though it has nearly healed. I found that I can stand without any pain or discomfort. It must have been something the doctors gave me while I slept. I catch myself wondering if this has all been a dream. Could it be that this was all just a terrible nightmare?

    No…no, it cannot be a dream. I heard Brayden speaking outside my room and I heard him mention my horse, Rupert, and how I may experience some hardship due to his absence; still, everything remains odd.

The doctors seem a bit put out by how well I have recovered. These doctors thought that the fever I had may never go away. They also suggested to Brayden and Papa that I might not be able to walk properly ever again, yet here I stand without any trouble, without any pain. In fact, my leg feels strong as though I could walk over endless pastures.

Shannon Maia Bishop

July 4, 1815

Dear Diary,

I write today with sinful confessions. My darling Brayden stopped by my room today to pay a visit and confirm that I was still recovering well from my ordeal. As he spoke of his business dealings and the world that I have missed over the past several days. I could not help but be drawn to him. I have always found him to be quite attractive, but today was different. Today, I wanted him...I wanted every part of him. The dress I was wearing seemed too constricting across my bust, and I could feel my breathing intensify as he looked into my eyes. Brayden's smell was intoxicating, and his manner of dress caused me to finger the buttons around my collar, hoping they would come loose. I longed to reveal myself to him...to take him in my arms, kiss his neck and taste his lips.

Shannon Maia Bishop

July 7, 1815

Dear Diary,

The moon was out again, and I had to see it. For most of the night, the moon remained hidden behind the tree line. I found myself walking alone in the pastures behind the estate, gracefully with not so much as a falter. I stayed out until it was completely visible. The night seemed different. No one else in the manor knew I was out, but I had to see it. I had to see the light it cast and watch the shadows of nightfall dance all around. I was captivated by its brilliance. It was only a crescent moon, yet something was very strange about it. I cannot explain the feeling I had, except that I was drawn to something. It was as though the darkness took on a different shade of black.

Brayden said that I have been acting unusual. He claims that I am warmer than I should be and that the fever I had a week ago may have returned. He and Papa have been insisting that I be seen by the doctors again. Mother said that this may be an illness that is brought on by an animal such as a wolf. The strange thing is that I feel normal, better than normal. A little warm...yes, but nonetheless better than I have ever felt. What do they know? None of them are doctors. They must think I am going mad! But I am not mad. I know what I saw, and it was not just a wolf. They should stop this nonsense, for this has no doubt bothered my two younger sisters. Anna avoids my gaze and trembles when I pass her in the hallways. Martha went so far as to say that I was deranged when she thought I could not hear her talking in the other room. Both have refused to see me.

Shannon Maia Bishop

July 9, 1815

Dear Diary,

Though I have gotten better each day from my encounter with the strange beast, oddities have continued to materialize within the manor. At first, I thought that everyone was acting strangely towards me because I was so ill and that their reactions to the fever were a bit over-done.

Yet recently, I have come to realize that their strange behavior may have been warranted. Yesterday, I found myself in the kitchen. Most would not think anything of this, but I was drawn to the raw meat that lay on the butcher table awaiting preparation for the evening's meal. I could not help myself. I took the raw meat in one hand and bit cleanly into it. A sudden rush of satisfaction spilled into my mouth. I closed my eyes chewing the meat slowly, enjoying every moment before swallowing. I turned to find myself not alone but in the company of my younger sister Anna, who stood staring at me aghast at what I was doing. Without saying so much as a word she turned and fled as though she had seen a ghost.

It came as no surprise that I was visited later that evening by the doctors who looked after me when I was attacked. They claimed that I still had the fever and that it was making me delusional and that I was unfit to wander the halls of the manor alone. Delusional, possibly.

Strangely enough I felt in total control, as though I was merely indulging a food craving. Never once did I feel unwell.

Shannon Maia Bishop

July 12, 1815

Dear Diary,

Brayden stopped by today. In his hand was the charm that I gave to him in the first days of my sickness. I love him so much, but I sensed a great distance between us. He said he loved me and hoped that I get well, but our conversations, once plentiful, were short and lacking. No doubt that my illness has caused great fatigue and trepidation in him. Perhaps, he has been made aware of my sinful fantasies; perhaps I gave myself blame to such acts while I slept. With my strange and erratic behavior, what was once farfetched has become more of a reality.

The moon is out again tonight, and it is a little more than half full. I have found myself staring at its brilliance every night from the balcony attached to my room. Sometimes for hours on end. Since I have been confined to bed rest very few people have come to visit. Brayden and the doctors who are tending to me are the only visitors I have had as of late. Though, they do not stay long. No matter. I happily return to gazing at the moonlight.

I do believe that when all is quiet in the manor, I may risk another walk in the pasture. No one will know.

Shannon Maia Bishop

July 15, 1815

Dear Diary,

I woke the morning of the 13th of July out of sorts. I remember climbing down from my balcony with relative ease the night before. I walked into the pasture to get a better view of the moonlight. It was captivating beyond anything I had ever seen in my lifetime thus far. My thoughts must have betrayed me. Staring up at the magnificent sight placed me in a state of hypnosis. It is the only way I can explain how far I actually walked. I glided through the dew-soaked pasture, taking in all the sights and sounds of the night. Perhaps it was just the moonlight or perhaps it was the confinement to my room, but I remember feeling completely free and one with the night.

At some point I must have stopped walking and lay down along a creek bed. The gurgling stream gently nudged me awake and I found myself in an unfamiliar place. It was early in the morning because the sun had not quite made it into the sky. It took several hours of walking, following the footprints I left in the soft ground, before I reached the manor. Naturally, everyone was concerned for my well-being. I showed up close to mid-day covered in mud with my clothes tattered from the terrain I covered the night before. Brayden and Papa had rallied a search party on horseback and spent the vast part of the morning looking for me. I can understand their frustration with me and their demands for me to stay in the manor. I tried to explain that I must have lost my way, but they became even more convinced that I was fully delusional.

They gave me a heavy sedative to make sure that I stayed inside my quarters. The doors to my balcony have been locked. Many people come and go just outside my door to spy on whether I am keeping to my quarters and not trying to venture out again. I can actually smell when people switch turns. Even though the soft moonlight is pouring through the window coverings, my walk the other night was equally frightening to me as it was to the rest of the family. I dare not attempt to do such a thing again. Something is truly different about me. Something I cannot explain. I will pray tonight for help. With all the hysteria surrounding my actions, with the diagnosis of delusional tendencies brought on by fever, I cannot help but realize that I have neglected my prayers for several weeks now. Perhaps this will be my source of release. Dear God, please be with me.

Shannon Maia Bishop

July 17, 1815

Dear Diary,

I feel anxious today. I do not know why. Deep inside my being is full of uncertainty. Sickness fills my heart and clutters my mind. I slept for most of the day and when I awoke everything seemed different. Simple things, such as the sweet smell of jasmine has changed. It is as though I can smell the very dirt from which it grows. I can see things from a great distance without any trouble, when before simply reading or writing for long periods of time were enough to cause my eyes to strain. Worst of all, I feel hungry. Hungry in a way that is more than a feeling that can be quickly remedied by sneaking into the kitchen and swiping a piece of fresh bread drizzled with the baker's honey. It feels as though I have not eaten in days. Such the agony it is, such the way that it has consumed my way of behaving. I do not want any porridge or stew or soup. I fear what is happening to me. I am not normal. I fear I am becoming something else, but what? What was that thing that attacked me? What will come of Brayden should I expire before my time, and what of my family. Papa, mother, Anna, and Martha? What?

Shannon Maia Bishop

July 19, 1815

Dear Diary,

Something is happening. Something is wrong. I feel pain throughout my entire body. I have felt it all day long. I am writing now to try to distract my mind from the torturous pain that has consumed me. It began in my stomach and has spread through my arms, legs, into my neck and down my back. Several doctors have tried to help with their cocktails and remedies. They tried to bleed me earlier, thinking that whatever disease I have might be flushed from my system. It proved ineffective. They tried to sedate me, but the concoction did nothing, it merely sent a cold rush down my arm. It feels as though my skin is too tight for my body. My legs are shaky, and my hand keeps losing grip on the quill that I hold. Night has fallen over the manor. Some light is coming through the window

July 22. 1815

Dear Diary,

I write today with lament, from a place that is strange to me. This diary is the only part of me that I have left. I must make sense of this. Tears roll down my face as I write these words. I have become the unspeakable. I am a monster. I do not even know what to call it. All is lost. All is gone. All have been laid to rest by the hands of a demon, by me. My family is gone. The words that follow come with great difficulty, but I must get them to paper. I am not sure if I am going to be able to describe what has happened. I awoke on the 20th day of July feeling stiff and unable to move, but aware of my surroundings. Horrible images filled my head. Pictures of death and suffering. People rushing towards me and some were running in terror. Slowly, my eyes gave in to the soft light that was pouring through the windows of the manor. I found myself in the main lobby of the manor, unsure as to how I got there. No one was around, all was quiet. That is when the terrible reality fixed itself into my mind. My hands shook as I lay naked, covered in a sticky crimson colored substance. Blood...Blood covered the floor as well as the stairwell and surrounding walls. Body parts, hands, fingers, and parts unrecognizable, rested in various spots across the lobby. A terrible pain still lingered in my stomach. I screamed, screamed so that I may wake from this dreadful nightmare, but it was folly. For as much as I screamed, the more awake I became, the more this hell became a reality. God what have I done?

Naked and weak, I struggled up the blood-soaked stairwell, stumbling every couple of steps as I made my ascent. I held my body tight as more images raced through my mind, but I could not be sure if they were real. I had to find out. As I crested the top of the stairs, I was met with more pools of blood and body parts. Overwhelmed by the sight of such carnage, I became sick in the hallway and fell to my knees. Laboriously, I crawled down the hall, over the different pieces of what was once a living person. Each time I passed blood and viscera, images of what had happened assaulted my mind.

A couple of house servants swung wildly at me with makeshift staves from displays in the hallway as they tried to escape without any luck. I could see firsthand how scared they were and then the blood and the unsettling sound of tearing flesh just before they died. Next, I came upon two bodies lying in the archway of the room. Each of the bodies rested mangled on the floor with their throats ripped out and completely bled dry. I screamed and recoiled in horror as the images of them both wriggling in pain flooded my mind. These two bodies were that of my parents. My father's unmistakable merchant log was still clenched in his hand. It was obvious that he had stopped his business transactions to come to the door because of the commotion. My mother dressed in her favorite lounge wear, once black and grey striped with sleeves that extended to the wrists, now dark crimson. I killed them. Both Papa and mother had a look of absolute terror frozen onto their faces. What have I done?

Tears were constant upon my face as I continued past several other rooms, all wrecked and disheveled as if some massive beast had crashed through the walls with the intent to destroy everything in the room. Weak from the repulsive sights that littered the manor, I made my way towards my quarters. The lavatory, just before my quarters, had its door torn from the hinges and lay in the middle of the hallway. I peered inside only to be struck still, dizzy with another image of the massacre. Dead, leaning against the far wall with a vast majority of its torso eaten away and its left arm severed at the shoulder was a body. I could only whimper as I crawled into the narrow room and touched the unidentifiable face of the victim. Had it not been for the long, brown hair, I would have never known it was my sister, Anna. Parts of her nightgown were strewn across the floor and mixed with the river of blood that led out of the room. She was preparing for bed when it happened. I wonder where Martha is?

Light from the day spilled through the windows of my room, showing the devastation. The curtains were torn from the rods that held them, the desk from which I wrote lay in ruins. More images pierced my mind. I remember…I remember the light that came through windows that night. I remember the moonlight, so bright, and then the excruciating pain.

The floor by my desk was also covered in blood. I touched it and felt a shockwave of images, images of my love Brayden. He was outside my door that night and came into my room. He ran towards me, then at first look recoiled. It was as though I was looking down at him, as though I was standing on a stool. I picked him up in the air and brought his face next to mine. I bit him, hard. I could feel his neck break under the strength of my jaws and the warm rush of blood over my teeth. His screams stopped as the last bit of air escaped the hole in his throat. I can still hear the sound of the tearing and ripping of his flesh.

All I could recognize on the floor near my desk was a small, metallic charm. The charm of the Archangel Michael, the one I gave to Brayden. Nothing remained of my love except the bits of the body across the floor. I looked into the mirror. It had been cracked at some point and several shards had fallen to the floor. I was accosted by another image, the image of the horrible beast that did this, the horrible beast that killed my horse Rupert, the horrible beast that attacked me, the horrible beast that committed these atrocities and the horrible beast I had become.

Shannon Maia Bishop

"My God…She killed them. She killed them all!" I whispered. An old *The Morning Post* article fell from the diary. I stopped reading and picked it up.

Massacre at the Bishop Manor!
All Dead Except One!
23ᵗʰ of July, 1815

```
Martha Bishop was reported to be the sole
survivor of a vicious onslaught that left the
rest of her family dead. The remains of the
bodies were found early this morning as a courier
came to the manor to deliver statements from
local merchants. It was clear that these deaths
did not happen on this morn, but were sometime
earlier in the week. The authorities believe it
to be the work of bandits, while church
authorities believe the deaths were sacrificial
in nature and that witchcraft may be involved.
Suspects of this heinous crime are being
collected and questioned, while the young girl
from the Bishop estate is recovering under the
care of the sisters of St. Mary's Church at the
local voluntary hospital. Due to her silence,
doctors cannot make a diagnosis but hope that she
will recover fully in the coming days.
```

I closed the diary and laid it across my lap still holding the news article in my right hand. I rubbed my temples with my left hand. Stiff from sitting so long on the hard ground, I rolled my neck once again to loosen the muscles on either side along with the ones that stretched down my back. The darkness was starting to fade from the small window as bits of dawn poked into the cellar. I glanced towards the cage and received a sudden shock.

"Holy shit!" I quickly recoiled to my feet and pressed against the wall. Mya's diary fell to the ground along with the article. The area behind the cage was still dark but there was enough light to see a figure hunched over with its arms wrapped around its legs, staring at me with vibrant green eyes that stood out despite the dimness. It took a minute for my heart to stop racing and realize that the figure was small, feminine, and made no abrupt movements towards the entrance of the cage.

"My apologies, you startled me. I was expecting to see you still lying on the ground. How long have you been watching me?"

"For a while," Mya said calmly from within the cage. "I have no memory of last night, did I change?"

"No, despite the moonlight, you stayed as you are now." She gave no response, as if she was waiting, expecting something from me. Her gaze fixed directly on my eyes. I picked up her diary and tucked the newspaper article back inside.

"I wanted to go see her at the hospital...Martha, but I couldn't. I couldn't bear the thought of seeing her in that mental state. I caused that. It was later when I remembered that she had seen me as a werewolf just before I attacked the servants in the house. She ran and hid but went into a catatonic state from which she never recovered. Martha died at only fifteen. It's my fault." Mya's voice wavered and a tear rolled down her face.

"I'm going to try to help you. I need to have some of my other equipment shipped over from Australia, and it's going to take some time to develop a process. I'm used to studying things in the natural world, not the supernatural. I'm going to try."

"Thank you. The rest of my diary?" Mya asked softly.

"I read enough."

"Now you know the truth." She looked away from me.

"Yes...yes I do."

PART II

Chapter #8

Robert Osborne
Friday, November 13, 2009
2:00 p.m.

"You have to understand, Mr. Osborne, a tax increase during these times isn't going to be very popular. Though economic prospects look favorable in the upcoming months, people are still cautious from the recession." Hugh Bennett shifted in the chair to adjust his suit. From his ferruled eyebrows I could see the irritation spread across his face.

"Look, our party is ready to introduce a new policy in the upcoming year that will include double the operational bonus for troops serving in Afghanistan. These are not tax dollars that are going to be wasted on some frivolous public services." My response wasn't to his liking. Henry, my assistant, sat patiently at a small desk by the door of my office recording the minutes of this meeting.

"Robert, I came here today to reason with you, so that we could talk as gentlemen." His voice was stern, direct, but lacked in fortitude. "The financial state of our country cannot sustain the spending that your party is suggesting. We need to come up with an alternative!"

"You're right. We should come up with an alternative. Perhaps we can cut back on the income tax proposals that your party have suggested and supported for years. This would be more appropriate. We would then be able to support the individuals that have pledged service to our country and sacrificed their health, even their lives, to protect the sovereignty that you and I both enjoy." Again, Hugh was not happy to hear this response and shifted to the edge of the chair and pointed his chubby finger in my direction.

"This is ridiculous! Our troops are well tended upon their return home. Besides what do you know about the sacrifice that our soldiers make?"

"My son, Grayson, is currently serving in Afghanistan…"

Hugh interrupted, "I'm sure that he'll have no financial problems upon his return…and you say that my party's spending is frivolous."

I stood from my chair and took a more authoritative posture. My voice was laced with anger: "I will not stand here to be lectured in my own office on the sacrifice my son is making for our country. I worked my way from nothing through smart business tactics to provide my children with an opportunity to be educated. Grayson has chosen to serve our country to give back what has already been provided for him. What he's doing is more honorable than anything you or I could possibly do. The least we could do is provide adequate compensation for his sacrifice, and the sacrifices of his comrades so that they may live out their days in dignity should they not be fit for service upon their return. Now with all due respect, Mr. Bennett, our meeting is through!

Hugh Bennett stood from the chair and buttoned his suit coat. He was shorter than me. We were of the same age and same resolve when it came to matters of our party, but he did not have much of a foothold when it came to matters of income tax and his party was losing ground in the House of Commons. "Damn Tories! This isn't over, Robert!" he said before he turned and walked out of my office.

Henry closed the door behind him and walked over to my desk. "Sir, I really think it's important that we take some time now to develop a strategy for the upcoming meeting with the European Union leaders. They haven't been your strongest advocates." My assistant, Henry, continued to ramble about the upcoming meetings and the items that were going to be discussed. Being a part of the Conservative and Unionist Party, Henry was always preoccupied with the implications of what a poorly run meeting may have upon those that did not line up with our beliefs. I glanced out the window of my office. "Sir, sir, have you been listening to what I've been saying?"

"Henry, give it a rest for a moment," I said with a tang of irritation.

"Robert, I'm merely trying to stay on top of the events for next week," he responded. "If we do not prepare properly for your engagements and your speeches, we run the risk of…"

"Henry, Henry…I'm well aware of my speaking engagements and meetings. We'll deal with the prep work over the weekend, but for now I would like to go to my daughter's competition."

"But, sir…"

"Henry, you already know that my daughter is more important than anything we need to discuss. I don't get to see her much, except for on the weekends, since Daphne and I divorced." I pointed outside as I put on my suit coat. "So, Henry, please at least try to enjoy this beautiful day and stop pestering me about things that don't matter."

"It matters to our party; besides, it's wet and muddy out and any proper establishment would have postponed this engagement for when the climate was more appropriate." Henry turned up his nose for a moment before returning his attention to his smartphone. I smirked knowing that Henry, in his own way, had conceded on the conversation.

We arrived a few minutes late for the competition. It was no matter; we only missed the pre-announcements. I stared at the horse track. Being outside in November was much better than the stuffy meeting halls of Parliament or even my office. Henry was right; the ground was wet and muddy. Yet, as muddy as it was the air was fresh and clean and bits of sunlight poked through the grey clouds as the wind pushed them along. Henry could never appreciate such things and he would never allow himself to enjoy anything outside of his proper realm. He was a good assistant, though. When it came to discharging the duties of our office, I would have no other person assisting me.

Laryn's academy, the Westminster School, had gone to great lengths to keep the horse track well-tended. All the obstacles were clean, bright white with red markings comprising of the school crest and were properly positioned at their designated heights. Despite the puddles from the rain earlier in the day, the grassy stretches still held together and remained a lush green. I shifted in my hard seat among the other spectators as I saw Laryn mounting her horse in the preliminary section of the course. Her hair was neatly tucked into her riding helm and her black coat was neatly pressed and buttoned to the brim. Daphne was traveling out of the country for business and would be gone for nearly a month. It was only logical that Laryn stay with me during this time. All my children had Daphne's dark hair color, but only Laryn had my blue eyes and a kindness that would soften the hardest of soldiers. I loved all my children, but she was my heart.

Sometimes I thought that I chose the wrong career by going into Parliament. I have always held the House of Commons in high reverence, and I admired my colleagues for the work that they performed for the betterment of the land. Perhaps if I would have chosen to stay a businessman instead, I would've been able to salvage my marriage and it wouldn't have put such a strain upon our three children. I could've stayed at home more often, I thought. My financial planning business earned a decent income, but it was small. It was not until I put in the hours of my legislative work that I afforded many opportunities for our children. Grayson, now twenty-four years old and a graduate of the Royal Military Academy Sandhurst, was currently serving as a Lieutenant in the British Army. Codie was nineteen years old and a student at the University of Cambridge. They may not have had these opportunities if I hadn't acquired the position that I did. I still own the financial business, except I don't see clients anymore and most of the day-to-day dealings are under the control of my former partner, Ashland Simmons.

On less formal terms, my sons and I have been blessed with many hunting trips and vacations. I am happy knowing that I have been able to indulge my children's passions, especially with Laryn. She was only eleven when her mother and I separated. I know it was hard on her, but I have always been impressed with how well she has been able to compose herself at the age of fifteen, especially with her horse. Most adults that have been trained in equestrian have not been able to match her accomplishments on the track. In the case of my wife, I promised myself that I would not alienate my children the way I did my wife. They will only know the caring and compassionate side of me. I've *never* missed one of Laryn's competitions.

"Henry, I think she's about to ride," I stated, nudging him to pay attention.

"I-see-her," he said, barely looking up from his phone.

Many of the horses were having trouble with the wet conditions. It caused them to be slow and occasionally throw their riders to the ground as they landed from a jump. I could feel my heart quicken as I saw the quarter horse lead Laryn and her horse to the release point of the track. The starting signal sounded, and her horse sprang into action. Cheers erupted from the crowd as the horse cleared the first obstacle with ease. The seconds climbed as they quickly turned over the first minute of her time. Laryn urged her horse to pick up speed as she maneuvered through the course. Hastily, she approached the portion of the course that fostered most of the difficulty for the other riders. She spurred the horse as though she knew none of the troubles the riders before her had had with this particular jump. Only seconds after her horse made its final canter, it bounded into the air, clearing the four-foot obstacle, and landed with a thud from its front hooves safely on the other side. Again, cheers burst from the on-lookers and I, myself, was also standing and cheering. With Laryn crossing the finish line, I could feel the tension in my chest start to subside as I breathed a long, satisfying breath. Though the time on the clock was not her best time on this particular course, it was enough to move her into the lead since her horse was such a good mudder.

"Bravo!" I shouted. "Well, done! Come Henry, we shall meet her by the stables."

Henry, without saying a word, simply stood and followed me as I made my way towards Laryn. Much of the crowd knew that Laryn had made a good run, good enough to possibly win the competition. Many were massing around her. This made it increasingly more difficult to get to her in a timely fashion. Ultimately, the sea of people parted and standing before me was my beautiful daughter, virtually covered from head to toe in mud. Her black riding coat was now a dark brown color as well as her white pants. The only thing that was not completely covered in mud was the small patch of skin around her eyes that was covered by her goggles. Her vibrant blues eyes shone through all the filth and lit up like lamp posts when she saw that I was there. A great smile beamed forth as she moved towards me.

"Father!" she shouted. "I'm so glad you could make it! Did you see me ride?"

She wrapped her arms around my torso completely ignoring the fact she was covered in mud. "Yes, of course I saw you ride. You were brilliant! I wouldn't have missed it for ANY-thing!" I said as I glanced at Henry.

He did not appear to notice my look or simply chose not to acknowledge it. He merely stared at his smartphone, obviously enthralled with an important text message or e-mail.

"Do you think it will be enough to win the competition?" Laryn asked in a hopeful manner.

"You know, I think it might. But there are still two more riders that have to run the course," I responded, just as hopeful.

The first of the two riders lost control of her horse after the first hurdle and veered off the course, resulting in an automatic disqualification. The second horse and its mount managed to work their way through the course, safely completing obstacle after obstacle. The crowd held its breath as the rider spurred the horse to go faster as it neared the finish line; however, the effort of the rider wasn't enough. She finished two whole seconds behind Laryn's time. The crowd cheered wildly. Laryn could hardly contain herself as she jumped up and down, screaming with joy. Her dark hair fell from the back of her riding helmet causing her to pause for a moment to make it proper again. My heart pounded and I felt emotions welling up inside of me. I, too, was overjoyed by her victory.

Several of Laryn's classmates and onlookers swarmed her. She looked up at me and through a mud-covered face beamed a glorious smile. "Go my dear…enjoy your victory! I am very proud of you." I said.

Henry clapped as though he did not want to abandon the proper etiquette and risk being called upon for such. As if routine, he pulled a handkerchief from inside his suit coat and gestured to wipe the mud from my suit, "Sir, may I?"

"Henry, piss off! I don't need you to wipe my bum every time a speck of dirt lands on my clothing."

"Sir, I'm only worried about the image that you may portray since it is more than a speck of dirt and since we are still in the public spotlight," he responded.

"I'm not worried about my suit or my image. Lord knows the photographers have captured me in much worse. We'll stop at the office, if it makes you feel better. I have dozens of suits and pullovers there. Better yet, how about we just wait 'til we get back to the estate; I bet I've got plenty of clean clothes there. I don't believe we have any other engagements today, except you can take my suit to be dry-cleaned at your leisure, since you are so concerned about it. For now, I'm more concerned about tending to my daughter and sharing in her victory." I gave Henry a disapproving glance. We turned away from the track and walked towards my car and the driver that was waiting.

"Very well, sir!" he responded without much of a fuss, ignoring my sarcasm.

"Does Laryn know to meet us at the limo?" I asked making sure the trivial business about my waistcoat and jacket was over and that we should move on to more pressing matters.

"I'll make sure she knows," he responded quickly. One thing about Henry, even though he was apt to share his opinion, which I did appreciate at times, he also knew when to leave a situation alone. Henry walked towards Laryn where she was being showered with praises and awards, but stopped, "Oh and sir…I nearly forgot. Grayson had phoned into your office to inform us that a week from Thursday next he will be home on holiday."

"Excellent!" I responded. "Place a call to Codie at Cambridge to see if he will also be able to come home. We'll arrange to go to the resort home and make an extended weekend of it."

Henry nodded in acknowledgement as he turned to walk back towards the crowd of onlookers that praised the medal winners. The sun finally made its way passed the dark clouds overhead. It made the temperature feel warmer than it was. Warm enough to cause me to take my coat off and drape it over my arm. The muddy spots on the coat were already beginning to dry and crumble off. I stared from a distance as the course judges draped a golden medal around Laryn's neck, announcing her name to the crowd one last time as their champion. A smile spread across my face as I crossed my arms with an overwhelming sense of pride.

CHAPTER #9

Father Preston Mathew's Log

Saturday, November 14, 2009

Over two weeks have passed, and I find myself still intrigued by Dr. Mya Bishop. I wonder whether she will be present for her monthly confession. Her state of mind the last time we talked had more emotions than our usual discussions. Though I had resolved to be patient and wait for her next visit, I have tried phoning her office line at the university. I am afraid to say that I was not fortunate enough to talk with her.

After two lengthy voice messages, I resigned myself to visit her office to see if I could speak with her in person. It was my hope that her busy lifestyle simply did not afford her the time to respond to my voice messages. Upon arriving at the university, I was met with disappointment, but I did have the good opportunity to be confronted by a gentleman by the name of William Garris. Being the Dean of the College of Arts and Humanities, he informed me that Dr. Bishop has not been back to her office in over two weeks. He also stated that she had cancelled her lectures on the Friday before Halloween and has not been seen at her office since. Paperwork indicated that she had put in for medical leave. Dean Garris indicated that he has known Dr. Bishop for an extended period of time and seemed just as concerned about her as I was. He claimed that he has tried to reach her by e-mail as well as by phone at her estate. Both were unsuccessful.

I fear that Dr. Bishop may have slipped into a state of depression or anxiety. She continues to blame herself for things that I feel were beyond her control. However, I still believe she has not been forthcoming with all the details surrounding the death of her family. Despite my continued efforts, I was still unable to gather any information about the accident she speaks of except for a funeral announcement for her mother Cassandra. I shall call the local medical facilities and if I am unsuccessful, I shall be steadfast in making time to visit her at her home. I don't want to intrude on her private life, but I find it very odd to abruptly sever all communications with one's work associates as well as friends. I pray that God has mercy on His servant and that I may be used as a vehicle to help her with the struggles she faces.

- Rev. Preston Mathew S.J.

CHAPTER #10

Diagnosis
Mya
Sunday, November 15, 2009
8:20 a.m.

I watched carefully over the past several days as Marcus made his observations and collected his data about me. At first, he seemed hesitant and overly cautious, avoiding much of my gaze. He insisted that I sleep in the cage at night. The hard floor has been dreadfully uncomfortable. I guess I could not blame him. Who wouldn't be nervous around me, considering what I was and what I have done? I was pleased to see over the past week and a half he has grown more and more secure with the notion that I was only going to change into a werewolf if the full moon was out. *Fortunately, we have a couple more weeks before that happens again,* I thought. I could tell that he too has not been sleeping well. Dark circles have formed around his eyes, and his mannerisms seem slow and laborious.

We were lucky that Marcus brought with him his laptop computer and recording devices. I purchased for him two different microscopes which have allowed him to begin analyzing my blood. He is still going to have other items flown in from Australia; specifically, a device that he and his team of researchers developed to collect information about the wild dogs they have studied in the past. He mentioned that he wanted to try out the device on other animals since they were so successful with collecting information on the Australian dogs. I have a feeling though, that he did not have the intention of using it on something like me. Nonetheless, I am hopeful that this will yield some sort of understanding, some sort of pathway for us to follow. He sat in the chair across from my desk looking a bit contemplative before saying, "My belongings should arrive in another day or so. Then I'll be able to collect more information about your vitals on a more consistent basis."

"What've you found so far?" I asked, realizing that he had not shared much with me since he began collecting data.

"Well, unfortunately, not much at all. I checked your heart rate, body temperature, the chemical makeup of your blood and your sensory responses to stimuli, but nothing has really come up that we didn't already assume or know."

"Meaning...?" I probed.

"We already knew that you have stronger senses and enhanced strength, yet there is no understanding as to why. On the other hand, it is clear that your heart rate is constantly elevated," he started. "It stays in the range of 120 to 135 beats per minute. I've observed this for about a week at various times. In humans, this would be cause for alarm. If a human gets a heart rate that high it's usually brought on by some sort of stimuli, something that has made them afraid or very angry. Perhaps even a genetic condition that would require medication. With you this isn't the case. Your high heart rate is consistent; however, with the many canines I've personally studied, it's not that odd for them to maintain the same heart rate. This adds to the reason why canines of all sorts are better hunters than humans. Having such a high heart rate produces adrenaline, making the senses more acute."

"So, in other words, you are saying that this is why my senses are enhanced all the time?"

"Possibly," he responded. "In addition to your elevated heart rate, you also have an increased body temperature. When considering all aspects of your...your condition, it's important to note that your body temperature may also contribute to your high heart rate and vice versa. Again, in humans, having a high temperature indicates an infection. Thus, it produces a higher heart rate."

"You don't believe that me being a werewolf is a...disease?"

"I thought it might be at first. When I analyzed your blood, I was looking for abnormalities, parasites, anything that would seem unusual or indicate a disease. Everything came back normal. There were no signs of infection or abnormalities at all. I even checked your blood against what I know about that of a dingo's..." he paused before continuing. "I'm afraid to say that the two had no similarities whatsoever. I'll be able to know for sure when my equipment arrives, and I can cross-reference other samples I've taken of dingoes in the past. Even though you're experiencing a high heart rate, high body temperature, and even increased senses, much like that of a canine, your blood...as far as I can tell, is 100% human. Like I said, it isn't anything that we didn't already know or assume and we're no closer to finding out why you change into a werewolf. The only clear thing is that you take on internal canine characteristics despite remaining in human form."

Marcus got up from the seat and walked to the opposite side of the den, pacing, as though he was deep in thought, trying to figure out the answer to an unsolvable problem. "Have you been getting enough sleep?" I finally asked to break the silence.

"Nah, it's difficult to sleep when we're no closer to a solution. I suspect it's going to be like this for a while," he responded rather solemnly. Marcus turned to face me as though something had occurred to him that had previously escaped him. Without saying a word, he promptly made his way over to the chair he was sitting in and pulled from his satchel my diary and began thumbing through the pages. Several moments went by before he spoke, "This doesn't make sense. Mya, after you were bitten you wrote in your diary that you experienced strange occurrences. Do you still experience these episodes of strangeness?"

"Are you referring to when I went for long walks and didn't remember them, or when my sister saw me eating raw meat in the kitchen of the manor?" I asked.

"Yes, those incidents. Do you remember feeling a heightened sense of anxiety or adrenaline? Have you had any other experiences like those?"

"No, I don't remember and…no, I haven't had any more." I answered. "Since then, I felt as though I have had more control over myself; except, of course, when the moon is full."

"It would be fair to assume that whatever makes you change also made you stronger every month thereafter, more in control?" he half asked, half told.

"Yes, I suppose so," I said matter-of-factly. "What are you getting at?"

"I don't know. I was just wondering why that was the only time you had those kinds of experiences. Why is it that only the moon causes you to lose control now?"

I hesitated before I answered. I wasn't sure whether he was legitimately asking or simply thinking aloud. "I have my theories," I finally said.

Never before had I talked with anyone so directly about this subject. So many times students in my lectures would flock to me in order to hear what I had to say about this particular topic. I would avoid these inquiries most of the time, or provide answers that I did not really believe, but this time was different. I had to explain my thoughts.

"Please, tell me…nothing at this point should be considered out of the question." His voice was intense.

He sat staring at me, listening to what I was about to say. I took a deep breath and began, "Throughout history, the moon has captured the imagination and curiosity of most living things. Wolves, from what I know, are no different. They hunt ferociously during the full moon because it provides better hunting conditions and most nocturnal prey are moving about more so than normal. I've come to find out that wolves are very efficient hunters and when they reach their prey a sort of frenzy occurs, a bloodlust so to speak."

"Yes, I've observed the same with the dingoes in Australia," Marcus cut in.

"Humans are no exception to this. Ask anyone who works consistently with the public for any amount of time; they'll tell you that bizarre things occur that don't normally happen unless the moon is full. It even affects the tides. With the human body being 70% water, how do you think it affects us? Considering the full moon's effect on human beings, it's fair to assume that a sort of frenzy may occur with us too."

"By frenzy, I would think that it involves an adrenaline rush of some kind. Heightening the senses of a person and causing them to act out in ways uncharacteristic to their nature?" Marcus asked.

"Again, this is just my theory, but based on what you have confirmed over the last couple of weeks it seems more plausible."

"Then if the frenzy, or adrenaline rush, that a wild dog feels is combined with that of a human you would get a stark raving lunatic, completely incapable of controlling their actions."

"Precisely," I said, confirming his notion.

"If this is actually the reason why you become out of control during the full moon, then there would have to also be some kind of aftereffects."

"After changing into a werewolf, it usually takes a day or so before I regain my strength fully."

"I would suppose it would be from the amount of adrenaline that is flowing through your body at one time and sustaining it for an entire night means you expend a lot of energy," Marcus added.

"I agree. I also feel that this is how silver may affect werewolves more so than anything else."

"How so?" he asked.

"Well, if a person is experiencing an adrenaline rush, as you pointed out, their heart rate is going to increase, body temperature may become elevated thus increasing the amount of energy the person expends. The same must be true with wild dogs," I explained.

"It is. I think I follow. Go on."

"When energy is used in the body, our brains are directing it to our bodily systems via chemical neurotransmitters through neural impulses. These impulses control heart rate, lungs, brain activity. The heart, lungs, and the brain are essentially controlled by these impulses even when the person is not experiencing a surge of adrenaline." Marcus nodded in agreement. "In order for me to even change into a werewolf, I would have to have a lot of energy stored in my body. So, if a silver bullet passes through my heart, lungs, or brain it would disrupt the neural impulses causing brain death, the heart to stop beating, or a collapse of my lungs."

Marcus sat processing my theory. A look of intensity spread across his face. "What you're referring to is the parasympathetic and sympathetic nervous system responses. The sympathetic responses occur when the body's in danger or experiences an adrenaline rush. All the blood and energy gets directed to the vital organ systems…fight or flight syndrome. But wouldn't a normal copper or lead bullet do the same thing?" he asked, his curiosity increasing exponentially.

"In humans, yes…in wolves, yes…the combination of the two species…I don't know. I haven't been willing to test this theory in its entirety for obvious reasons. I can still be harmed as a human. I conducted a small experiment on my hand." Inquisitive, Marcus leaned forward. I pressed on before he could respond to my abnormal statement, "After the time I tried to overdose on tranquilizers and failed, I was desperate for something to work. I poked my hand with a normal letter opener. It pinched, but wasn't excruciating like one might think. A second attempt was made, only this time I used authentic silverware. As I poked my hand with a fork, the pain was something that I couldn't bear. My entire arm felt a shock wave and a burning pain that took several hours to recede. I know that we don't have electricity pulsing through our bodies, but when I poked my hand with the silver fork, it felt like there was. Both times I poked my hand it left a scar. I didn't attempt any other experiments involving silver thereafter."

"Perhaps we need to look at that situation from a physics and thermodynamic perspective."

"You're not suggesting that electricity is actually inside of me like the power lines, are you?"

"No, I was thinking more so of thermal conduction. Though silver is the best conductor of electricity, it's also the best thermal conductor, too. What may have happened with the fork was that you conducted the heat energy within your arm. Since your neural impulses resemble electrical pulses within the body, it would feel like an electrical shock if you interrupted the pathway. Added to that, the burning sensation you had probably was the result of heat conduction. May I see the scars on your hand?"

"No…strangely both marks disappeared completely the next time I changed into a werewolf. It was as though it had never happened."

"Hmmm…perhaps it's also something with cell growth." Marcus sighed and brought his hand to his chin, letting his eyes drop towards the ground. Several quiet moments passed before he slumped back into the leather chair in my den. Without looking at me, Marcus began rambling questions, "Does the moon cause all this energy? Where does the energy come from? Why a wolf? Why do you change into a wolf-like creature instead of something else?"

I paused again for several moments before interjecting, "As history would have it, the wolf has been man's top hunting rival for centuries. Wolves have also invoked more fear in humans than any other creature. Ultimately, I don't quite know. It's an answer that I've been seeking for nearly a century. It's the supernatural element I can't explain. I'm sure when we fully discover the answer to that question, we'll also be able to explain most of everything else I've experienced."

"Have you ever run into any other werewolves?" Marcus asked, skillfully guiding the current line of thought back to something I could address easily.

"Not since I was attacked," I replied. "I suspect some are out there, but my fear is that as time rolls by all written records of such creatures and their origins will be lost. The more humanity can discredit happenings of the past with scientific facts of today, the less likely it becomes that I'll find the supernatural answers I seek in written form. Marcus, if for nothing else than to properly record the facts about me, this is why I sought your help."

Chapter #11

Two years now…for two years I've been fighting this war in Afghanistan. Most think there's no real end in sight. Bullocks! I thought. As a Lieutenant of a special-forces platoon in the Royal Army, my team and I carried out some of the riskier missions, some of which were not exactly reported. Our term of service had reached its end, but my crew had opted to extend it to continue to carry out these kinds of missions. If they were all unanimous with their decision to press forward in this war, I had pledged to remain with them. *Many of my best mates had fallen for unworthy causes. My platoon's commitment isn't only worthwhile it'll yield favorable results with the war effort.* I recommended that the chaps take a long weekend of much needed R&R and a good drink at the pub to think matters through before committing to such a feat.

The air was much cooler than what I was normally accustomed. Bits of sunlight tried to take their place in the sky, as I took in a deep breath of foggy London air. It felt good to be standing on my home soil. I positioned my military cap upon my head, tucked the remaining bits of my dark brown hair under the rim, and slung my duffle over my shoulder before making my way from the tarmac to the outdoor terminal. Glancing back at the military cargo plane we rode in on, I noticed that some of my mates were already greeted by loved ones. For me, I suspected that my father had already made arrangements for me to be driven from Heathrow to his estate just outside of London, in Hertford. Once inside the terminal, I steadily made my way passed several individuals in suits, reading the morning paper, waiting to catch their flights.

Despite the morning hour, many people were entrenched in conversation. Most of the different languages being spoken I didn't recognize. The ones I did came from being in Afghanistan, others by simply observing their outward nationality. Most were looking to travel during the holiday time. The smell of coffee and other breakfast items permeated the inside space. Though I was hungry, I pressed passed the various breakfast stations, knowing full well that a car was probably waiting on me and punctuality had been and always will be a virtue my father respected.

I had no need to go to luggage claim, one of the advantages of being on a military transport. Besides, I was not going to be home for that long and all my belongings I needed were in my duffle. On the other side of the airport, taxis raced to and fro, dropping off and picking up passengers. It was quite a change from the hectic trafficking in Afghanistan. There we had to check every car that went through a road checkpoint with sniffer dogs to make sure they weren't carrying car bombs or looking to plant Improvised Explosive Devices. On the same note, the likelihood that some fearsome force was going to try to overthrow the checkpoint was drastically reduced here in London. It was at this point that I heard a familiar voice, "You scraggly bastard! What the hell are you doing show'n up all fancy in your uniform?"

I turned to see a young bloke with the same dark hair as me, casually dressed, walking in my direction. "Well, I wouldn't expect a civy like you to understand. For the record, I know who both my mother and father are, and just 'cause they're not together doesn't make me a bastard! But since you insist on calling me that, the same must be true of you…brother!" I said with a bit of a smirk.

"Some things never change. You always were the calculated one!" he said as he embraced me.

"Always good to see you too, Codie!" I accepted his jovial comment in stride.

He offered to take my duffle and I was more than happy to oblige. "Dear God, what on earth do you have in this thing? I would swear it has got two, maybe three bodies in it. No wonder you've nearly doubled in size since I last saw you."

He waddled over to a BMW that was parked along the curb with its flashers on. Though five years separated Codie and me, I have always had a playful affection towards him. Different than my comrades I serve with in the army, but no less significant. It was the difference between friends and family. I sat down in the front seat of the car, placing my cap across my lap as he secured the duffle in the trunk. Moments later we were speeding away from the curb, enough so that it caused me to grab the handle above my door. "You're right Codie, some things never change. You always were the crazy one!"

"Dah!!! You just need to learn how to relax!" he spat back at me, continuing to speed along the road. "All this military stuff has got you wound too tight."

Ignoring his comment, I tried to change the subject. "So how have you come to bear this terrible burden of picking me up at such an early hour?"

"Dad thought it would be better than the normal driver. Besides, I was happy to volunteer. It has been quite some time since we have seen each other; nevertheless, it still took three cups of tea before my eyes could open properly. Even though I'm home on a brief holiday from school, I've not adapted fully from the college life," he explained.

"Dad mentioned in his last letter that you're a student at Cambridge?" I asked. "That's pretty good, right?"

"Yeah, I am…more so because dad wanted it. I don't mind though; it's a good school and I'm having a lot of fun. Did you know there are lots of pubs like Bird in Hand and Corner House on Newmarket Road by the school? I've been to just about all of the others too," he said proudly.

"Isn't the point of schooling to *learn* rather than to drink?" I responded, knowing full well that there is nothing on the planet like a good drink of hand-crafted English ale at the pub.

"Hey, I'm learning…I can tell the difference between most English and Scottish ales, porters and stouts." He chuckled. "Ah! It's not as much as you think. Most of the time, my mates and I go after football, which only occurs on Tuesdays and Thursdays. Besides, Political Science is as an area of study that doesn't require much, at least not at this point."

Codie had always admired dad for his work and no doubt his lifestyle. Rather than pursuing reasons for his choice of study I merely changed the subject again. "Are you planning on playing with your mates today?" I asked, half hoping to maybe play in a match. After the plane ride, it would be good to get out into the cool air and run a bit. I also wanted to have some more time with Codie. Playing football has always been a common ground between he and I.

"No, dad said we're heading to the weekend estate. He said that we have much to celebrate, with you coming home and Laryn winning her competition. He also said that he's hoping to do some hunting with us," he uttered as he continued to beep at cars moving much slower than we were.

"Competition, what kind of competition?"

"Equestrian…you know, horse-back riding."

"Yah, I know what it is."

"Apparently, she has become quite good. Good enough to compete at a regional level. MOVE OUT OF THE WAY YOU BLOODY ASS!" he shouted as we moved close to the tail end of another car.

So much had changed. Laryn was only eleven years old when I left for basic training and was just learning how to ride. Now she was winning competitions. Codie was only part of the way through his public schooling, whereas now he was a college student at Cambridge. Worst of all, mum and dad were still together. *Perhaps if I would've been around and helped out more when dad was gone for work…nah, it wouldn't have done a bit of good. Mum left for her own reasons, it had nothing to do with me.* I could not blame dad either. He did all that he could to try and work through things. Unfortunately, it was not enough in mum's eyes. I was glad they were still on amicable terms and that he still got to see Laryn a fair amount.

It did not take long, especially with Codie's driving, before we pulled in front of Dad's large brick estate. The morning light was now full in the sky, and the day had the makings of being clear and pleasant. I stepped from the car noticing everything was in good order. A chilling breeze blew across my face. Before I could even place my cap back on my head, out ran a dark-haired girl, shouting, "Grayson! Grayson, is it really you?"

Laryn wrapped her arms around my waist and squeezed tightly, knocking me off balance. "My goodness Laryn, you've grown!"

She stepped back and did a bit of twirl as if to show how much. Laryn was no longer the little girl I had left behind so long ago. Standing before me was a beautiful young lady, full of spirit and happiness. "Have you heard, Grayson?" she asked.

"About your competition? Yes! Codie told me on the way here. I'm so happy for you!" I stopped as I glanced upwards to catch another figure making his way towards me.

"Welcome home, Lieutenant!" the gruff-looking man said. I stood upright as we shook hands, and he placed his other hand on my shoulder. It had been almost four years since I had seen him. He seemed calmer, though aged. More silver spread across his hairline than before. I could only speculate it was from the absence of my mother, more so than the nature of his work in parliament. "Do come inside, all of you! We've a wonderful breakfast prepared and after such we'll be heading to the resort estate for the weekend," he said with a smile and distinct level of excitement.

"Sir!" I said, not realizing that I was so formal. Dad paused as if taken back; perhaps he sensed that I had already traveled a very long way and would be content to stay here. "Is it best to go to the resort estate given that it's so late in the year already? Isn't the community closed for the season due to unpredictable weather patterns?"

"Nonsense!" Codie blurted out. "Boy, they really got you balled up in knots, don't they?"

"Knock it off, Codie," Dad thwarted his effort to verbally abuse me. "My assistant Henry has already made preparations for us to be there. Horse wranglers have already been sent with Laryn's horse so that she may get some riding time this weekend. Henry also checked the forecast and mentioned that we are in for a clear, but cool, weekend."

The fact that most sensible people wouldn't think to go north to a heavily forested region this late in the year never occurred to him. My father has always had a knack for arranging special privileges for his family, sparing no expense in most cases. I felt that he sometimes gets blinded by the excitement of his family members all together.

My father continued his ramblings about how fantastic the weather was going to be. "We may also have the good fortune of hunting during the time of the full moon. This actually makes for wonderful conditions, since most things stir a bit more in the moonlight," he finished.

Despite the weariness of my trip home and the reasons behind my trip, I reluctantly agreed to go.

Chapter #12

<pre>
The Charm
Mya
Thursday, November 26, 2009
11:00 a.m.
</pre>

Since the arrival of his equipment from Australia, Marcus has not referred to our conversation we had last week. He only explained briefly that he had to cross-reference the discoveries about me with regular wolves and dingoes and that it was going to take some time to be sure about his conclusions. For the past week and a half, Marcus had hardly moved from his computer. When he did move it was only to continue staring through the microscopes that were set up in the main library.

I suspected he still had not slept much. I caught him nodding off at his computer or momentarily dosing at his workspace on the table. Many times, I have awakened Marcus from a sound sleep to bring him a brew of tea. At first, he seemed to be apologetic for not working or even startled that I was awake, and he was not. However, fatigue had finally started to take its toll. Instead of being startled or even apologetic, he simply rubs his face, thanked me for the tea and continued working.

"Marcus, I think you need to take the rest of the day off from your work. You're no good to me if you burn yourself out." I sat down across from him at one of the tables in the library. I placed the tea pot by the edge of the table.

He nodded in appreciation and slowly began to sip the hot tea, blowing on it to cool the liquid before it touched his lips. After a few sips he said, "Mya, you know I can't stop working. I'm no further than I was a week ago and this weekend there's another full moon."

"I understand," I responded, accepting the fact that he was not going to give into rest. "Have you at least been able to confirm some of the things we discussed last week?"

"Yes. Your heart rate, body temperature, and even your increased abilities and senses all line up with that of the canine species. Nevertheless, your actual blood remains human and does not resemble the DNA makeup of any kind of canine that I've observed, studied, or even referenced over the last couple of weeks. I still can't fully prove the thermal conduction theory either." He placed his teacup on the large wooden table as he stood. Marcus slowly walked around the library, looking up at the many volumes shelved from the floor to the ceiling. He mumbled as he scanned the books, "I just don't know…there has to be something we're missing."

The books contained much of the history I had been studying for nearly a century. Many of the books had not been touched in years and were covered with a thick coating of dust. He continued walking around the library as if pondering which volume he wanted to pull from the shelves, yet still he was obviously preoccupied with his immediate dilemma. Marcus paused momentarily to glance at a particular book before shooting me a look. He pulled the book from the shelf and slammed it down on the table. A bang echoed up to the top of the vaulted ceiling followed by a relatively large cloud of dust. The title simply read Medieval Curses. Marcus thumbed through the book. "I'm approaching this all wrong." After several pages and pausing to read a few here and there, he slammed it shut and yelled, "DAMN!"

"What were you looking for?" He did not respond. He merely sat at the table with his hand covering part of his mouth, staring away from me deep in thought. "What is it?"

"Do you still have the charm you spoke of in your diary?" he finally asked, ignoring my questions. "…the one of the Archangel Michael?"

"Yes, of course. Like my diary, it's one of my most valued items," I said solemnly. "Why do you ask?"

"Well, a thought occurred to me that perhaps the supernatural element we're looking for pertains to a curse. Being an Aborigine, I've a few memories of the elders from my tribe that spoke of curses. Most of the time it was for simple things. Natural remedies and man-made amulets were used to ward off unwanted things, like bug infestations of crops, pollution of our water source, and the like. Occasionally, there would be curses to keep dingoes away from our livestock, but only rarely was a curse geared towards humans."

"What do you mean rarely? What kind of curse?"

"Bone pointing…I only saw it once before I went on my walkabout. I was too young to understand the ritual. An elder pointed a thin sliver of bone at some people believed to be the same extremists that had been harassing my tribe. What kind of bone…I don't know. I learned later that the ritual was supposed to be full-proof, never supposed to fail…it's kind of a mark of death. Only the *Kurdaitcha* could do it."

"The *Kurdaitcha*…you mean ritual killers?"

"Yes…" Marcus sipped his tea. "It was ironic that when I was on my walkabout, my tribe was virtually annihilated by the group of extremists that was supposedly marked for death. At first, I thought the curse failed or that it was performed wrong since it was 1974 and most of these practices had died out earlier in the century. On the other hand, one could say that the curse did work; just not on those who were being condemned. There were a lot of people that didn't want to see equal rights for the aboriginal people, but most of the activist movements were completed in the 1960s. Many people were practicing tolerance, and were innocent of the crimes performed by the extremists…May I see your charm?"

I slid my hands around to the back of my neck and unhinged the golden clasp of the thin chain that held the charm. Hesitantly, I extended my hand to give Marcus the charm, "I have studied many things involving the *damned*. Why do you think this has something to do with a curse?"

"I'm not sure. I remember many people, children, and adults, at my orphanage praying to Michael for protection. I would assume that would include protection from curses, too. Praying to the Archangel Michael is not too different from the practices in my tribe. Besides, it was Michael who threw Satan out of heaven, and it's widely believed that Satan is the source of all the curses in the world."

"Are you Catholic?" I asked.

"Me, nah. In fact, I've never been very religious. The orphanage I was taken to for medical treatment after my dingo attack was run by Father Joseph, a Catholic Priest. My beliefs come from what I've been able to study and observe, only just recently have I started to consider there is something more. Besides, I didn't stay long at the orphanage before I was adopted by my white foster parents. They named me Marcus and said that having a Christian name was good enough in terms of religion. I did learn that there were some good people in the world outside of my tribe, both religious and non-religious. My foster parents owned a cattle ranch and didn't put much faith into anything other than their cattle," he rambled on as he inspected the charm with great interest. He handed it back to me, "I don't know what I was looking for; perhaps I was just hoping for something. Thank you…why do you value this charm so much, is it for sentimental reasons?"

"Yes, that is part of it. The last person to touch this charm other than you was Brayden, my fiancé. He kept it safe," I said as I trailed off from the subject of Brayden. "I also treasure this because of my beliefs as a Catholic."

"Do you think it gives you protection?" Marcus asked.

"After the death of my family, I spent many months and years traveling as a nomad, fleeing every time the full moon came around. Eventually, I made my way across many parts of Western Europe. This continued until I found refuge in a monastery in Germany. Not fully understanding my condition, the sisters of the monastery encouraged me to have faith in God and to pray to the Archangel Michael for protection on my journey since I wore the charm. I did for a while. Some say that the battle between the Archangel Michael and Satan is going on even today. I thought that perhaps the Archangel Michael would help rid the evil within me though I have trouble believing in it anymore. To me, the battle lines have become blurred. I was wearing it when I was attacked…this is the most common depiction of him, holding his sword high above a demon," I said pointing to the charm. "I wasn't supposed to become the demon."

"Perhaps because you were wearing it is the reason why you're still alive."

"Alive! There isn't a day that goes by that I don't wish I would've died that night in the stables. My family's DEAD because of me!" I slammed my fist to the table.

Marcus scampered to his feet and quickly backed away from me. "Please, I didn't mean to offend you. I'm merely pointing out that there may be more of a reason as to why you're alive."

At that moment, Marcus had a complete look of fright on his face. I could hear his heart beating faster and I could smell the fear-induced perspiration on his body. It took several more moments before I turned away from him, realizing what had just happened. "Marcus, I'm sorry…please, sit back down. I don't know what came over me."

During my outburst, I had spilled the remaining tea that was in Marcus' cup on the table and the pot had fallen to the floor. I walked out of the library, across the hall to the closet, to get some rags. Upon my return, I found Marcus still standing away from the table watching me closely. I quickly wiped up the tea and placed the metal teapot back on the table, but before I could do anything else, Marcus said, "I understand why you can't talk about that, and I won't bring it up any further."

Cautiously, he walked over to where his equipment was set up in the library and rummaged around for a moment or two before walking back towards the table. Still very guarded, he held out a small device in his hand. It was no bigger than a small paper clip with an oval shape. "This is the device that my team of researchers has helped develop. When inserted into the body, it acts as a tracking device, but it also sends back readings of all the vitals systems within the animal to this central monitor." He pointed to a netbook device. I listened intently as he continued, "We used these on the Australian dingoes so that we could track a packs whereabouts, but also to see what excited their behavior. Naturally, this information can be used for a number of reasons, mainly for farmers and cattle ranchers. I would like to insert this under your skin to see what kind of readings it produces…"

He paused, as if what he was about to say was going to be met with opposition, "I want to see what kind of readings it produces after you've changed into a werewolf. To see what excites your behavior while in that form."

"I don't know…" I said before he interrupted.

"I'm going to have to get a complete reading, one that is more than just a few moments long."

"Marcus, even though the cage is strong, if something happens and I get out then you won't survive," I explained.

"I know I won't survive it, that's why I'm going to be a good distance away when you change."

"Will it still work the same if no one is around to excite my behavior?"

"I thought about that, and the answer is probably no."

"Then it won't do any good…"

"Unless you're out in the wild when you change," he said, avoiding my gaze. "I could bait you into an area and then shoot you with the tranquilizer gun from a safe distance. We've done this sort of thing before in Australia."

"No, absolutely not! There are too many things that can go wrong. What if someone happens to be around for whatever reason and I go after them instead of the bait?"

"That is a risk, so we're probably going to have to go to a secluded region to avoid any contact with other humans. Do you know of any places that we can get to within a day? We could leave tonight since the full moon won't be out until about 9:00 p.m. tomorrow night?"

"Marcus, this is crazy. I respect your methods and we're making progress, but this is out of the question!"

"Mya, by doing this we may gain a better understanding as to why you change into a werewolf. As of right now, if we don't do anything different, we're going to be stuck with the same results we've gotten over the past three weeks or so. I need to study you in your supernatural state." A confident authority escaped with his words. "The second night I observed you, there was no change because you were heavily sedated and there was nothing to excite your behavior, not even the moon because your senses were too dull to recognize it. You said yourself that the times you avoided the moonlight you were able to avoid changing into a werewolf. There are pieces to this puzzle that are missing. We need to know what happens when the moon is full, and you're not caged. That information could lead us to answers that aren't in any of the books in your library. You also said that you wanted me to properly record the information about you being a werewolf; without this data, there will be nothing new to document."

"I have committed too many atrocities during the time I've been alive. My soul cannot afford to take any more risks that will condemn it to hell." Tears welled up in my eyes.

"There has to be some place we can go? It's late in the year and I'm sure that not many people are going to be looking to go for a nighttime stroll in the woods," he said, somewhat ignoring my plight.

As much risk as there was with this proposition, I knew Marcus was right…we had to do something different to yield different results. I stood up and turned away from him, hanging my head as I rubbed the charm of the Archangel Michael, "Please tell me no one will get hurt and that you can actually pull this off?"

"I have a night vision scope that I've already mounted to the tranquilizer gun that will be able to see you in the dark for up to a half a kilometer away and by inserting this device into you I'll be able to know exactly where you are," he explained as he loaded the small device into a pressurized mechanism. "Once you get close enough to the bait, I'll be able to drop you within twenty yards of it. Since we already know that the tranquilizer formula won't kill you, I'll also increase the dose of it so that all I need is one shot to bring you down."

"What are you going to use as bait?" I asked, turning towards him.

He gently grasped my left wrist causing me to expose the inner part of my arm. The mechanism was cool to touch against the muscle but caused a stinging sensation as he pressed the button that shot the smaller device under my skin in the middle of my forearm. Marcus looked up at me as I rubbed the spot of the injection. "Me. I'll be the bait. You're risking everything by doing this; it's only fair that I have just as much to risk for coming up with the idea."

"Marcus, you can't!"

"I said I'll help you, so unless you have a better idea…"

I paused a moment before I replied, "I might."

The next day we drove six hours to a remote location in Northeast England known as Derwent Gorge and Muggleswick Woods with a full quarter of beef. We agreed that this would be enough to produce a good scent in the air. This region was approximately 360 kilometers from Essex and was common for hiking. There are several resort estates in the area, but the likelihood of anyone being present was low given that it was so late in the season, and national nature reserves such as this tend to implement strict policies due to the sudden onset of bad weather. Permit-carrying hunters may be in the woods, but we figured all of them would be out of the woods before 9:00 p.m. at night when the moon was scheduled to rise high enough to be visible.

Marcus positioned himself in a tree so that he would be able to shoot down at me from multiple angles. The quarter of beef was mounted to a tree directly adjacent, but no more than 10 feet from the one Marcus was perched. The time was now creeping towards evening, and the daylight was beginning to fade. With nighttime air fast approaching, it carried the scent of blood. Soon, the moon would reach high enough into the sky to cast its light below. Coolness from the dark was setting in on the land. Before leaving Marcus, I gave him the charm of the Archangel Michael. "I pray to Michael that he provides enough protection that you survive the night. Godspeed, Marcus."

Chapter #13

It was pleasing to know that Henry was completely accurate about the weather, and we had a beautiful clear day for hunting. The day was grand. With all his piss and ginger, Codie managed to bring down a fairly large red stag with nine points upon his rack. *He's going to be rather unbearable for the remainder of the weekend,* I thought. *He has bragged about nothing else since we returned from the woods, taking every opportunity during dinner to point out the size of the dead animal hanging upside down from the game post.* Laryn, however, found the idea of a dead animal hanging from the game post repulsive. Codie's display of egotism may have been primarily aimed at disrupting the gentle nature of his sister. I could not blame her reaction, though. Coming back to the estate from riding an awe-inspiring gorge to find a large, gutted carcass hanging outside the house would startle anyone. Nonetheless, I was happy for Codie; he has become a skilled hunter. I watched him cleaning the wooden stock of the .450 Rigby rifle he used to kill the animal. The gun was gorgeous, especially since I had acquired it from an English lord who claimed that a member of the royal family had previously owned it. True or not, it was a privilege to have seen my son use it.

I, on the other hand, had found great pleasure that I was surrounded by family. I had drawn a pleasant sense of satisfaction knowing that both Laryn and Codie have experienced an abundance of happiness despite the mistakes I made with their mother. Grayson has been a different matter. He seemed a bit preoccupied and aloof most of the day. *I'll talk with him later when Codie and Laryn aren't around; perhaps the burdens of his affairs are weighing heavy on his mind*, I wondered, gazing into the fireplace in front of my leather, wing-backed chair. The fire continued to crackle as I sipped a glass of 18-year-old Macallan Scotch. The whisky burned as I swallowed but left hints of wood smoke with a bit of clove. A thought dawned on me, *He may hold bitterness towards me for the divorce. This is the first time he has seen me without the company of his mother.*

These thoughts were interrupted by Laryn parading through the room with a concerned look upon her face. She was quite composed during dinner despite her brother's attempts to unhinge her with his hunting stories, but by the continued way she kept looking out the windows suggested that something wasn't right.

"Are you sure the weather is supposed to remain calm, dad? Are there going to be any storms?"

"No honey, the weather will remain clear for the next two days. In fact, we should be able to see the full moon above the tree line. Why, is there something wrong?" I responded, concerned yet poised.

"Winston seems restless in the stables. He was odd earlier this afternoon when I was riding him, but I just figured he was a bit put out from the ride here. I keep hearing him banging around and neighing as if something has startled him. He has done this before, but usually it meant the weather was going sour."

"I think your first assessment was right. He's probably still stirred up from the trip up here. Are the horse wranglers still tending to him? They might be making him nervous," I asked in return.

"No, they left after they brushed him down and they're not supposed to return until morning. It could be that bloody carcass of Codie's hanging on the post!" she said sharply, glaring at him.

"Hey, what do you expect? You knew we were coming here to hunt. Where else am I supposed to hang my trophies?" he said defensively, chuckling some, realizing he finally broke down her defense mechanisms against his gearing.

"I'm going to go check on him." Laryn began to pull on her boots.

"Laryn, be careful. A fox or something of the like may also be walking around outside. Do you want one of us to go with you?" I asked.

"I'll go with ya, sis'," Codie said before she could respond. He got up from the table where he was sitting and placed the nicely polished .450 Rigby Magnum Rimless on the wooden rack beside the door. Codie handed Laryn her coat as he slid into his own. With a clank of the door closing behind them both, Grayson came into the sitting room from upstairs and sat down in the chair beside me.

"Is everything okay with Laryn and Codie?" he asked.

"I believe so. They just went to check on Winston. He was stirring a bit in the stables. I suspect it has something to do with the trip here." I shifted in my chair to better face Grayson. I was nervous to approach him about his affairs, but I was not going to let an opportunity to speak with him individually slip away. "Grayson, have you been feeling all right since you got home? I know things around here may be very different from what you've experienced in the last couple of years. I'll understand if you prefer to keep your own counsel on specific matters."

Grayson looked over at me and sighed deeply before he began, "Things are different for me. Everything has changed so much with Laryn and Codie, even you. Our family isn't the same anymore."

"I'm sorry that I bollocksed things up with your mother and I know that you may hold some resentment towards…" I began before he stopped me.

"No, dad, you misunderstand. I know mum left on her own accord and I don't hold any resentment towards you. The problem that's weighing on me has to do with my time here," he explained. I was somewhat relieved to hear this, but still concerned about his troubles. I listened carefully as he continued. "I'm proud to be a soldier in the British Army, but I feel I've missed out on a lot of time with everyone here. My term of service is up and this weekend I'm to decide whether or not I'll re-up with my company. I told them that if they all decide to re-enlist that, as their Lieutenant, I wouldn't abandon them and I too, would follow suit. But, I don't want to abandon my family either. I don't want to miss out on their lives, their accomplishments, and even their defeats. I want to serve my country, but I also want to serve my family."

"I'm proud to hear you say this. Know this…by serving your country you are serving your family. Your family all supports what you're doing, and we all anticipate the day when you can come back to your home country for good. For now, you must uphold your commitment to your mates, but with a better knowledge of why you're truly fighting in this war. I manage to throw around legislation and policy, but what you do is making an impact on a global scale. Do not grow weary in the good that you're doing."

Grayson folded his large arms across his chest and sank back into the chair as if he seemed content with this rationale. He had left barely a man by the world's standards, but has returned wise beyond his years, noble and just. Nothing more really needed to be said about the matter and we both sat enjoying the warmth of the fire and the softness of the atmosphere. The moment of quiet was broken as Codie came back through the door. We both turned to look.

"Laryn said that she was going to walk Winston around in the pasture. I told her to stay within the fence line of the estate. She said she won't be long. According to Laryn, the horse needed to get familiar with its surroundings," Codie explained.

"Did she take a flashlight?" I asked. "The pasture can be tricky at night even though it is fenced."

"No, she didn't. But you can see quite well with the full moon out. The whole fence line is visible," Codie replied.

"Dad, from what I've heard, Laryn can handle this," Grayson added.

Both Grayson and I settled back into our chairs as Codie went into the kitchen to get a glass of water. We sat staring at the glowing embers of the fire and listened to it crackle. I stood to stoke the fire when I heard Winston neighing in the pasture as though he was injured. It was followed by a high-pitched scream of terror and agonizing pain that could only be from Laryn. I dropped the fire poker as Grayson stood from his chair and ran to the door. Codie came running behind us, yelling, "Did you hear that? That sounded like Laryn!"

I made my way through the door as the screams and horrendous cries for help continued. Grayson followed closely behind with a flashlight in hand. "Grab your gun!" Grayson said to Codie.

We made our way through the pasture following the horrible screaming sound, calling out Laryn's named as we ran. I stopped suddenly as Grayson came to my side. The screams had stopped and standing about twenty feet from us was the silhouette of an animal. We approached with caution as Grayson shined the flashlight on it. Codie came running to join us, gun in hand. He pointed it at the animal as we watchfully closed in on the dark figure. "Oh my God! It's Winston!" Codie said in horror.

The horse had a look of alarm on his face and would not let us get within a few feet of him without standing on his hind legs, thrusting his hooves uncontrollably in our direction. Winston whinnied as Grayson shined the light on his side. The horse was covered in blood from where various parts of his shoulder muscle and hind quarters had been torn open. Flesh hung from the horse as blood pooled beneath him. "Where's Laryn? LARYN! LARYN!" I yelled repeatedly, but there was no reply.

"Dad, listen!" Grayson stated.

A faint snarling sound was coming from the fence line. Winston continued to neigh out of fear and pain behind us as we closed in on the sound. The closer we moved, the more distinct it became. Biting and tearing of flesh and muscle and the cracking of bones. Hunched over, devouring something on the ground was an oversized wolf-like creature. It had a massive structure, arms like that of a well-muscled human covered in fur, with bulky shoulders and a giant wolf's head. The canine teeth shimmered in the moonlight as they sunk into the flesh of its prey, twisting, and thrashing until the piece it wanted broke loose. It chewed hungrily as we watched, awe stricken at the sight we were witnessing. The creature paused for a moment as it stuck its snout into the air as if it caught the scent of something new. With a quick turn of its head, the beast was now focused in our direction. Grayson shined the light on it illuminating bright green eyes that cut through the darkness like lanterns. The thing stood on its hind legs with its head nearly two feet above the five-foot fence surrounding our estate. At its feet, I could make out Laryn's coat soaked in blood. "LARYN!"

"Codie, SHOOT the damn thing!" Grayson yelled.

The beast let out a ferocious growl with its head pushed forward and its fur covered arms splayed out to either side. It began advancing towards us with great speed. Codie quickly squeezed off three rounds in the beast's direction, but it did nothing to stop it. The brute lunged forward towards Codie, crashing headfirst into him knocking the gun from his hand and rendering him unconscious. The beast slashed at Codie, catching his left shoulder and across his chest. Grayson grabbed the gun from the ground and managed to squeeze off two more rounds at the beast. The monster turned, unflinching, and swung its massive arm against Grayson, knocking him backwards into me and breaking the gun in half at the stock. Both Grayson and I fell to the ground dazed. I struggled to watch as the wolf creature stood on its hind legs, silhouetted against the clear moonlit sky, muzzle pointed upwards and let out a triumphant howl before bounding over the fence line, into the darkness of the forest.

Grayson staggered to his feet and ran to where Codie lay, calling his name. He placed his fingers on his neck to check for a pulse, his head on a swivel to confirm the whereabouts of the creature. He sat Codie up against one of the fence posts as he began to come back to consciousness. Grayson tore a portion of his shirt and tied it around Codie's shoulder that was bleeding profusely. I slowly crawled towards Laryn's coat. I forced myself to my knees, tears streaming down my face as my mouth hung open aghast at the sight. Almost nothing remained. Her entire torso had been eaten away. Only fragmented bones and bits of fleshy muscle made up her limbs. Blood soaked the ground. Laryn's neck had been completely shredded. Frozen on her face was the look of horror and suffering that no child should experience. My screams echoed into the night.

CHAPTER #14

Saturday, November 28, 2009,

Dr. Bishop did not show up during confession yesterday. I made a special point to be present during all the appointed times. I have been anticipating her arrival, if nothing more than to ask about her sudden disappearance from the university and lack of returned phone messages. When she did not show up, I resolved to visit the local medical facilities, but none had a Dr. Mya Bishop registered as a patient. I placed a call into the office of her department, but no correspondence outside of her office address and phone were allowed to be given out. Having no luck with that I visited Dean Garris, whom I met a couple weeks back. We talked and he explained that Dr. Bishop has had no communication with him or the university. He mentioned that he went over to her estate and again was met with disappointment. Apparently, William also knew her mother quite well, well enough to have a picture of her standing with him and his wife outside the college offices. He informed me that Dr. Cassandra Bishop had died 11 years ago in a car accident. I could not help but comment on how much Mya looked like her mother. Before I left him and despite the policies of his department, he gave me the address to her estate, under the condition that I would communicate with him about her current whereabouts.

I left our meeting feeling put out and very uneasy. In all the times that I have met with Mya, she spoke of her family as plural, rather than just her mother singularly. This confirmed the suspicion I had that she was harboring more about this event than she wanted to tell. I took it upon myself to look into the accident further, but only managed to come across the same small funeral announcement in a local newspaper that I had found before. I cannot fancy a reason why she would hide the truth about her mother, even with me.

I arrived at her estate earlier this morning, taking leave from my duties at the church to do so. I classified it as a matter of outreach. Though the drive leading to her home ended with several spots for cars to park, none were there. I was met with a darkened manor. I knocked several times, but only found myself standing alone at the entrance. Inside appeared to be well tended to, or at least from what I could see through the windows. The remoteness of her estate was astonishing but left me with a chilling sense that one could get lost very easily in such a vast space. I feel as though I have overstepped my bounds by visiting her home. I pray that God offers her the protection she needs to overcome the challenges that lay ahead of her. Darkness surrounds this child of God. For now, I shall remain patient and have faith that God will watch over his servant.

- Rev. Preston Mathew S.J.

CHAPTER #15

Nightmares
Mya

Pain came with the morning. Stabbing into my gut, pain was everywhere. I tried to move from the spot where I lay, but every muscle in my body tensed. My vision was blurry, yet I could see the outlines of several tall trees and could hear the sounds of a couple of quarrelsome ravens hoping for an opportunistic meal. I guessed I was still within a forest, but where was unknown. The sound of leaves crunching and small twigs breaking, suggested something was walking in the distance yet it was too far away to make out what it was. I managed to roll onto my backside and stare up at the blueness of the sky. Coolness in the breeze quickly reminded me that I was naked, and it was late November; however, this did not explain why my body hurt the way that it did.

It had been many years since I allowed myself to roam freely after a change. I could only guess this was the reason everything was so different this morning. Without warning a sudden burst of nausea came over me. Struggling greatly, I managed to push myself to my side before I got sick. My stomach wrenched and my eyes watered as the contents from within emptied onto the forest floor. It seemed endless, one heave after another. As I finished, a coppery metallic taste resided on my lips. I placed my arms across my face and fell to my back as visions from the night before began to assault me. *First was darkness, the fullness of the moon soon followed and then there was the scent of blood, an overpowering scent of a fresh kill.*

Another violent episode of vomiting interrupted these recollections. More blood with each heave. The sound of the footsteps that were once in the distance were now closer and moving with some speed towards me. My blurred vision was made worse by the gagging that caused my eyes to water profusely. Panic was also beginning to set in. I had no real way of identifying what was coming towards me. Smelling the air was useless with the smell of blood and bile all around. My body began to quiver as the pacing of whatever it was slowed near me.

"Crikey Mya, there you are!" a familiar voice said. The silhouette of the man leaned over me. "To make this easy on both of us, I've gotta give you this tranquilizer. We gotta get you out of here!"

I was relieved to hear his voice, to feel his hands touching my face and arms. A blanket was wrapped around me as I was forced to sit up. The prick of the needle in my right arm and the sudden rush of coldness through my veins was a welcomed feeling, one I knew all too well. Rapidly, the world around me spun into darkness as I drifted out of consciousness. Familiar, yet different, images began to accost me.

Anna stood in the lavatory; her face pleasant then immediately struck with fear. Screaming...her heart beat wildly and echoed inside my head...blood covered the manor floors...her body ravaged, fear frozen on her face...a pasture, unfamiliar, dark but still a dim light...fog, haziness...a body torn apart, different...young like Anna, but not...dark hair and bright eyes that shone blue despite the darkness...her heart beat fast...slowing to a stop...her face terrified and twisted with suffering... dark pools of blackness contrasted sharply with her fair skin tone.

The image faded just as quickly as it came. I blinked several times at the bright light that was pouring over me. It was painful to see. I remained still, trying to piece together where I was and what was happening around me. Landscapes changed rapidly from what I could make out and the revving of an engine suggested I was riding in a car. Wrapped from head to toe in an itchy, wool blanket, I lay across the back seat of my Land Rover. A dark figure was driving, seemingly unaware that I was waking up. His hands tightly gripped the steering wheel as I felt the engine being pushed to higher speeds.

Groggy and nauseous, my breathing labored, I closed my eyes again, allowing myself to slip back into darkness.

Running through the forest…fast…a deep crevasse…a stream snaking through the forest floor…rippled without Sound…drinking…feeling myself breathing in the night…reflection…glowing green eyes enshrouded by a massive wolf's head…canine teeth that extended over the bottom portion of the mouth. The entire mouth was poised, snarling back…wanting to bite, wanting to kill.

Startled, my eyes blinked open. I was no longer in a car. I lay on a cement floor and the smell of trapped moisture filled my nose. Kneeling over me was the same dark figure that was driving the car.

"Marcus…" I said as I my voice trailed off.

"Mya, we're at your estate in the lower level. It's getting close to evening and I'm going to have to sedate you heavily to make sure that you don't change again. Something has happened, Mya, and I need some time to piece things together," Marcus said as he lowered a large syringe to my arm. I could not feel the prick of the needle this time, more than likely due to the weariness that I was already feeling. Even so, I did feel the cold rush again climb through my arm and before I could respond to anything that was said, I had fallen into a heavy sleep. Sleep with no dreams, without the presence of any emotions, and totally devoid of life.

Chapter 16

Funeral
Robert Osborne
Wednesday, December 2, 2009
10:00 a.m.

Clouds had rolled overhead bringing a cold rain that fell heavy at times with only a drizzle for the rest. The atmosphere was bleak, and I found myself surrounded by sadness. Pictures of my children were placed throughout the sitting room of my home. They showed Codie and Grayson on various holidays and school events, Laryn with her horse. Captured at all ages, their smiles were bright and loving, not showing for a moment the slightest hint of unhappiness or contempt for things around them. Tears streamed down my face and spilled onto my waistcoat as I looked over them. On this day, no one had a smile to give. Most were wrought with emotional pain, expressionless and hollow looking.

Laryn was dead, her joy of living was gone, her last moments alive stolen by a demon. A demon to which could not be placed with a name or origin. I sat there pouring over the pictures, filled to the brim with sorrow, awaiting the dreadful moment when I must lay to rest what was left of my beautiful daughter.

"It's time," Grayson said as he entered the room. My heart jumped and I let out a quick breath. I had not heard him come into the room. I wiped my face clean of the fresh tears and stood. "Codie's already waiting for us."

We shared the same look as we walked next to each other down the corridor into the main foyer of the home. Codie stood with his coat in his right arm and the other bound by a sling. He was still unable to use his left arm from where the claws of the beast ripped into his left shoulder, bicep, and part of his chest. Codie ended up having over two hundred stitches to close the wounds. No one spoke as we made our way to the car parked in the drive. Grayson sat in the front seat, while Codie and I sat together in the back. Henry, my assistant, took the liberty of driving us to the church for the service.

Westminster Cathedral stood tall, silhouetted against the grey sky as Henry drove up to the foot of the front steps. People were muddling up to the church with grief-stricken faces. Some women, including my ex-wife Daphne, wept loudly and openly, without care of anyone seeing them. I walked over to console her. She looked up at me between sobs. "This is your fault!"

"What…what do you mean?" I reached to give her a hug. Daphne pushed my arms away and stepped backwards.

"Why did you go north this late in the season? You were supposed to be watching over her!" Tears continued to stream down her face as she pointed her finger at me. "How could you let this happen? You abandoned her! She was only fifteen, Robert! How could you have abandoned her?"

I turned away from Daphne as two other women rushed to her side. She continued to wail loudly as she walked towards the church entrance. Tears flowed again as I put my hand over my eyes. An ache in my stomach moved into my throat as the emotional wound of Laryn's loss was made deeper. I felt a hand on my shoulder. "She just upset Dad. We all are."

I turned to face Grayson. Codie stood a few feet behind him. There was nothing I could say. Daphne was upset, but I felt some truth in her words. It was my idea to go to the resort. Many of my colleagues walked past me into the church to pay their respects and to support my family. Moments later, a black hearse slowly rolled to a stop in front of the church. As much as I loathed the day and despite the amount of pain I was in, I took my place on the right side of the coffin that bore the remains of Laryn. Grayson and Henry were opposite of me, and Codie was behind me on the same side. We lifted the coffin from the hearse and made our way towards the church, not caring about the cold rain that pelted our faces and dampened our clothing.

The coffin was placed at the end of the center aisle, just below the altar. I sat in the front pew along the edge with both Grayson and Codie to the left of me. Daphne sat to the left of them. She continued to weep but said nothing more to me. The smell of incense permeated the space around us. It seemed to burn my nose and stick to my face from the tears. For the next hour we listened to the designated readings from the New Testament, followed of course by the reading of the Holy Gospel by the priest. I heard none of the homily. My mind was transfixed on the night Laryn died. *What was that goddam thing?*

After the Mass had ended, Laryn's coffin was again carried to the hearse to where it was transported to her final resting spot in St. Mary's Roman Catholic cemetery. The procession of cars stretched nearly four kilometers down the street from the church. In a way, I felt blessed by the amount of people willing to show their support and offer their condolences. Alas, this torturous ceremony came to a close as I watched, amongst many others, Laryn's coffin being lowered into the ground beneath a shimmering headstone that marked the dates of her short life. I felt numb to those around me. I could hear them chatting and whispering about how Laryn had died. No one was quite sure of their comments. The papers had labeled it an animal attack. If asked, I would not have been able to describe it even though I was there and I saw it with my own eyes. I was the last to leave the grave site, reluctant to leave my little girl to this forlorn setting. *How could God have let this happen? How could he let my family suffer in such a way?* I thought, despite knowing full well there was no possible way I could understand the workings of God.

We returned to the estate. I changed out of my dress clothes. When I came back downstairs to the sitting room, Grayson and Codie had already started a fire and were quietly talking. They stopped as I entered the room. The fire was very comforting against the cold from outside. I had not realized how chilled I was until I found myself standing next to the yellow and orange flames as they licked at air escaping through the chimney. Grayson stood next to me and handed me a glass with Scotch over ice. I sipped the drink letting the caramelized, smoky flavor of the whiskey wash over my tongue and spill down my throat. It stung against the dryness of my mouth but warmed my stomach. "What were you two talking about?" I asked in a solemn, but curious voice.

"Nothing really," Grayson replied. I must have given him an, *I don't believe* you look. Before I could inquire further, he continued. "Dad, I don't think now is the time to discuss this. It's been a long day so far. Codie and I were just chatting, that's all."

Grayson had a keen sense of situational awareness. Codie, on the other hand, has been and always will be less apt to this kind of tact. His lack of patience and anger shown in his eyes as he began, "We were talking about that thing that attacked…"

"Codie! I said now isn't the time for this. We agreed not to bring it up," Grayson snapped.

"It's okay, let him finish. I want to know," I said firmly, but calm. I sipped my drink and listened to Codie.

"As crazy as this sounds, I think it was a werewolf," he said. A hush fell over all three of us. Before that night, I would have found the answer he gave to be rubbish, a mere figment of the imagination, and illogical; however, knowing what all three of us saw it was the most logical answer. Codie rubbed his temples to subdue a headache that was brought on from the concussion he sustained that night. "I don't know how it's possible, but we all saw it. The size of the beast, its eyes, its teeth, the way it moved, and the way that five rounds from the Rigby didn't bring it down."

"What do you think Grayson?" I asked.

Reluctant to engage in this conversation, Grayson sighed deeply, "I can't disagree with Codie, even though I would like to. I have replayed the night over and over in my head and I've no other explanation for what happened. Not in all the combat that I've been in, have I ever seen the like. I've seen some pretty awful stuff, stuff that makes the hair on the back of the neck stand on end. Frankly speaking, it scared the shit out of me!"

"That's a fuck'n understatement!" spouted Codie angrily.

Normally I would have said something to Codie about his language, but this time I almost said the same thing. We were all saddened and unnerved by this. The logs on the fire crackled and dropped ash to the bed of the inner hearth. A feeling of sadness swelled and mixed with anger from Daphne's words. *I loved Laryn, I didn't abandon her.* We all sat quietly listening to the sound of the rain as it pelted the windows. No one said a word until Grayson broke the silence, "Is there anything you need me to do before I leave tomorrow?"

The question caught me off guard. "What do you mean leave?" Venom laced my response.

"I – I have to report back to my company. I've already extended my stay under the conditions of a family emergency, but I must report back to confirm…"

"No, you're not leaving! I need you here! Confirm nothing! I'll have Henry place the necessary calls to alert those who need to know that you've decided to not re-enlist for another term of service. There's no need for you to leave just to come back home in a week or two," I demanded.

"I wish it were that simple, but if my company has unanimously decided to re-enlist for a second term of service…I told them, I would too. I gave them my word and I owe them my service."

"You owe service to your family!" I yelled as I threw my drink against the floor. It broke into several pieces and the remaining liquid splashed across the wood floor. I knew what

I said was wrong even before I said it, but my anger was growing too strong for any inhibitions. Grayson's face hardened as I continued, "Laryn is dead, Grayson! Don't you understand that? DEAD! SHE WAS TORN TO PIECES! I couldn't even hold her dead body in my arms and kiss her forehead…I need you here! I need your help with…whatever that thing was. Werewolf or not, I'm going to hunt it down and make sure that every last bit of it is wiped out!"

Grayson wanted to say something else, a look of insult on his face, but turned instead and walked out of the room. Codie sat rubbing his temples, as if the commotion strengthened his already pounding headache. I turned away from him not wanting to confront anyone after what I had said to Grayson. I leaned upon the mantle above the fireplace and stared at the glowing embers that fell from the logs.

"Are you actually going to go after it?" I heard Codie say from behind me. His voice was lower but was seething with anger.

"Yes…I have to Codie. I can't let something like that continue to exist after what it did to Laryn." I remained fixated on the fire.

"I want to help."

I did not answer at first. Under no circumstances did I want Codie involved with this thing. His future was bright and full of possibilities. I did not want it ruined the way Laryn's future had been ruined; however, he was there that night. He saw the beast and he shared my pain. Without looking at him, I mumbled, "Not too directly."

"Not too directly? What's that supposed to mean? If you're going to hunt this thing, I want to be involved. You said yourself that I was becoming a great hunter. I don't want to sit on the sidelines while everything's happening around me!"

"Look! I don't even really know what that thing was!" I turned to look at him. "You and Grayson seem to think that it's a werewolf; outside of a few stories I've read and several half-rate movies I've seen on the television, I don't really know what that constitutes. I don't even know how I'm going to hunt it. I'm not going to have you get involved with something that could harm you again or worse, harm you the way it did Laryn. That's for *damn* sure."

"What about Grayson? Just a minute ago you were practically begging him to be involved with this. Why is it that he has more of a stake in this than I do? I know…" Codie trailed off and began rubbing the bridge of his nose with his free arm. His headache apparently had gotten the better of him. A touch of panic had also set in. "I've seen the movies, too…and that thing dug its claws into my shoulder. I don't know what that's going to do to me."

Not wanting to make the same mistake I just made with Grayson, I softened a bit knowing that Codie was right to some degree. "Codie, Grayson is a military Lieutenant. He was trained at Sandhurst in the Department of War Studies. Being a member of the House of Commons, I have a great deal of political power and influence, but I have no combat experience. Grayson, on the other hand, has been in combat for years and I need him to help coordinate my efforts. You have to understand Codie, there are things I may have to do that I just don't want you to be a part of."

"I miss her too!" That was all he said as he stared at me with a look of fury behind the tears in his eyes. I hoped to dissuade him from his original notion; however, I could see that there was no convincing him otherwise, but I still did not want him involved. It was too dangerous.

"Help me to figure out what we're up against. Your university is bound to have a few experts that can give us some useful information. I mean, it's Cambridge for God's sake," I pleaded. "Now, let me go make amends with your brother."

Part III

Chapter #17

Mark of Darkness
Marcus Holland
Wednesday, December 2, 2009
1:35 p.m.

I worked frantically for the past four days, analyzing, and sifting through the data from the device in Mya's arm. *I need to speak with her about my findings,* I thought, but I let her lie on the concrete floor as I watched and waited for her to wake. Mya stirred in her sleep as though she was being plagued by awful nightmares, the ones that cause the inflicted to wake from a sound sleep screaming with fright, drenched in a pool of sweat. Outside the day was dreary and dismal. Rain poured down and the sun was covered with darkened clouds. Inside the manor was equally drab. Water seeped into the lower level and pooled at various places throughout the space. There was not much air flow. Mildew caused my eyes to water. Every now and then I would have to cough from the irritation. The levels above were not much better. Dust had begun to build up on the wooden furniture since our time over the past month had been consumed with research. Equally likely is that the normal caretakers, if any, were probably told not to come to the estate for an undisclosed amount of time; nevertheless, things in the manor were starting to take on a feeling of neglect.

From behind the bars of the cage Mya, fitfully opened her eyes and she sat up quickly with a gasp of air. Underneath the blanket I had wrapped her in she hunched over holding her chest, breathing very rapidly. The cage door was open and had remained open once I determined the full moon was complete and that she was *not* going to change. I quickly made my way from my chair into the cage and knelt beside Mya. "Let's get you to your feet." Placing one hand under her arm, I helped her up. She was still feeling the effects of the tranquilizer I had given her. "I cleaned you the best that I could, but you might want to take a bath and get some clean clothes. I'll start some tea."

She didn't say anything in response but allowed me to guide her up the stairwell to her chamber. I sat her on the bed, and she directed me to the wardrobe where most of her clothing resided. I pulled what I thought were undergarments, a pair of pants, and a pale blue long sleeve top and handed them to Mya. "I'm going to start a brew of tea. Are you going to need help into the lavatory?" I asked.

"No...I'm all right," she said weakly as she sat on the edge of the bed, rubbing her eyes with one hand and the back of her neck with the other.

It did not take long for the pot to whistle. When I returned, Mya was clean and completely dressed. She sat on the edge of the bed continuing to rub her neck with her eyes closed. She sensed that I had come back into the room, "My eyes are still blurry."

"Sorry about that. I gave you one hell of a dose of the tranquilizer. You've been asleep for four days," I stated.

"Jesus...Marcus, what happened? My thoughts are clouded and mixed with old memories. My body hurts terribly, and I've no sense or sequence of time with anything." Her eyes continued to blink rapidly to stave off the grogginess.

"It worked," I stated, apprehensive to tell her my findings.

"What worked? What are you talking about?" Her voice was filled with lethargy.

"The device implanted in your arm..." I trailed off, interrupted by the sound of the timer I had set for the tea to brew. "Crikey, hold on a minute."

I came back into the room with a cup of tea for Mya, not bothering to bring the entire pot the way she normally did when I was deeply involved with my work. After a couple of sips, she took in a deep breath and said, "Go on."

"The device in your arm recorded all the data I needed. It gave us your body temperature, heart rate, increases in chemical and brain activity. We were able to record all that was occurring inside your body before you changed into a werewolf as well as after. I believe the power inside of you is what has kept you alive and young for all these years. Every time you change your cells are replaced with new tissue. My thought is that any dying cells get replaced with new ones."

"How do you know they are being replaced?"

"The device also sent back an analysis of your blood. The readings before you changed were human; however, after the change your blood cells had a completely different genetic make-up. Curiously, it did match a wolf, but not entirely. My findings have suggested something completely new, not seen before. Hair is the only exception. Your grey is caused by the cells *not* being fully replaced. Though the follicles are replaced, your hair is essentially *not* alive, so it retains its grey look like the rest of us. I'm also convinced that if you sustain an injury as a human, it won't carry over to your werewolf form. This is why you have no scars on your hand from when you jabbed them. The tissue was completely replaced. I would think the same is also true if you sustain an injury in werewolf form. It won't carry over to your human form…unless it's silver." I explained. Again, I was very guarded in my speech.

"If this is true, why do I still have a scar on my leg?"

"I don't fully know. Since that was the initial bite, perhaps there's something more to it. It's your mark of darkness, so to speak. It's part of the supernatural elements we haven't fully uncovered yet."

Mya glanced at the ground, contemplating my findings. "Do you have something I can look at…a graph or chart of some kind?" she finally asked.

"Certainly, follow me." Mya stumbled at first, spilling her tea a bit when she tried to walk, but assured me that she was fine. We walked down the long hallway to the library. She sat down at the table and placed her hand over her eyes.

"Something's wrong. I have…terrible images in my head." Her voice sounded laborious.

"Are you all right? Do you need to go lie back down?"

"No, no tell me what else you found. This feeling will eventually wear off," she said, only slightly composed.

I hesitated for a moment before I continued, "All of the readings at about 8:50 p.m. show normal…meaning nothing happened that we hadn't already discovered." I showed her the printout of the graph that was recorded. "As you can see on the graph, at 8:58 p.m. all of your vitals began to spike. I can only assume this is when the full moon was visible in the sky. This is the moment when you changed into a werewolf. Eventually your vitals plateau off. Your heart rate stopped climbing at 180 beats per minute, your body temperature went up to 44.4 degrees Celsius, and there was also a significant increase in brain activity and chemicals such as adrenaline and epinephrine. This confirms that the full moon truly does trigger this reaction inside of you. When it's out everything increases. The amount of energy your body was not only giving off but that must have been contained inside of you was extraordinary. This certainly builds a good case for why silver affects a werewolf. Any silver passing through you may conduct the heat away from the point of entry, which may disrupt the path of your neural impulses. Needless to say, it would cause a great deal of pain and, in your werewolf state, may render various parts debilitated."

"I'm glad that this device worked so well, but what does all this mean?" she asked. "We're still no closer to a solution than before."

"I agree with you. We still don't know why you morph into a wolf-like creature. My gut feeling still believes it has something to do with a curse, witchcraft or even some other religious element. What this information does suggest, Mya, is that the full moon is a trigger for heart rate, body temperature, and chemicals inside of you. This helps to explain why you were acting so strangely when you were first bitten. The moon wasn't completely full but was visible enough for you to have some kind of new reaction. For a human, if your temperature goes above 40 degrees Celsius, you may be subject to hallucinations or blackouts. Having never experienced it before, you were less apt to control yourself, therefore causing you to go for long walks where you have no memory, eating raw meat, feeling lustful, or the other oddities you wrote about in your diary. However, this also suggests that you may not need the moon at all to change into a werewolf." When I said this Mya became increasingly more intrigued. "You have spent most of the two hundred-plus years avoiding people out of fear for what you have become. Fear is certainly an emotion that can cause an increase in heart rate and so on, but a stronger emotion that you may not have had a lot of since you have become esteemed at avoiding people, is anger."

"I have been angry since then! But I've never changed when the moon wasn't full!" she protested.

"I'm not referring to simple frustration or even deep sadness that can sometimes mask itself as anger. I'm talking about full blown rage! The day in the library when…" I carefully paused not to elicit any unwanted emotions. "…when you spilled the tea, I saw something in your eyes that was different. They appeared as though they were glowing bright green, if only for a moment. I thought you were going to change right there in the library. The only other time I saw your eyes flash like that was when you actually did change into a werewolf the night I arrived."

Mya looked as though she wanted to say something. I could tell that she was taking everything I said under careful consideration. Mya sunk her mind back into the information I gave her, pausing every so often to roll her head from side to side in order loosen her neck. It was clear that the effects of the tranquilizer were finally wearing off. She continued to sip her tea and read the graphic representation of the information I gave her. She looked up from the papers with an inquisitive look. "These graphs show a constant range of my vital signs before and after changing into a werewolf throughout the entire night, except here," she questioned as she pointed to a separate spike on the chart. The time on the chart indicated 9:13 p.m., a little over fifteen minutes after her initial change. "What does this spike mean?"

I did not even have to look at the chart. I knew what she was referring to and had been trying to determine what exactly it meant. My only conclusions were that she, as a werewolf, became more excited by something else other than the bait we had displayed on the opposite tree from me. I was nervous to discuss this fearing that something unspeakable had happened. "Mya, you never reached the bait we had set up," I finally said.

"What do you mean? I – I thought you had shot me with a tranquilizer?" she said, pausing to catch her breath. "That is the only way I can explain the way I felt when I woke in the forest...Please, please tell me you shot me with the tranquilizer...please."

"I can't...because I didn't. After you left me that evening, the device in your arm immediately registered you on my screen." I showed her the netbook computer that I used. "You walked about one and half kilometers away from me before you stopped. You stayed in one position for about two hours, then at 8:58 p.m. you began running at a fast pace back in my direction. I made sure the tranquilizer gun was loaded and I readied myself as you approached. You stopped your advancement though. You stopped for about a minute or so at 9:12 p.m. At first, I thought you lost the scent or maybe a small animal had crossed your path, but then you began to move fast again. Fast in a different direction. Panicked, I began making noise, screaming at the top of my lungs, hoping that you would follow the sound and the scent of the bait. But you didn't and you kept going. You finally stopped about five kilometers away from me. I don't know what happened the rest of the night. You were all over the place. I stayed in my spot until the first rays of light began to show in the sky. I used the tracking device to locate where you had stopped. I made my way back to the vehicle and drove to the closest spot to your location. I ended up hiking nearly four kilometers before I found you in a pool of bloody vomit."

Mya held her hands over her face as she let deep heaves of breath escape. Her body shook with each one. I had been watching the news broadcast since we returned to the manor. Almost every report spoke of a prominent member of the House of Commons losing his daughter to a vicious animal attack. They announced the funeral services on the morning report. I did not know how to tell Mya that she may be responsible for this, but I was not entirely sure she did it. She could have attacked an animal of some sort. "Mya, there's more. You may have killed something." My voice was grave.

As soon as I said this, I watched her face grow cold and stone-like. Most of the color fell out of her already pale skin and she became ghostly white. Before I could suggest the possibility of an animal, she blurted out, "A young girl! Dear God, it was a young girl!"

She dropped her teacup. It hit the table and fell to the floor where it smashed, splashing tea all over the wood panels. "Mya it could've been…."

"NO! I did it, I remember! She was on horseback…no, no she was walking her horse. I attacked the horse first. When she screamed, I turned on her. Oh my God! She's dead! She's DEAD!" Mya wailed, with deep sobs of sorrow and torment. She stood from the table, with her face in her hands again and backed away.

I made my way towards her. "There has to be another explanation."

"No, no, no…this is why I got sick. This explains the blood, the terrible pain. I didn't recognize it at first, but it was the same feeling I had when I killed…when I killed my family! I ate my fill as a werewolf! That is why there was so much, so much blood! What have I done? I can still hear her screaming in my head!" She was in hysterics.

"Mya, we'll figure this out. There has to be another…" I said as she pushed me away from her.

"This was wrong…we should've known better. I should've never been set loose!"

"There was no way of predicting that she would be out that late at night. The odds were in our favor," I tried to reason.

"Dammit Marcus! You aren't hearing me! A girl is dead because of me! Everything was hazy because of the tranquilizers, but I remember now! I can see her face as I bit into her neck! I can still taste her blood, hear her screams, and…and there were others present…there was gunfire…someone else got hurt. Oh God! Did I kill someone else? No, no I didn't, something pulled me away…something distracted me… no that's not right, I stopped! Just for an instant I could control it, I don't know!" she yelled with one hand over her forehead, while the other stabilized her against another table in the library. "This was your fault, Marcus! It was your idea to let me loose! You said the plan would work! I never wanted to do this! I knew something bad would happen. DAMN YOU!" Mya roared in anger.

Mya stumbled forward. I tried to help her, but in a fit of rage she backhanded me. I felt a dizzying sensation as I moved backwards and then the sudden crash into the shelves of books. As I hit the ground several volumes fell from their spots on the shelves around me. Blood trickled from my nose and mouth. The room spun and my vision went blurry. Just before everything faded into darkness, I caught the outline of a figure and a split-second glint of green from its eyes.

Chapter #18

I had decided to take leave from my duties as a member of the House of Commons. Though it was an uncommon practice, even after a death in the family, to take a month leave, no one questioned the decision to do so, not even Henry. In fact, Henry had been most helpful during this difficult time, and I felt fortunate to have him around. Whatever I asked for or had him arrange, he did it without question. Quite different from his normal standoffish self. I suspected that he too had been disturbed by Laryn's death and that questioning me would only add to the anguish we all felt. I had not shared any details with him about Laryn's death, but the rumors of what did happen have circulated around the estate and had probably festered into facts. I was sure he had drawn his own conclusions about what happened.

He turned a blind eye to my research over the past two days; loads of articles and books dealing with any kind of beliefs about werewolves. Everything from the fictionalized accounts to mythological origins to occultic reports and adaptations. Most people would have deemed this manner of obsession as madness; however, Henry remained steadfast with his duties and kept his own counsel, regardless of his personal agreement with the task.

"Henry, what time is our meeting today?" I asked.

"12:15 p.m., sir. They should be arriving at the estate in approximately 45 minutes," he responded methodically.

"Make sure Codie and Grayson join us at the meeting."

Henry nodded in agreement without saying anything else. Codie, I knew, would be happy to be a part of this meeting,

Grayson was another matter. He was still peeved about our conversation the day of Laryn's funeral. I had gone back on an assertion I made to him about serving his country. I tried to make amends, but deep down he felt as though he has abandoned his company and that I was to blame. I admired Grayson for his nobility, a character trait I often found lacking in myself. I love my son, but I must be selfish, *I need him,* I thought. Grayson was used to working with men of character and dignity, not mercenaries. I had to go this route. I could not involve local law enforcement. Too many people would view the notion of werewolves as insanity. Mercenaries, if they were paid enough, didn't care about the type of job. This meant secrecy.

Outside the weather was cold and cloudy, but dry. Inside, the manor was quiet, except for the dull hum of the air vents blowing heat into the room. I sat at my mahogany desk, pouring over a mythology book about witches, werewolves, and vampires. A cup of tea rested off to the side of a stack of books but remained half-full and had grown cold from neglect. After finishing a piece about the links of werewolf-ism to that of witches, I flipped to the bibliography to see what other titles were used when writing this book. Several names were listed of people I had never heard of from all over England and various other countries. One name in particular stood out, Dr. Cassandra Bishop from the University of Cambridge. *With Cambridge being so close she might be very helpful. I wonder if Codie knows anything about her?* My thoughts shifted to Codie's injury. One of the drawbacks to reading large amounts of information about one particular subject was that the very nature of facts and theories lent themselves to the reader to form their own conclusions, regardless of how accurate or inaccurate they were. *What if his injury causes him to become one of these beasts?* I hated this line of thought and was happy to be disrupted by Henry entering the room.

"Sir, the gentlemen you requested are here to see you."

"I thought they weren't supposed to come until 12:15 p.m.?"

"That's correct, but it appears they have arrived a bit earlier than expected, sir. I would think with the rather large sum of money that we've offered them; they don't want to displease you in any way. If I may say sir, I find them to be totally barbaric."

"Thank you, Henry, for that assessment. You, of course, are welcome to stay, but I assume you've already decided against that idea," I responded.

"That's correct. If there isn't anything else that you will need, I shall show them in and retire to my quarters?"

"Just make sure that both Codie and Grayson know that we're starting. Thank you Henry."

He simply nodded and exited the room. Moments later, four brutish fellows entered my study. The first of the four was bald, stood tall, wearing a leather coat with a black, tight fighting t-shirt underneath. His pants were baggy with pockets on either side and were tucked into military grade black boots. The other three were dressed similar.

"Well boys, it seems we're move'n up in the world. Would ya get a load of this fuck'n office? At least now we know the check that was written isn't going to bounce." The bald man laughed as he took off his leather coat and slung it over the desk where I had been sitting. Both arms bulged with muscles. Tattoos stretched from under his t-shirt down to his wrists. On his left arm was a naked woman, kneeling with her arms above her head. On the right, it was the same pose only the figure was a skeleton. Both had various other symbols and markings of which I was not familiar. He extended his right hand and said, "Me name's Jinx."

He had a heavy Irish accent. His hand was incredibly strong, and it nearly crushed mine. Another small tattoo resided on the webbing between his thumb and forefinger. It was an Irish flag with the letters C.I.R.A. "Robert Osborne. Jinx is it? Does your mother not like you or something?" I asked, trying to make light of the situation.

"No, sir! She fuck'n hates me!" he said turning to the other men, laughing loudly. "Obviously, it's not me real name, but given the nature of me business Jinx suited me betta'."

Codie and Grayson entered the room. "These are my two sons, Codie and Grayson." Codie seemed tentative and cautious, though Grayson remained unshaken, never losing eye contact from Jinx.

"Ah, well isn't this sweet. It must be fuck'n family photo time. Hold on! Where're me fuck'n manners? Behind me over here this old biddy's Snake! He's called that because he likes to use venom from pit vipers in his work. Don't let him bullshit ya though, he likes to brag and say it's because of his bellend." Jinx laughed. The dark-haired man called Snake had a big tattoo of a snake's head that came up from beneath his shirt and stopped at the base of his neck. The mouth of the snake was open, fangs out and it looked like the snake was trying to swallow his head. "Over here, these two bad bastards go by Kap and Rex."

Rex had red short, cropped hair that made his head look too small to be on top of his massive body. Kap was equally as big but had brown hair that was slicked back into place and greasy looking. "Now that we're all one big happy fuck'n family, why don't ya tell us how we can be of service to ya?" Jinx crossed his arms and flexed a little, trying to keep up his persona.

Codie sat in one of the leather chairs in front of my desk and Grayson stood back a bit, both watching the interaction. Codie simply listened while Grayson, I could tell, was itching to engage in the conversation. Before he could say anything, I spoke up, "Well first off, nothing that we discuss or do goes beyond anyone standing in this room. Got it?"

"As long as ya keep paying us, we stay quiet," Jinx said in a more serious tone.

"Are you good at what you do?"

"Well, I've been doing this shit two years shy of a decade, since the disarmament began in '01'. I'm still alive and I get paid well. What do ya think?" Jinx responded.

"You were in the army, in Ireland?"

"Yeah…yeah we were. All of us…Bloody fuck'n shame if ya ask me. We never should've stopped."

"Have you seen some real action? More than just toy soldiers?" Grayson piped in.

"Look Dickbrain…" Jinx said menacingly moving towards Grayson. He stopped directly in front of him, staring in his eyes. "I've seen more shit, been in more fucked-up situations, and have come out cleaner than yer pampered arse could imagine. Don't question me about me work."

"That's enough!" I yelled. "Grayson's a Lieutenant in her Majesty's Royal Army, educated at Sanhurst and has been fighting in the Afghanistan war. You would do well not to insult him or me!"

"Yer lucky daddy's paying the bills, otherwise this may have ended differently. English Gobshite!" Jinx taunted as Rex moved in front of him.

"Not here! Our day will come," Rex said. Jinx backed away from Grayson, blowing him a kiss with his mouth.

"Back to my original question, are you any good at what you do or am I just pissing money away?" I was cold and serious.

Jinx paused for a moment still looking at Grayson, but it seemed that I was finally speaking his language. "Between the four of us there isn't a weapon that we can't use. I personally am good with close range combat. Knives, pistols, ya name it. This also comes in very handy if you want to get information out of someone, if you know what I mean. Snake's a communications specialist. He can set up anything ya need to spy on people or retrieve information. Shifty little bastard, always try'n to live up to his name. He's also damn good at looking at video recordings and manipulating video if ya need something covered up. Both Rex and Kap are sharp shooters just in case ya don't want to get too close."

"Do you have weapons?" I was naïve to even ask.

Jinx smirked, "Sure thing, we gotcha covered."

Snake finally joined the conversation, "What exactly are we going to kill or is all this for your protection?"

His voice was low, more English sounding than that of Rex and Jinx. He was keen to pick up on the fact that this was not going to be some stroll through the meadow. "I don't know for sure. What I do know is that it is very dangerous, and we have to investigate some things first to gain our footing. Any of you four know how to make bullets?"

Kap raised his hand, "I can customize any bullet to fit any gun. What did ya have in mind?"

"We need to make bullets out of silver," I said.

"Silver? Personally, I've never used silver. I prefer armor piercing, hollow points. That way if the little babby is wearing body armor they still come tumbl'n down," Jinx interjected making a hand gesture to go along with his words.

Every bit of mythology and facts that I had read over the past two days indicated that silver was the only way to get rid of a werewolf. I was not putting much belief behind this notion, but I didn't want to take any chances. Before I had an opportunity to explain this, Grayson chimed into the conversation. "They won't do any good. We shot it five times with a .450 Rigby, and it was as though we were shooting blanks."

Before Jinx could respond, Rex asked, "You referred to our target as an IT. Does this mean we're looking fer some kind of animal?"

"No sir, our target's a werewolf!" Grayson replied with a stone look on his face. Codie shifted in his seat and rubbed his left arm.

For a moment, no one in the room spoke. None were expecting that kind of response. A sudden fit of laughter broke out among the four men and Jinx picked up one of the books lying on my desk. "I think ya three have been read'n too many of these faerie tales."

"Ya don't actually expect us to believe that rubbish, do ya?" Snake hissed.

"You can believe whatever you want. You will find out the truth soon enough. Are you gentlemen willing to do this?" I asked, expressionless and unflinching from their laughter.

"Sure, we'll play along with yer little game. A lot of shite if ya ask me, but like I said before, ya keep writing those checks and we might even sit down for a tea party." Jinx's sarcasm and disbelief were obvious.

"Very well then. When the job is complete, you will each receive an additional fifty thousand pounds on top of the hundred thousand you've already received. If you happen to die in the process, your earnings will be distributed among the remaining members of this group. Remember, these conversations are to remain confidential. If something were to get out about what we're doing it would be very damaging to my political career and current campaign. I'll make sure that all of you are tried for extortion and locked away in a prison that is designed to wipe out your very existence." For once I had to completely agree with Henry, these men *were* barbaric. But they were perfect for what we needed to do.

"Well sir, it looks like ya got yourself a squad of soldiers," Jinx said with a chuckle. "So, what's next?"

I walked over to my desk and pushed Jinx's leather coat out of the way and grabbed the book I was reading before the men had showed up. I flipped directly to the back of the book, to the bibliography page where I had found the name Dr. Cassandra Bishop. "Codie, have you ever heard of this person?" I said as I pointed to Dr. Bishop's name.

"No, I haven't. Should I have?" he asked.

"She's a professor at Cambridge that contributed to this book involving werewolves. She may be of some help to us. Can you login to the university's website and pull up her contact information? Try and get us an appointment to see her this afternoon."

"Wow, ya fellas are really serious about this werewolf shite, aren't ya?" Jinx asked.

"Afraid so, you can back out if you like?"

"As loony as this whole thing sounds, I'd be fuck'n stupid to pass up a hundred and fifty thousand!" he replied.

"Good, then start unloading your gear and make any preparations you need. Kap, get started on making those silver bullets," I commanded.

"You got it boss. Do we have the silver already?" Kap asked.

"Go shopping, I don't care where you get it from," I said.

Without another word he turned and exited the room with Jinx. The other two remained behind. Grayson walked over to me, "Are you sure you want these men involved with this? IRA was and still is a formidable group associated with terrorism and they certainly aren't trustworthy."

"What would you have me do, use regular law enforcement, the military?" I asked. Grayson didn't respond but merely pursed his lips tightly as if to say that he didn't agree with any of this.

"Dad, it doesn't look like there's a Dr. Cassandra Bishop at Cambridge anymore. There is, however, a Dr. Mya Bishop in the college of Arts and Humanities. Apparently, she is the professor that teaches the class every fall about lycanthropy. I tried to get into it, but it was already closed out when it came time for me to register. She might be a relative, but the only contact information listed is for the college itself," Codie explained.

"Is the dean of the college listed?" I asked.

"Yes, Dean William Garris, but it's nearly 1:00 p.m. He's probably not in his office."

"Have Henry make the call to set up an appointment for us this afternoon. I'm sure there will be at least someone to take the call and contact the dean if he's not there. Also, tell Henry to stress that we'll be happy to make a generous contribution to the college for his assistance. I don't think the *Dean* is likely to pass up an opportunity like this with a member of the House of Commons, either." I fully intended to use my position and wealth as a means of getting my tasks accomplished.

Within a half hour, we were making our way to the University of Cambridge to meet with Dean William Garris, who Henry explained was quite refreshing to talk to after dealing with the brutes from earlier. Grayson opted to drive with Codie in the front seat and I sat alone in the back. Two of the mercenaries, Kap and Snake, stayed behind to make the preparations that I had requested. Jinx and Rex drove behind us in a white van, no doubt making light of the situation and boasting about making an easy hundred and fifty thousand pounds. It was about an hour drive from the estate to Cambridge. I said nothing the entire trip and only stared out the window thinking about how these men had no idea what they had signed up for. Maybe Grayson was correct. Did I want these men involved? No. It was too late now. To go back on a promise of money with these men may be equally as dangerous as the werewolf we're hunting.

When we pulled up to the building that housed the College of Arts and Humanities, standing outside was a middle-aged gentleman with silver hair and a pudgy belly. He was wearing a brownish-grey sport coat, with a white, button-up shirt and a bowtie, tan slacks with brown shoes. Standing next to him was a younger lady perhaps in her mid-thirties, with her hair pulled back into a bun and that wore a black, full length skirt and a puce colored blouse that contrasted with her pale skin. Both looked very astute, quite different from the barbarous men that were traveling with us.

As we stepped out of the car, the man greeted us with a smile and introduced himself as Dean William Garris. The lady next to him was the executive assistant for the college. Both were taken aback by the look of the two mercenaries that walked up behind us. "It's a pleasure to meet you Dean Garris." I shook his hand. "Thank you for taking the time out of your busy schedule to meet with us."

"Please, call me William. Believe me when I say that the pleasure's all mine. Margret has informed me that you're interested in making a contribution to the college?" he asked pleasantly, gesturing in the young woman's direction.

"Yes, I am. I'll have Henry, my assistant, make the arrangements when we're through. But before we get into all of that, may we speak with you alone about another matter?" I asked politely.

"Certainly, let us go inside to one of the conference rooms." Margret entered one of the offices across the hall from us. Grayson, Codie, and I all sat down at the large oak table in the conference room William had directed us into. Jinx and Rex simply leaned against the wall, one on either side of the door, both with their arms crossed. A dull buzz escaped from the fluorescent lights above us. Several portraits of professors were displayed on the cream-colored walls. All had the same framed oak that matched the table. William sat across from us. "How can I be of service to you gentlemen today?"

"We're actually looking for someone and we're hoping that maybe she would be able to join us if she's present in the building." I leaned onto the table with my elbows and crossed my fingers. "If not, if you could at least give us a way to get in contact with her?"

"Whom are you referring?" William asked. A concerned look appeared on his face.

"Dr. Mya Bishop."

He took in a deep breath and folded his arms across his chest, a look of distrust in his eyes. "She's not here. What business do you have with her?"

"Well then, is Dr. Cassandra Bishop here?" I asked, going back to the original name I had found, dodging his question.

"Neither one of them are here. Dr. Cassandra Bishop died a little over eleven years ago in a car accident. Her daughter, Dr. Mya Bishop, has been employed with us for nearly six years," William became a bit more defensive.

I already knew the answer before I asked, "What does she teach?"

"She specializes in Medieval Folklore and Mythology. What's this all about?" he inquired more assertive.

"Do you know where we could find her? We need to speak with her about the subject matter she teaches. My son Codie has explained to me that she teaches a relatively popular class that I would like to ask her about." Aware of his defensiveness, I kept my voice calm, yet direct.

He picked up on my calmness, "Is she in some kind of trouble?"

"No, not at all. We just know that she's an expert in the occult, specifically the history and origins of such things and…we would like to talk to her about it."

William was a man of facts. My vagueness and intrusive questions were not sitting well with him. His reaction suggested that he had a closer relationship to Dr. Bishop than just a faculty member. Perhaps he was a relative or a close friend of the family. Nonetheless, he was certainly the correct person to discuss her whereabouts. It also did not help that there were two very large individuals standing on either side of the door, who couldn't help but look menacing. "I don't know where she is," he said perturbed by the way the conversation had gone. "You sir, being a member of the House of Commons, already know that I cannot give you her personal information. What I can tell you is that I haven't seen her in nearly two months. I was trying to get her to give a talk about her subject matter, which was to be held on Saturday the 31st of October, but she declined the event as well as cancelled her remaining lectures and went on leave. Even with my efforts to contact her, no one in the department knows what has happened. I suspect she would like to keep her matters private," William explained.

I sat back in my chair, perplexed by the strangeness that surrounded this conversation. I was about to dismiss the whole situation, say thank you to William for his time and leave, when he stated, "You're not the only one looking for her. A priest by the name of Father Preston Mathew was also looking for her. Maybe he has had contact with her."

All of us in the small room took immediate interest in what he said. "Where can we find Father Mathew?" I asked very stern.

"St. Teresa's Cathedral."

As I stood up to leave, I asked, "Has Dr. Bishop ever disappeared like this before?"

"She can be rather antisocial, a bit of a hermit you might add, but never like this. I constantly try to get her out of her stuffy estate to have dinner with my wife Mildred and me, but I've had little luck."

Jinx and Rex seemed to know exactly what I was thinking and were already making their way out to the van. Grayson, who had been frantically writing things down on a small pad of paper, also got up. "Since Dr. Bishop isn't here, where else does she spend her time?" I asked as we were leaving.

"If she isn't at her home, church, or here, then she's probably in some damn library." William said, irritated by the situation.

We left William bewildered and agitated. I did not really care. Henry would make him feel better with a sum of money. I wanted to find Dr. Mya Bishop. Laryn was killed by a creature my two sons and I believe to be a werewolf. Dr. Bishop, who appears to be the leading expert on occult literature and folklore, may be the best person to help us. I knew these types of people all too well in parliament. They would quite frequently take a medical leave so that they could finish some obsessive research, only to spontaneously get better and publish a new book at the same time. I smirked as this thought crossed my mind.

"What's our next move?" Grayson asked as we got back outside.

I acknowledged Grayson but ignored his question and walked straight over to the backside of the van where Rex was standing. The door was open, and Jinx was talking on his cell phone. "I want to find out everything we can about Dr. Mya Bishop. I have a feeling she is avoiding the public to finish another book or something."

"I'm already talking to Snake, and he says that his system will be up and running in ten minutes." Jinx was all business now. He also knew that finding Dr. Bishop may prove to be helpful at completing this task, putting him closer to the extra fifty thousand pounds.

"I think we should make a sweep of the libraries on the campus and in the area. Since we're here it doesn't hurt to check; perhaps someone has seen her recently," Grayson said as I turned to face him again. He too, was also thinking along the same lines.

"I agree."

"It may also do us well to check out the security cams and doors. Lots of universities have card keys that need to be swiped before they unlock. Snake might be able to track her recent card swipes." Grayson was talking more to Jinx who was still on the phone with Snake. He had, obviously, performed this kind of search in Afghanistan.

Jinx relayed this to Snake before ending the cell phone conversation. Both Rex and Jinx holstered a sidearm.

"I don't think you blokes are going need those. I mean, she's just a professor," I claimed with a look of cynicism.

"Better to be prepared then to get caught flat footed. We always carry them," Rex added. Jinx just maliciously grinned as if to say, I do what I want. I was not going to argue with them or even try to reason that this was a place of academia and that a more plausible threat to them would be that they would actually learn something.

CHAPTER #19

Three days ago, Marcus lay in a heap of rumble. Books were strewn all over the floor of the library along with some of his equipment. Before leaving him, I checked his pulse to see if he was still alive. I wondered what he would think when he regained consciousness. Would he stick around and continue his work, or would he simply flee? *No doubt he had an awful headache when he woke and more than likely a broken nose, but thankfully he's still alive*, I thought. *He must go. This situation has become too dangerous, and I need to go back into hiding.*

Thankfully, I had grabbed my leather coat as I left the manor. It was December, and though it had been mild and relatively clear, it would have looked odd not having a coat of some kind. I needed to blend in the best I could. The only thing I should have had with me but did not, was an umbrella. Populated areas were too much of a risk, so I only ate at secluded pubs or fast-food restaurants. I slept in my Land Rover, huddled in the fetal position, crying mostly. I thought about going to church but realized that a weeping woman would draw too much attention. Though I had not changed my clothes in three days, a new question was swirling inside my head: Had I been searching for answers in the wrong places? I had read nearly every fictional account about werewolves and have studied in great detail the origins of lycanthropy, witchcraft, and even satanic practices, desperately hoping to find a clue that would lead me to the solution, a way out of this affliction. It was not until Marcus had talked about his tribe being annihilated after trying to curse some extremists and asked to see the charm of the Archangel Michael that I realized the curses I had studied through witchcraft and Satanism may have been the wrong ones.

Curses, I had learned, were not as simple as people would like to believe. Curses have been classified as spells, that a person or entity cast to cause harm to another individual for a designated amount of time whereas a true curse comes about in direct response to someone's malevolence towards another human being, especially one who is innocent. The whole idea of Karma has been based around this notion. What goes around comes around. *Marcus said it himself, many of the people in his region were practicing tolerance and Aboriginal curses may have been cast upon the innocent,* I thought. *Perhaps curses are God's way of teaching humanity the difference between right and wrong.* The curse, in theory, would be lifted when the person does right in the eyes of God, finds grace and asks for forgiveness. However, a curse would endure the test of time and spread like a cancer among humans if it was not forgiven and was forgotten.

As a Catholic, I spent a great deal of time asking for forgiveness so that I may be just in the eyes of God. It never occurred to me that I was the victim of someone else's curse that never had the opportunity to rectify their wrongs with God or even the knowledge that they were even doing wrong.

I found myself back in the one place that had always brought me a sense of peace, where answers could be found if a person were willing to put forth the effort. I found myself back in the library stacks of Cambridge University, seeking not the curses of witches, voodoo priests, or even that of Satan, but instead the curses instilled by the priests and holy men in the name of God. The rare ones, the forgotten ones, the ones that the church wanted to erase from their history. Throughout Europe and into the Americas, many people were accused of being heretics, believed to be in league with the dark lord, mostly on the grounds of spectral evidence. Many people that were innocent of such things were burned at the stake, hanged, or tortured to death. I had also become familiar with the common practice of damning the accused before they died so that their soul would not make it to the kingdom of God. These acts were performed by priests and holy men. Such a ritual was carried out if a heretic was found guilty of the more heinous crimes. These crimes included violent murders, cannibalism, and the destruction of holy relics. Many of these incidents remained undocumented for obvious reasons. Judgment did not belong to the priests. God was the only being that could issue such a fate. In their ignorance, they were left vulnerable to the very curses they were trying to inflict on others.

I knew what kind of writings I had to find. If they still existed, they would be held in the private book depository, which required an access card to view the artifacts contained. Fortunately, being an employee of the university granted me such privileges. I always kept the card in my SUV, so that I would never be without it when I was doing research.

I parked behind one of the buildings adjacent to the main library. It was Saturday and most of the campus parking was open. I got out of my car and looked at my reflection in the window. My hair was untamed and needed a wash. I pulled it into a ponytail and made sure that any straggling hairs were pulled into place. Behind me, I could see a few people walking to and fro. Most paid no attention to me as they continued to text and walk on the paths between the buildings. Yet one person stood out. He was sitting a good distance away from me on a bench, dressed casually, but from the reflection he appeared to be looking in my direction. I turned to face him. Though I could not make out his facial features, he was African. *The man from the corner that day with William,* I thought. Distracted by a couple of students laughing nearby, I looked back to the man on the bench, and he was gone. A light breeze sent a chill through me. I shook off the nervous feeling and made my way towards the library. Who was he and what did he want?

Inside the library was warm and quiet. "Good afternoon." I tried to sound as cheerful as I could to the student worker behind the information desk of the main library. It was difficult given the emotions that were coursing through me and the strange encounter with the man on the bench. I looked around to see if the man had followed me into the library as I said, "Uh, yeah…I would like to have access to the book depository for the next hour."

"Do you have an access card?" the student said in a monotone voice. She had several books splayed out in front of her and it was clear that she was working on something that she didn't want to be distracted from.

I handed her my card and waited nervously, hoping that I would not run into or be seen by any of my colleagues. That would warrant an explanation that I was at the time not prepared to give. I continued to watch for the man outside, but there were only a few people meandering around. Most of the student body had finished their fall courses and were more than likely on holiday. The student behind the desk took the card and swiped it through the magnetic reader that registered my number in their system. She handed it back to me and had me sign the registry log of people that come and go. I gave a weak "thank you" as I placed my card in the pocket of my pants and waited as the student pressed the button to unlock the door to the climate-controlled portion of the library. This was where all the older books and writings were kept for preservation and restoration. With a low buzz and a loud click the door unlocked and I was free to enter.

I walked down a long corridor passing an air exchange unit that every two hours sucked out the stale air and replaced it with fresh air. It was the same technology that was used in hospitals and medical facilities where the air needed to remain sterile. It helped to prevent mold and mildew from building up which can be potentially bad inside a place that had items susceptible to this damage. As the mechanized door behind me closed, the door in front of me unlocked. I walked through and was greeted by several large shelves of the oldest books, writings, and artifacts the world had produced.

Dr. Reynolds, the curator, greeted me as I entered. "Dr. Bishop, what a pleasant surprise to see you today!" He was an immigrant from South Africa with a heavy accent. As usual his smile beamed wide and bright as he shook my hand warmly with both of his. He was tall, bald with deep ebony skin. I had always had a great fondness for him. It troubled me that I never allowed myself to get to know him better, outside of research. Dr. Reynolds was a very learned and interesting man and had helped me locate numerous items throughout my recent years of research. "It has been a while since you've come to see me."

I was relieved somewhat by his comment. It meant that he was not privy to my absence at the university. "Yes, it has," I responded again trying to disguise my emotions. Never was he caught underdressed for any occasion, and today was no exception. He wore a button-up white shirt with a black tie under a burgundy, woolen vest, dark slacks and black shoes. "I was wondering if you could help me locate a particular type of document, pamphlets specifically?"

"Dr. Bishop, you're one of my favorite professors. I would be more than happy to assist you with your research. What time period are you looking for today?"

Everything in this facility was classified by period and then arranged accordingly. "Thank you for your kindness, I was hoping to look at items from the 15th, 16th, and 17th century," I responded.

"Well, that's pretty broad. Is there something more specific, a particular type of writing, author, category?" he asked.

"Catholic writings," I replied. "Rare ones, specifically dealing with the accusations against heretics and Satan worshipers. These writings were probably not mass produced as common literature or there may even be writing about how these events never occurred. Anything related will serve me well."

He whistled loudly in amazement. "That may take a little time to locate. The Catholic Church hasn't been too diligent with preserving those kinds of documents, at least not for the public viewing. I'll check our records. This may take a while in our facility if we have anything at all. Did you want to wait, or shall I send word when I have located something?" he asked.

"I'll wait if you don't mind," I answered back. Dr. Reynolds must have noticed that I was out of sorts.

"Are you feeling okay today, Dr. Bishop?" he asked. I lied by saying I was fine and that I was just tired from teaching this past semester. Before turning away from me to return to his office computer, he gave me a concerned, worried look. I could see into the small offices to the right of the entrance. They were behind a row of windows that allowed Dr. Reynolds and his team to look out to monitor the artifacts during hours of operation. This is also where they worked on the restoration and preservation of the artifacts. It acted as a security measure to help discourage people from stealing anything from inside. I saw Dr. Reynolds glance back up at me twice, each time with the same distraught look on his face. I averted my attention from Dr. Reynolds' worried glances by taking in my surroundings. One of the few pleasures that I allowed myself in my exceptionally long life was that of the libraries and museums of the world. Most of the time I was visiting them for research purposes, but I still found the grand structures awe-inspiring and comforting. The ceilings here were high with exposed oak rafters that arched downward along the support beams. This repeated every so often for the entire length of the depository. Several air exchange units lined the walls, venting upwards between the rafters. The flooring was a marble pattern, with a high-gloss finish. Easy to clean.

Not quite a half-hour passed before Dr. Reynolds rejoined me in the waiting area. He looked pleased with himself as he glided across the floor. "I didn't find any from the 15th, 16th, or 17th century that fit your criteria exactly, but I was able to locate a few very old books and some documents that discuss events from the 16th century that may relate to your search," he said, handing me a pair of latex gloves and motioning to me to follow him. "These aren't exactly primary documents and most of what I found was written in the late 18th century and early 19th century, but I think you'll find them useful nonetheless."

Perhaps this was the reason I had such affection towards him. Any task placed before him he would approach with multiple solutions taking great care to come up with the best answer, given the circumstances. If the answer was not as forthcoming as it needed to be, he would select the next best thing. I admired that trait in him. "I'll take a look at anything you have. Might I ask, what are we going to be viewing?" I started to pull on the latex gloves, a requirement when handling older artifacts.

"As you and I both know, witchcraft and Satanism were believed to be one in the same. Practitioners were persecuted exactly the same with hangings, burnings, and torture of unspeakable means. Some of it was justified at the time; not having knowledge of mental illnesses or even the effects from drinking polluted water or eating poisonous crops led many to believe that a person was bewitched or was under the influence of the devil. With the advancement of farming methods, better storage of food and science in general, many of the earlier accounts of heretics were discredited. However, no one likes to admit their mistakes, so lots of the written accounts were destroyed, if they were even written at all. What I've found though, are some good writings about the events in question by a Catholic priest that was looking to recount the history of the church to demonstrate how the church has used science without sacrificing faith. It came to us in the last year through a donation," Dr. Reynolds explained as we walked.

"I appreciate you taking the time to find these items for me. What else were you able to find?" Again, I tried to cover up the anxiety and regret that was written all over my face. Dr. Reynolds remained steadfast ahead of me as we walked and did not even look back when I asked the question.

"The secondary search I did turned up some artwork, a pamphlet to be exact, that tells of a particular individual that is mentioned in the priest's writing. The language is in German and most of it was handwritten along the sides. I know you speak German, but if you need some help deciphering the penmanship, please let me know and I'll have one of our specialists assist you. Is there anything else I can do for you, Dr. Bishop?" he asked as we arrived at a small table where the resources were already spread out, waiting for me to peruse. He must have had one of the stock managers pull the resources as he found them on the computer.

"No, I'm fine. Thank you again for your help, it is always appreciated."

"My pleasure, Dr. Bishop." He gave a curt nod of his head before he turned to leave me to my work.

I picked up the book written by the priest. It was titled Modern Thought and Faith by Father Bentini. I thumbed my way through to the table of contents to preview the chapter headings. The time from the clock on the wall was approaching 2:15 p.m. and I had to work fast. I did not want to overextend my stay and again draw attention to myself. The first chapter heading read *The Heretics of the East and West*, which I deduced was an introduction of sorts. Following this chapter were the chapters titled *English Heretics*, *Heretics in France*, *Romanian Witchcraft*, and *German Witches and Fiends*. I stopped there, taking into account what Dr. Reynolds had mentioned about the other resource being written in German. I flipped to page eighty-eight, careful not to damage the pages in any way.

The first name that appeared on the page under the chapter heading was Kabona. I quickly skimmed the first couple of pages to discover that a slave man in 1753 was accused of witchcraft and satanic practices after he was found lying near the dead bodies of his owners that were brutally murdered. Despite his injuries, he was imprisoned for a month before his trial was scheduled to take place. *They were probably waiting for him to die from his injuries so they wouldn't have to give him a trial,* I thought. Many times, this happened to slaves when there were more pressing issues that required the attention of the local magistrate.

It went on to reveal that he supposedly used magic to keep himself alive and to later escape from the prison that held him by breaking the metal bars of his cell. The priest noted that early prisons may have been built poorly and that the stone may have come loose that held the bars in place, thus allowing him to escape. The priest further explained that rats among other vermin trapped in his cell probably allowed him to eat, giving him sustenance, which helped him to heal from his wounds. More importantly, he described that this slave was not a part of German folklore and that he probably was imprisoned somewhere near London. The priest used this fact as part of the rationale for the falsity of the story.

I wrote on a small pad of paper that Dr. Reynolds had also left for me, the name of the slave and date to do further research on him at a later time. I kept skimming the pages of this chapter until I came to an account of another individual by the name of Johan Stich. This one caught my attention because after the name it read: *A Witch Turned Wolf.* Before reading what it said about this man, I cross-referenced it with the artwork that Dr. Reynolds had found. Sure enough the name Johan Stich, written in German, stood out on the page. I had read this story a few times and knew it well; however, I was looking for something else this time. It was one of the stories that did not get much attention because it was so like the infamous story of Peter Stumpp the supposed Werewolf of Bedburg, which turned out to be a glorified story of cannibalism. Most people thought of Johan Stich as the same, especially since it also took place in Germany, east of Bedburg in the Sachsen-Anhalt region. What was intriguing was that there was no mention of Peter Stumpp. The two stories were usually told jointly because of their similar nature.

The artwork, which I had also seen referenced before in books, was a set of individual pictures placed on a display together to give a full retelling of what happened to this man. The first picture showed a primitive sketch of a wolf attacking cattle with their bowels being pulled out; another one illustrated a wolf standing on its hind legs and walking like a human. The wolf was then depicted running into the forest with a child pointing his finger, then a man strapped to a table as two other men were poking his body with what appeared to be hot iron rods. The sequence then showed the man's stomach cut open followed by a picture that represented his hanging and later dismemberment. The last image revealed a man in holy garb, holding a cross aloft above the convicted. This is what I wanted to confirm!

I immediately flipped back to the account written by the priest because I didn't have time to translate the writing on the artwork and began reading. It read:

> *Alas, is the case of Johan Stich, a man accused of witchcraft and consorting with Satan and put to death in late 1500's. The exact date continues to be a subject of debate amongst scholars. It was believed that this young man made a deal with the devil at an early age to gain immortality. It was also believed that in exchange for his soul, the devil gave Johan a piece of hide torn from a wolf's back and was told to wear the hide over his shoulders and nothing would be able to hurt him, and he would be strong.*
>
> *Livestock were most of his victims. These cattle were torn to pieces with most of their entrails pulled*

from their bodies and half eaten. Most of these accounts were written off as standard wolf attacks. It wasn't until Stich attacked a man, making several bite marks on his neck and torso, that the locals began to think these attacks were more than just random wolf encounters. The man's young son was later found half eaten, like the cattle. It was passed on that five other children were found dead in a similar fashion a short time thereafter.

These horrible deeds came to an end when a young farm boy came across upon a large wolf devouring its prey. Frightened, he called for help. The locals followed a trail of blood into the nearby forest where they found the remnants of something that had been eaten and a uniquely cured hide on the forest floor. Johan Stich was later seen walking near the small town by the forest's edge inquiring about a piece of hide that he had lost. Stich was immediately imprisoned for his suspicious nature only to be accused later of witchcraft and Satanic practices. Many days of imprisonment led to his confession to the brutal murders. Johan Stich was sentenced to death.

The means by which his execution was carried out began with the removal of his tongue. Some accounts say that his tongue was removed so that he would no longer be able to taste the blood of his victims, whereas other accounts state that it was so he could not cry out for God. It was claimed that his death was modeled after those he gave death. His limbs were broken, his body scorched with searing hot iron rods. His stomach was cut open and his entrails were pulled from within so that he may not feel fullness ever again. Some also stated that this released the souls of his victims. Just before his

hanging and dismemberment a priest uttered a
curse, damning his entire bloodline to hell.

The last line seemed to leap from the page. The other accounts of this story weren't explicit with this information. No priest had the power to condemn a soul to hell and damnation. This power only resided with God. In fact, priests were supposed to grant the soul a chance at redemption through the confession of the tongue. There, as plain as day, was a lead I had missed throughout all my years of research. More intriguing was that fact that the priest did not just condemn this one man, but his entire bloodline, the innocent. The intent was to destroy his entire seed. If this was documented, then surely other accounts were, too. I turned the page and read further:

Like most witches, the remains of Johan Stich were
burned. Some say that his daughter was also burned
alive. However, many claim that his daughter was so
grief stricken by the atrocities her father had
committed that she ran off, never to be seen again.
Others say that the Satan, provoked by the priest's
curse, imbued the daughter of Johan Stich with
immortality so she may bear the curse of her father
forever, yet still carry on his sinister deeds.

The priest never had a chance to ask for forgiveness because he must've thought that he had performed God's will when in fact he went against God's will. Since the evil stopped near the town, I bet he had no idea the terror he had unleashed for punishing the innocent, I thought. Moments into the next page, I stopped reading as I heard approaching footsteps. Half expecting to see Dr. Reynolds when I looked up, I was surprised to see a middle-aged man with silvering hair. He had an inquisitive look upon his face but walked with authority. Several other gentlemen walked behind him. I glanced back at the clock, and it read 2:51 p.m. *Damn!* I thought. *I should've left sooner.* A familiar scent filled my nose that made me feel very uneasy. One that was too familiar, one that was recent. I did not recognize any of the men, at first, but when the middle-aged man stopped at my table, I was immediately assaulted by visions in my head of the same man screaming, screaming a name, a name that was not clear.

"Excuse me," he said politely. "We don't mean to disturb your work but we're looking for a Dr. Mya Bishop, do you know her?"

The other men that were with him stood a short distance away from my table where I was sitting. "Who wants to know?" I asked knowing that I should not have said this, but I was too caught up in the uneasy feeling in the pit of my stomach to think clearly.

"Are you Dr. Bishop?" he asked in a guarded tone, aware of my nervousness. Something was wrong with this situation. Not waiting for my reply, he said, "Dr. Bishop, my name is Robert Osborne. Please forgive our intrusion, but the young girl behind the counter stated that you were here. We're interested in your research and would like to talk with you about it," the man said with a controlled fierceness behind his words as he sat in the chair opposite me at the table.

"I'm sorry but I can't talk with you now. If you would like to make an appointment with the College of Humanities, I would be more than happy to talk with you at a later time." I stood from the table, leaving the artifacts behind. I took my latex gloves off and began walking back towards the entrance, but one of the large men stepped in front of me and we collided. He crossed his arms, making a point to show off the large muscles on his arms. "Where ya going, cutie?" His voice was low, contemptuous. I looked up at him as I stepped backwards. He blew a taunting kiss at me.

"We've already tried to make an appointment with you, but no one in your department has seen you for nearly two months. Yesterday, Dean Garris seemed particularly put out by this." Irritation filled Robert's words. I did not like the way his polite posture changed to a more serious one. As he spoke, I understood the familiar scent. It was one I had encountered in the field a week earlier. I closed my eyes tight as an image of the man screaming in the darkness pierced my conscious mind. "I find it odd that a prominent member of the faculty of a prestigious university would just cancel all of her lectures, file for leave, and disappear only to reemerge here."

Simple nervousness turned to fear, and my breathing began to quicken, "What do you want with me?"

"First off, we understand that you're doing research, and this is probably why you've taken leave. We would like some help with questions we have." His voice was cold. Fear continued to build inside of me. "We also understand that us finding you here does not bode well with your employer..."

Robert's words seem to trail off, becoming muted. I could only hear my heart beating faster and faster. I tried to push passed the large man, but he grabbed me by both arms so tightly that my skin began to burn. Adrenaline coursed through his body; I could smell it.

Gripped with my own fear, I thrust my arms upwards with great force. He was obviously caught off guard by this and he released his hold on me. A surge of energy spread through my body like a wildfire. I grabbed the man by the lapels of his leather coat and lifted him off the ground. I threw him with an incredible force into shelf of books. It tipped backwards, spilling the artifacts all over the marble floor. I began to run towards the entrance. I could not stop, I had to get out. I had to get away from these men. I heard one of them yell "Stop!" but I did not listen. I could hear shouting behind me as well as the pop, pop, pop sound of a pistol. Several bullets wisped passed my head.

I was at a full sprint when I hit the entrance door of the depository. The massive metal structure came completely off the electronic hinges with ease. Several sparks flew into the air as I glanced back to see a horror-stricken Dr. Reynolds. I knew that after this moment I would never be able to come back to this place again. I would never get a chance to explain the strangeness of this situation. Part of me felt a twinge of remorse for all the kindness that he had shown me, but I did not have time to feel it fully.

Several pistol shots echoed behind me along with shouts of profanity and anger. I made my way quickly to the next door, taking care to open it fast without damaging it and before the security system electronically sealed it. Once on the other side I pushed it closed and heard the electronic lock snap into place, knowing that it would buy me some time from my pursuers. It would not open again since the other door was compromised. I glanced over at the student working behind the desk. She had a look of shock as she stared back at me. Without even a second look back, I turned and ran as fast as I could. *They know who I am now!* I thought. *They will search for me…Marcus…I must warn Marcus.*

Chapter #20

Dangerous Departing
Mya
2:56 p.m.

Once outside, I slowed myself to a fast-paced walk. Though my pursuers may be close behind, I did not want any more attention from onlookers. There was also no sign of the man on the bench. I looked one last time for him as I reached my SUV. My hands were shaking so hard it was difficult to press the key fob to unlock my vehicle. I could feel my heart rate pulsing through my neck and the warmth of blood rushing into my face. I needed to get away from the university. I needed to disappear again like I had always done in the past. *This time was different though; they knew who I was. They would be able to find me easier. The world wouldn't forget me this time.*

Only as I pulled away from the university did I take a moment to look back to see if I was still being followed. Thankfully, nothing indicated that the chase was going to continue at that moment. This thought rattled around inside my head for a while as my breathing slowly returned to a normal pace. The sound of my heartbeat echoing in my ears eventually slowed as well. Outside, the landscape passed by quickly with an occasional acceleration of my vehicle's engine. The sun was beginning to retreat from sky as the late afternoon began to creep up on the day. I did not bother to stop, despite the need to fill my car with petrol. *I can make it back,* I thought. *I need to warn Marcus if he is still at the estate. No one else can be harmed by me.*

There was still daylight, but the sun had fallen behind several dark clouds as I pulled up to my manor. Shadows covered it like a grim shroud. Instead of the handsome, old structure that I once called home, a monument of darkness with painful memories of evil deeds stood in its place. A sharp cold bit at my cheeks and the tip of my nose. I quickly made my way from the Land Rover to the foot of the steps and through the large double-hung oak doors. No lights were on at the front of the house. Some light passed through the windowpanes, but the foyer was mostly dark. I called out, "Marcus! Are you here?"

I glanced into the parlor where I first talked with him. It too was dark, and there was no sign that anyone had used the room in several days. The air was dusty smelling and dense. I turned away and walked to the first doorway of the many rooms that stretched down the hall. Taking a quick look from one corner to another, I was again met with disappointment. *He must be gone*, I thought. A strange sense of relief filled my insides. It did not last long though. Leaving the doorway, I was met with a man holding a gun with its barrel pointed directly at me. I froze.

"You stay right there, Mya!" Marcus said. "I won't hesitate to bring you down if you make any wrong move!"

Fear filled his voice, and I could hear the gun parts rattling as it shook in his hands. "Marcus, please put down the gun. I'm not going to hurt you," I said. "I can't stay long. Something has happened, and I have to go into hiding again."

Marcus did not respond at first. I could see the gun was the same tranquilizer gun that he had been using since the first night. Although he would not have been able to kill me, being rendered unconscious would have been equally as destructive, leaving me vulnerable to being found by anyone searching. Slowly he lowered the gun. "I've been tracking your whereabouts since I came to. I also saw a spike in your vitals about an hour ago and I was afraid you might return in werewolf form."

I looked at Marcus' face and across the bridge of his nose was a deep gash with a fair amount of swelling. His eyes were black and blue from the blood that must have drained into his sinus cavities. "Marcus, I'm sorry for what I did…I lost control." I paused to collect my thoughts before I continued. "I've come back to warn you. Marcus you're going to have to leave, you're in danger if..."

"I'm already leaving," he interrupted. "I've scheduled transportation to the airport this evening. I have a flight that leaves at 9:05 p.m. nonstop to Sydney, Australia."

An assortment of emotions flooded my mind. Much included sadness from the damage that I had caused, but also worry for Marcus. "Marcus, you can't wait until this evening! You're going to have to leave sooner than that. People know who I am. They were able to find me in the library and they'll be able to find where I live. They'll find you here!"

"What people? Who are you talking about?"

"Robert Osborne. He's the father of the girl I killed." My voice cracked with sadness and fear. "I don't know how they found me so fast, but I recognized the scent when they first approached. I couldn't place it, but the more Robert spoke, the more the memory of that night became clear. He was screaming that night, screaming at what he saw me do. He has men that are helping him, mercenaries by the looks of them. I must move fast. I was at the library, I panicked. I threw a member of his group into the shelves...they shot at me!"

"Jesus Mya, how long do you think before they get here?" Marcus asked.

"I don't know, but I have to leave soon."

"Where are you going to go?"

"I have to..."

"Crikey, you're bleeding!" he interrupted. I looked down at my shirt that was once a pale blue, it was now dark crimson. Quickly, I took off my leather coat and rolled up my shirt as Marcus came closer to have a look at it. There was a wound on my left side just below my ribs.

"I didn't even know I was hit." The wound must've happened when the men shot at me as I made my escape from the book depository. "Is it bad?"

"No. You're lucky. I suspect it may hurt for a bit, but it's only a flesh wound. I can do a quick patch if you like?" Marcus disappeared into the lavatory only to return moments later with a wet towel, tape, and some gauze pads. "Did they know you're a werewolf? I mean…were they using silver bullets?"

"I don't think so. It doesn't feel the same as silver." Marcus continued to patch my side.

"Well, based on what we've found this should heal the next time you change into a werewolf." I hated the casual demeanor of his comment. It was as though he knew I was going to change and there was nothing that could be done to prevent it. Marcus stood upright.

"Does this mean that a normal bullet would kill me?" I asked.

"As a human, maybe. You didn't feel it this time because of your heightened adrenaline from your panic. When you're a werewolf, this chemistry is at its peak and the bullets would probably pass right through you without as much as a scratch to show for it. Call it what you will, Mya, but you're a remarkable species," he stated.

I did not like being called a remarkable species, but I was not about to challenge Marcus on this notion. Instead, I focused on the immediate situation. "Marcus, do you still have your computer up? I have to use it."

"Yeah, just my netbook I was tracking you on, and my laptop. Everything else is packed up."

Again, I flinched at this. I knew it was too dangerous for Marcus to stay, but part of me had come to appreciate our interactions and was sad to know that they were coming to an end. If nothing else, during our conversations I was able to catch a glimpse of my humanity. "That'll be fine."

We walked down the hallway into the library where we had spent most of our time together. His equipment was packed up and pushed off to the left side of the entrance. Sitting on one of the large tables and still turned on was the small device that registered my vital signs and whereabouts. It beeped loudly as I got close to it. Next to it was Marcus' laptop. I touched the navigation pad at the bottom of the computer to release the screen saver. I pulled up a search program that I used when doing research at the university. The software did not bring up people who were still living, mainly due to privacy issues, but if someone was supposedly dead from two hundred and fifty years ago it would be able to bring up any records or writings about the person. I began typing immediately and while it was searching, Marcus slid a chair over to me. "What are you looking for?"

"I came across a name while at the book depository that really caught my attention: Kabona. He was a slave that was accused of killing his master and his entire family. Though he claimed that he was innocent, Kabona was imprisoned and was waiting for a trial when he escaped. Evidently the door to his cell was torn completely from the wall. He was accused of witchcraft; however, I feel that there was something else involved; a werewolf to be specific. The manner in which the attack occurred at the estate doesn't reflect witchcraft. Satanic witchcraft is more ritualistic, carries more ceremony. The people at the estate were supposedly torn to pieces. He also sustained a severe injury in the process. His method of escape, being that the cell door was ripped from solid stone, indicates something very strong and powerful came into the cell or left from the cell. It would make more sense that he became a werewolf since he didn't die from his injuries despite being probably treated very poorly. In the small account I managed to look over, it mentioned that he was imprisoned for nearly a month before his escape, which would indicate he changed at the first full moon after his initial attack. More noteworthy is that this escape supposedly happened in London," I explained.

We both sat for a moment while the software processed my request. Several matches popped up, but after sifting through many bogus ones I came across one titled Kabona of the Paige

Estate. The document was the official statement ordering the death of the slave Kabona by way of burning to death at the stake. Though a common fate for those believed to be agents of witchcraft, the date for such practices was wrong. Stake burnings ceased under King Charles II's decree in the late 1600's. Certainly suspicious, but the document only recounted the tale I had just explained to Marcus. I quickly typed in the name Kabona Paige into the search engine. Sure enough several matches popped up on the screen of a person carrying this name and were all of African descent. Birth certificates were dated nearly a hundred years after the supposed time of his escape in 1753. Other documents told of his involvement with local merchants and businesses, positions a person of color would have had trouble holding. I managed to trace the history and genealogy of this person through the 19th and 20th centuries until the documentation ran dry, indicating that the members of this family tree were still alive. The final document was the death announcement of a man named Carris Paige that had a son by the name of Corbin who still resided in London.

Having practiced them for many decades, I was relieved to have such superior research skills. I had a keen eye for certain details and was fast at incorporating them into other research. This proved helpful since the afternoon was almost gone and the evening approached. The time was past 5:00 p.m. Marcus had moved all his equipment into the main hallway and had patiently waited while I did my research before asking, "Have you found anything?"

"Yes, I've one more search to do and then I'll be done." I responded. I typed the name Corbin Paige into the local listings and brought up an address in London of a night club. "That's where I need to go!"

"You're going to a night club?" he asked incredulously. "I thought you were going into hiding?"

"I am...I will, but I need to follow this one lead. I need to know if my suspicions about this person are correct. This man may have done the same thing I did throughout history," I explained. I excused myself and walked to my quarters down the hall and quickly changed clothes. Having a blood-soaked shirt was not going to be proper attire for a night club. I pulled a long sleeve, black, form-fitting shirt from my wardrobe. It had a v-neck that stretched to the middle of my chest exposing my endowments. I pulled the shirt gently over the wound in my side. Though, patched I did not want the wound to start bleeding again. Coupled with black leather pants and boots that went to mid-calf, I resembled every other young person looking to go out to a club. Though my true age was over two hundred years old, I still had the look of a young women in her late twenties or early thirties. When I reemerged, Marcus was standing in foyer. I looked into the library as I walked past and realized that he had packed his laptop and small tracking device.

"I could help you know," Marcus said. I sensed that even though he had packed his belongings and was scheduled to leave, if I had responded in a pleading manner he might have stayed.

"No Marcus, this'll be too dangerous. You've done more for me than you realize and for that I thank you, but you must leave soon."

"I called the transportation agency while you were doing your research and they have rescheduled to pick me up within an hour," he stated.

Trepidation was displayed across his face as I walked past him through the oak doors. I stopped and embraced the darkness of the early evening and the coolness of the season. Small flakes of snow, mixed with a light rain fell from the blackened sky. I turned towards Marcus one last time. Leaning forward on my toes, I gently kissed his forehead. "You're a good man, Marcus. I pray that God is kind to you and keeps you safe."

"I should hope that *He* would do the same for you," he responded.

CHAPTER #21

The Hunt
Grayson Osborne
Saturday, December 5, 2009
5:30 p.m.

I sat in one of the chairs in my father's study and watched as several grown men aggressively argue back and forth about the events that occurred earlier in the day. Codie sat at the desk staring at a computer screen, seemingly numb to his surroundings. The name Kabona was scribbled on the notepad that Dr. Bishop had left behind in the book depository. Codie was set with the task of trying to discover the significance of the name and to discover everything there was to know about Dr. Bishop. Jinx, the obnoxious, oversized mercenary, was cursing loudly at my father, while the other mercenaries stood behind him.

"What the *fuck* happened back there?" Jinx yelled. He was holding an ice pack on the back of his head where a fairly large gash and swollen lump resided, an apparent injury from being thrown into the bookshelf.

Not backing down in any way, my father spat back at Jinx with an equal amount of venom, "Look I never said this was going to be easy. Besides, I thought you blokes were supposed to be good at what you do! Maybe I hired the wrong men!"

"I mean this *fuck'n* princess was no ballerina! Fuck, I don't know what she is?"

"She's a werewolf," I broke in as I stood and walked towards Jinx and the other men. "I told you yesterday, we're hunting a werewolf."

"I thought yer little puppies were only supposed to change when the moon is out!" Jinx said half serious, half taunting.

"According to everything we've seen and learned, they do; however, they are obviously strong even when the moon isn't out. Oh…that's right. You weren't awake for most of that." I wanted to provoke Jinx.

This enraged the man even more, "Are ya start'n with me boyo? Ya prissy Brit, I'll fuck'n have ya right here!"

"I bet you will," I mocked him, daring him to carry out what his words already declared.

Jinx lunged forward at me, but I unbalanced him when I grabbed the seams of his coat and forced his momentum to the left. He tripped over my extended leg and hit the floor with a loud crash, as I rolled on top. I knew he was armed and that his first reaction would be to go for either his pistol or knife along his belt. But I was used to this kind of warfare and was much faster than him. I pinned his right arm to the ground, pulled the knife from his belt and pushed it hard against his throat.

"Enough!" yelled my father. "Grayson, let him up!"

I held the knife firm against his skin, ready to pull it fast across his carotid artery. I stared into Jinx's eyes and caught only the look of fury as he struggled against my hold. He reminded me of a man I killed in Afghanistan. He was our informant. He tried to betray our company on a recon mission. He acted out of fear and drew a weapon on my sergeant. It only took a couple of minutes to bleed him out.

Had Jinx been faster, he would have killed me. He had complained enough, though. I had learned long ago loud mouths were not productive to the mission and often times needed dealt with quickly before they put other members of the company in danger. With a quick motion, I flipped the knife in my hand away from Jinx's neck and stood to my feet. The other mercenaries were surprised at what happened and made no advances towards me. Codie had also stopped what he was doing and sat aghast. Rubbing the back of his head that had started bleeding again from the impact of the fall, Jinx rose to his feet. As tempered as he was, he made no indication that he wanted to continue this dance. He glared at me before turning to face my father again.

"I think given the circumstances and the hostility of the working conditions ya need to fork out a bit more pay; otherwise, find someone else to carry out this fucked-up mission," Jinx said.

"Listen to me, you slimy piece of Irish shit! The terms that were agreed upon aren't going to change, so deal with it or I'll make sure that you disappear permanently. I'm sure the world won't even ask a question about a murderous C.I.R.A. member found dead, floating in the canal!" My father was furious. Jinx spat on the wood floor before turning and walking to the far side of the room. Still angry, dad slammed his hand down on his desk. "Of all the fucking people, the first person we seek out for help ends up being the werewolf we're looking for!"

"Dad, we don't know that. Even though it's a good bet that she's something other than human, judging by how easy she was able to toss Jinx and the damage she caused to the electronically sealed door, we don't know if she was the same creature that attacked Laryn," I explained as I noticed Jinx shoot me a glance of disgust at the recounting of his mishap.

"Are you *fucking* blind Grayson? Didn't you see her eyes? The bright green color and the vehemence just before everything happened! I'll never forget those eyes! Those eyes were the same as the ones that night in the field! The ones that ripped your sister apart!"

I winced at the memory of Laryn's attack. I had endured several insults, unintentional, but still painful over the past week as I watched the sadness inside my dad turn to anger and rage. It had blinded him and may continue to do so in the future, but he had to understand that as a military officer I could not operate with the false sense of only facing a single enemy, "I remember Laryn's attack all too well, but you have to realize that Dr. Bishop may be one of many werewolves and that she may be in league with others." He did not respond. Instead, he turned away from me and placed a hand over his forehead. Diverting my attention away from him, I turned to

Codie. He was still trying to take in the whole situation. "Have you found anything out about Dr. Bishop or that name on the notepad?"

Shaken back into reality, Codie turned in his chair to face the computer again and said, "Uh, yeah, I found a few things," I walked over to where he was sitting and looked over his shoulder. Dad, without saying a word, paused for a moment before reluctantly doing the same. "I was able to pull up a picture of Dr. Bishop as well as a picture of Dr. Cassandra Bishop."

He minimized the two pictures so they could be viewed next to each other on the screen. The only difference in the two pictures was that Dr. Mya Bishop had a streak of auburn in her hair where Dr. Cassandra Bishop had a streak of grey. Other than that, the two pictures were virtually identical. "Bloody hell!" dad said from over my shoulder. "They're the same person!"

I could not deny it. They appeared to be the same. Same mouth structure, same nose, same jawline, and the same strikingly vibrant green eyes. Before I could respond to this discovery, dad turned towards the mercenaries that were standing across the room listening intently and said, "Kap, how are those silver bullets coming?"

Kap stepped forward, "I've got plenty of silver, some from the pawn shops nearby but mostly from items around your house," he said with a smirk. "All I need to do is melt it down, shape them, and they're ready to fly! I got me a propane torch in the van. I was just waiting on your say so to use your pieces from around the house."

Dad hesitated for a moment, but then gave him the okay to use the items mentioned. Kap nodded and left the room. Most of the silver products in the house came from dad and mum's wedding gifts. They had received actual silverware and plenty of silver platters. Most of the sentimental value was gone, at least I assumed. Especially after the accusations mum had of dad the day of the funeral. They clearly still had an effect upon him.

"Snake, I need you to locate where Dr. Bishop lives. I doubt we'll be able to track her scans from her library access card again, but we may get lucky at her home," I stated.

"I already have her address. I pulled her information as soon as Jinx called after your meeting yesterday with the dean. Her estate is about an hour and a half from here."

"Nice work. Codie, is there anything else you found?" I asked.

"This Kabona character apparently was a slave that was accused of witchcraft for killing his master and his master's entire family. He was imprisoned and waited for a month to be tried before he escaped. Seemingly, the way he escaped involved breaking through the metal cage door to his cell. After that, he was never seen again. The account on him is small, but it was the only one I could find."

"Well, Dr. Bishop had the name written down for a reason. Perhaps she thinks this guy is another werewolf?" I looked towards dad briefly as if to suggest evidence for my earlier point. I turned to look at Snake again. He was already typing things onto his laptop computer, when I asked, "You got him yet?"

Jinx finally emerged from the corner that he was sulking in, aware now that the petty squabble was over and that we were back to business. He looked over Snake's shoulder as he typed. "Alright, I've cross-referenced the name in my database with that of London's data base of personal listings and we have a match. A man of African descent carrying a name that stems from this one…owns and operates a nightclub in the Soho district, it's a bit north of Leicester Square. He's apparently the ancestor from an African named Kabona who lived roughly two hundred and fifty years ago. It's a long shot but out of the fifty-two possibilities this is the closest match to the story that Junior found over there," Snake said, not worried about whether Codie took offense to being called junior.

"As soon as Kap gets done with the bullets, we'll check out both places tonight. Kap and I will go to the club to see if we can find anything. The rest of you will go to the estate of Dr. Bishop," I stated. Turning towards Rex and Snake, "We'll need you both to scout out the location to see if anyone is home. Once it has been determined that it's clear, the rest of you can move in. Rex, they'll need your sniper cover when going into the house. Try to get a spot off the ground in a tree or something… you don't want this thing sneaking up behind you in the dark. Hold your position until I make contact."

Rex nodded in agreement. It took Kap less than an hour to melt down all the silver products that he had collected and to make several silver bullet cartridges, enough to fill the magazines for the pistols we had along with several spare magazines. He explained that it would take a bit longer to custom form the bullets to the AR-15s, but he was at least able to make several cartridges for Rex's sniper rifle. It was apparent that he had not only done this kind of work before but was also extremely good at it. Never in my service in the army had I known a man that was as skilled as Kap with making bullets. His accent was similar to Snake's, more English than Irish. I could not help but wonder where he got this kind of training. *Irish Republican Army probably.* It was a waste that he had become a mercenary instead of serving in the Royal Army; many of the former soldiers joined up, but many feared becoming targets of C.I.R.A.

We all made our way towards the front entry of the manor. Ferocity still lingered inside my father. I could tell by the look on his face and his silent demeanor as we stepped outside. Jinx was equally pissed off, but instead of being silent about it, he made a point to let everyone know by announcing to his crew that this gig was *equivalent to shit beaten up in a bucket.* I did not say anything to him. Jinx reminded me of a dog that pissed on the ground to mark his territory when another dog came around that had the potential of being meaner. It was not a pissing battle that I wanted to engage in at that moment; there was no point. I had to remain clear headed.

I stepped out into the early evening darkness. The air was cold against my face, and I could see my breath as I exhaled. Everyone was loading up the vans with guns and other equipment, making sure to double check the supplies before we left. Everyone except Codie. He stood at the top of stone steps staring out at the vans with a look of apprehension on his face. I looked from him to the vans and realized that he was feeling the same fear a new soldier gets just before they enter a combat zone. Over the years I had grown used to this feeling and paid it little attention, especially if I had other men that were counting on me to lead. Slowly, I walked towards Codie. He broke his stare from the vans and fixated his gaze upon me. His brow was creased with concern. Before he could say a word, I spoke, "Codie, I know what you're going through and I'm not the one that's going to deny you the opportunity to hunt this thing. You're man enough to make the decision on your own. Just know that there's no shame in being afraid."

Codie swallowed hard before asking, "Are you afraid to go after this…this thing?"

"There has never been a time that I wasn't afraid, it never mattered the kind of mission. It could be a routine patrol or the order to seek and destroy a target and I would have the same anxiety…the same fear," I said calmly. I could tell that dad was getting impatient as were the other men, but Codie needed to hear this.

"How do you get passed it?" he asked in a shaky voice.

"I always thought of my mates, of home, of you chaps here, of what I was fighting to protect. You can never really get passed it; you can only be distracted from it momentarily." Codie began to say something, but it tapered off before he could get it out. Even though he spoke boldly and with conviction several times before this, it was evident that he did not want to be a part of this mission, but he did *not* want to let anyone down or lose face in front of the barbaric men. "Codie, I need your help tonight. Can you stay behind to contact the priest Dean William Garris spoke of earlier? He may know things about Dr. Bishop that can help us. Have Henry help if you run into problems with access to information. We may be able to use dad's authority as a member of the House of Commons to get passed potential roadblocks. Off you go."

Codie seemed relieved by this request. Though he did not say it out right, he gave a nod of thanks before turning to go back into the house.

"What's going on?" dad yelled from the vehicle. I walked quickly away from the house and joined him at the door of the car. "Is Codie all right?"

"Yeah, he's fine. I need him to find out more information about Dr. Bishop, so he's going to stay behind."

Dad did not bother to question further. He too had a look of relief on his face and understood what I had done for Codie. I got into the van with Kap. He drove ahead of the other convoy but as we pulled away from the manor, they turned the opposite direction to go to Dr. Bishop's estate. Neither of us said a word. Snow mixed with rain making it miserable. I took a deep breath and exhaled slowly. My thoughts were filled with the events of the day and with the fear of the events yet to come. Darkness stretched out on the road before us.

Chapter #22

The Nightclub
Mya
Saturday, December 5, 2009
6:35 p.m.

When I left Marcus at the estate my heart was filled with sadness. He had been the only person that I could confide in my dark secret and the only one that helped me to try to understand why I'd become the thing I was. For this reason, I had to leave him behind. We both knew what I could do if I was pushed to my limits. *Even with Marcus' scientific notions and methodology, I must do things that are too dangerous for him to be involved*, I thought.

I let my head rest on the steering wheel of my Land Rover. I parked at the far end of the South Park and Ride at the Cambridge Station. On a Saturday night in London there would truly be no parking and I would spend most of my time driving around looking for a spot. I grabbed the identification card for the library and finally stepped out into the evening. *Time to go.*

I planned on leaving my vehicle at the park and ride. I removed the license plate and made sure that I did not leave anything that could identify me inside. I was careful to do this discreetly. Other people had a similar idea of taking the tube into London. Eventually someone would notice my vehicle was abandoned and call for it to be towed off, but I did not want someone to notice it now. When finished, I made my way to the entrance of the tube station, dropping the license plate and library ID card into a waste receptacle.

The wintery mix had picked up quite a bit from when I first left my estate, yet the loads of partygoers that poured into the tube station seemed undeterred from the search for London's entertainment. Some people were dressed appropriately in woolen coats and scarves, and carried umbrellas, whereas others, mostly younger people, were dressed to attract attention. They wore form-fitting jeans of all colors and skin-tight tops that revealed too much. It mattered not that the high temperature for the day was only eight degrees centigrade and that the temperature gauge at the station now read three degrees centigrade; they were out to attract a mate or would-be relationship.

Hmm! Methods of courtship have changed drastically over the past two hundred years, I thought as I waited for the train. Wearing clothing that revealed a woman's breasts was considered vulgar and was reserved for the tramps that worked the back alleys of the marketplaces or the kind of women that filled the brothels. No civilized woman would be caught in public in such attire. But who was I to criticize; I too was dressed in this manner; however, I was certainly not trying to attract a mate. I was merely trying to blend in with the crowd.

The train arrived on schedule at 6:45 p.m. Hundreds of people emptied into the exchange station as seemingly hundreds more piled onto the train. For some this was their final destination, for others it was merely a place to see before heading into London. The train was packed, standing room only, but I was fortunate enough to be pushed to the rear of the car where I could lean against the back panel. It was going to take about 50 minutes to make it to King's Cross. I needed to go unnoticed.

Most of the trip I was lost in thought about all that had happened, with Marcus, the young girl that I had killed, and what I was attempting to do. I paid no attention to the ramblings of those around me. I merely stared out the window of the train, watching the occasional flashing of the lights mounted inside the tube as the train passed by them. I arrived at King's Cross at 7:27 p.m. Tourists flooded the platform. Many were looking at the tube maps to locate their next destination, while others snapped "selfies" of each other posing as proof of their trip to this London landmark. I merely made my way to escalators. *I need to take the Piccadilly line to the Leicester Square station. This will put me south of the club.*

From the bottom of the escalators the theater advertisements that hung on the walls looked crooked, yet once I was on the escalator, they were perfectly positioned at eye level. *I'm the opposite,* I thought. *At first glance I look normal, but the closer someone gets the more crooked I appear.* I stayed to the right on the escalators, allowing those that were in a hurry to move past me without any trouble. I was in a hurry, but the less people noticed me the better off I was going to be, especially after the library incident. There was no doubt that I was going to be on the authorities watch list. Law enforcement was too strict for an event such as this to go unnoticed.

It was a short walk to the other exchange station. I paid my fee to ride and soon enough I was on the train headed to Leicester Square. I emerged from the tube station at 7:55 p.m. among oceans of people. A sense of relief washed over me. I took a couple of long deep breaths knowing that it would be nearly impossible to single me out, even with security cameras posted everywhere. Briefly I looked around. I hoped to fancy a look of the London Eye, but no good view emerged amongst the buildings. It was difficult to see much of anything because of the holiday *fun fair* that occupied the space.

The club was located on Greek Street. I kept my head low and walked north past several half price theaters, sex shops, pubs, and cafés, all busy with customers. In the distance, I could hear *Big Ben* chime the eight o'clock hour. A neon sign shone; *Club Red,* against the darkened night sky. Inside, I could hear the deep thumps of bass and the cheering from the patrons. A line stretched down the walkway and around the corner. At the front, a large man stood behind a velvet red rope with a clipboard in his hand. He wore a headset atop his slicked back hair. A wool trench coat, black in color stopped at his knees, but covered his black suit. His entire wardrobe for the evening was in sharp contrast to his pale white skin. Despite his dapper look, the man reeked of security. I knew that I would not be able to sneak past him, but I also was *not* going to wait in a line all night like some groupie trying to be a member of the popular crowd. I walked straight up to the large man, ignoring the jeers and taunts from the crowd of people and placed my arms around his neck, pressing my breasts against him.

"Do I really have to wait in this loooonnng line?" I drew my left hand down his chest and onto his stomach, while my right hand caressed the back of his neck.

Clearly the man was caught off guard, but responded the way I wanted him to: "Er…yeah, I mean no…I mean is your name on the list?"

"You know full well that my name is not on that list, but it should be." I pressed my breasts harder into the man and twirling my fingers around his hair on the back of his head. Normally this probably would not have worked if I was an ordinary woman, especially with this man, yet I was anything but an ordinary woman. I learned a long time ago that men respond to the animalistic nature of women under the right circumstances and under these circumstances are rendered powerless to the female advances. Though this man was strong he was weakened by the warmth of my body against his amidst the wintery mix and the cold night air. I looked directly into his eyes, breathed heavily before pursing my lips together. His heart rate quickened, and I could feel the nervousness in his body. We broke our embrace when another man standing within the doorway yelled, "BLOODY HELL, DANNY! Are you going to let some people in or not? I been hold'n this door for nearly five minutes and it's fuck'n cold!"

The large man named Danny looked slightly embarrassed, but nonetheless motioned me through with three other people that were at the front of the line. I entered through the doorway still able to hear the protests from the people I had just cut in front of and walked down a narrow hallway that was lit with red lighting only to end with another security guard and a young female sitting behind a metal cage. "That'll be ten pounds," she stated as I approached.

A sudden rush of panic washed over me as I realized that I had not anticipated paying to get into the club and had spent what I had on the tube fair. The girl from behind the cage had half her head dyed red that looked like blood stains from a wound. She stared at me with disgust as I fumbled around pretending to look for money. Several piercings in her ears, nose, and lips were all connected by a chain. Tattoos stretched up her arms disappearing below her sleeveless top. Knowing that I had spent my money, but not willing to forgo this venture by turning back I simply stated, "They got my cover!" as I pointed to the people who were walking behind me.

I did not wait for the girl to respond and pushed passed the security guard through the red curtain that marked the entrance into the club. Once inside it was easy to disappear with my black outfit. It was very dark with flashing strobe lights. I peered back only once to see the security guard coming down the steps that I had just taken, scanning the inside for me but without knowing where I had gone. The bass from the techno music was so loud that it drowned most of the cheering from the partiers and shook my insides. I was hoping to find the owner of the club, Corbin Paige, but truthfully, I did not know who I needed to find.

The dance floor was open with several stages spread around a center bar area. I moved through the crowd with relative ease. I glanced around and noticed huge speakers that rested on the ground along the walls and hung in the corners of the high ceiling. Each stage had multiple people on it all swinging glow sticks in their hands to the beat of the music. The glow was mesmerizing amidst the beams of red light that flashed from various spots throughout. Jetting out from one of the walls over the main dance floor was an office made of glass. Several people were in the space, and one appeared to be looking out over the people below. I figured that if the owner were in the club this was where he would have been. Under the office was another smaller bar that had glowing red lights that reflected off the mirrors behind the liquor bottles. Just to the right of it was an archway with a sign above that read *VIP Lounge*.

Access to the office above must be through there, I thought. I quickened my steps towards the archway but stopped to look at some commotion to my left. The security guard from the hallway pay station was moving in my direction, staring directly at me. I diverted my eyes and tried to blend in the best I could. It was no use. His gaze was fixed upon me. More panic filled my body and spurred me to move faster towards the archway. My thought was that I would be able to blend in with the darkness better once inside the lounge and that perhaps he would lose sight of me again.

I was fortunate that there were several people that still stood between me and the security guard. They were all unaware of the circumstances, which made it hard for him to push passed them. Being a bit smaller I slipped past those that stood before me and found myself standing at the archway. I was just about to enter the darkened area when a hand grasped my wrist and twisted it upwards.

Another large man in a black suit had his left hand over his left ear and he spoke into a headset. I could make out the words, "Got her!"

"Let go of me!" I wailed as I twisted my arm free from his grasp. "What the hell do you think you're doing?"

The large man was surprised by my ability to free myself. The surprised look was quickly replaced with anger as he yelled over the thumping bass, "Look lady, you didn't pay the fee to get in so we're going to have to escort you out!" He placed his left hand over his left ear again and spoke into the headset, "I'm bringing her out right now."

"I need to speak with the owner of the club. It's important! Please let me by!" I pleaded. It did nothing. The large man blocked my path and shoved me backwards. By this point, the first security guard from the pay station had caught up to me and began assisting the other man with taking me outside. They pulled me in front of the bar next to the archway. I writhed within their grip. "Please I have to speak with the owner!"

"Listen you dumb bitch! I don't give a shit who you want to talk with, you didn't pay to get in!" the security guard yelled. A menacing look spread across both their faces. Under normal circumstances, I would have let the men escort me out without drawing too much attention to myself. In fact, on normal circumstances I would have simply scheduled a meeting with the owner during the daytime. But this was not normal. Time was against me. Other men were hunting me. I felt my heart rate accelerate and the blood rush into my face. The fear inside of me swelled with the thought of what was happening. My muscles tensed against the hold the security guards had on me. I yanked my arms in tight, freeing myself from them both.

One of the guards reached out for me, but I grabbed the lapels of his suit and drove my forehead upwards into his mouth and nose. Blood streamed out and spilled down the front of him. Still holding the lapels of his suit, I lifted him off his feet and threw him over the small bar into the shelves of liquor bottles, shattering one of the mirrors! My breathing intensified as I felt a power surging through my body. The other guard grabbed me in a bear hug from behind and lifted me up. His crushing hold pressed down against the wound in my side. Pain pierced my body as I twisted and turned against his arms. I slipped down from his grasp, but his right arm momentarily remained draped over my shoulder, around my chest, still trying to hold onto me. I grabbed hold of his arm with both of my hands, my left at his wrist and my right at his elbow. Driven by fear, I pushed with an enormous amount of strength in opposite directions. His arm broke at the elbow like a twig under the pressure. The music came to a stop as the man crumbled to his knees screaming in agony.

Others that had realized what was happening screamed in terror at the injured man wriggling on the ground holding his dangling right arm. There I stood, fists clenched, arms shaking, trying to fight back an unspeakable force within, but it was too late. Fear had overwhelmed me. I watched my skin burst forth with brown fur as the muscles in my arms and legs increased in size. My back arched and my clothing ripped from my body. The bones in my face cracked and moved forward into a snout. Canine teeth protruded from either side. The screams of those around me grew louder and louder. I fell forward as my legs broke backwards against my knees to form the legs of a wolf. I watched my hands that were once small grow large as pointed claws pushed out from the tips of my fingers.

People were trying desperately to flee the club, horrified at the events that were taking place. I forced myself to stand upright, shook my head from side to side and let out a howl. The security guard that I had thrown over the small bar, a bit dazed, finally stood. He too recoiled and screamed in terror! My head whipped around and fixated on him. I leapt upon the bar and stared down. I now towered over the trapped man. His hands shook with fear as I growled and reached for him. Among the broken shards of the mirror, I caught a glimpse of myself and paused for a moment. Eyes stared back at me glowing green with fury. Staring back at me was my nightmare.

Chapter #23


```
The Werewolf
Grayson
Saturday, December 5, 2009
7:55 p.m.
```

"Bollocks! We should've taken the bloody tube!" Kap was not the most patient of individuals. We found the club with relative ease. The GPS in his van brought us directly in front of the establishment. Parking, on the other hand, was another matter.

"There's no way we would've been able to take our side-arms into the tube. If we were to be caught by the transit police…checkmate my friend. This game would be over." It took some time, but we managed to find a spot a block and a half away from the location of the club just north of Soho Square. There were *No Parking* signs posted with the threat of a fine unless we were a commercial vehicle. Kap assured me that even though we bore no markings of a commercial business, the van would look the part long enough for us to check out the club.

"Look, we'll be fit right here. Our vans have fake license plate numbers and by the time anyone figures that out, we'll be gone."

"It's a risk, but we don't have much choice."

As we both stepped out of the van, we were immediately hit with the coldness of the evening. Several people walked past us on the walkways. Most were too busy in conversation with one another or trying to stave off the bad weather to bother paying us any attention. I wanted it this way; we needed to prepare a few things before we went into the club. Kap opened the back door to the van and motioned to get my attention. I joined him at the rear of the van, and he handed me a harness. I took off my leather coat, slid my arms through the arm loops and adjusted it so that it laid flat against my back.

On either side of the harness there was a place to hold a sidearm.

"Do ya really think we're going to find out anything while we're here?" Kap asked as he adjusted his own harness.

"I don't know; I don't want to take any chances though." I examined the magazine that contained silver bullets. I had never seen bullets made of solid silver. They shimmered in the light of the streetlamps above. Not giving it a second thought, I jammed the magazine into the Glock G17 RTF2 9mm, pulled back on the action to make sure that the cartridge entered the chamber without anything jamming. Kap did the same. I placed the weapon in one of the spots on my holster and reached for the second Glock. "All I do know is that I want to get in, talk with the owner of the club, and get out as fast as possible. I feel that we should try and meet up with the others at Dr. Bishop's estate. Parking here also makes me nervous."

"I told ya already, we'll be fine and fit parking here. If ya were that concerned about the estate, why didn't we all go there first, then follow up with this lead after we established a safe zone?" Kap's question was genuine.

"In Afghanistan, I was in charge of a company of soldiers that would carry out highly complex search and destroy missions. I would leave my Sergeant in charge of locating the siege point while I and a few other mates in my company would confirm intelligence that we had received about the location or a secondary target. The other soldiers would hold their position until the information was confirmed then they would move in on the target. By doing it this way, the recon team was less of a threat to the local town's people, and they were more likely to offer up the information we needed. These missions were designed to be carried out fast, but with efficiency," I explained. "Our situation tonight is no different. I told Snake and Rex to hold their position until they had received word from us. This also gives them a chance to scope the area for other dangers. We're the recon team. Though my father is the diplomat, he unfortunately is blinded by his own anger to effectively extract information. Much like Jinx, he would be forceful rather than tactful. Should this be a false lead, then we'll be able to rejoin the rest within couple of hours or so without drawing too much suspicion to ourselves; however, if this information proves to be useful then we may gain a leg up on our adversary."

Kap nodded in agreement and continued to load his weapons. The harnesses that we both wore were covered by our coats. We looked like two normal blokes that were seeking excitement for an evening. I did not want people to know that we were armed. I had learned through the many military operations that the less threatening I appeared the easier it was to complete an objective. Kap did not say much else even as we walked down the street towards the club. I informed him that we would be able to use my father's authority to get into the club should we meet any resistance. Again, Kap merely listened. He was very aware of his surroundings and mindful of those who demonstrated expertise in areas that were foreign to him. *His talents are being wasted as a mercenary or even with the troubles in Northern Ireland,* I thought. *Big Ben* broke my train of thought with his eight o'clock chimes.

The night was miserable. Cold rain mixed with snow made the walk to the club almost unbearable. A line stretched down the walkway with people dressed in nothing more than light t-shirts or tops that barely covered their upper torso. Most stood shivering with skin bright red from the cold. *These people are idiots.* Deep thumps of bass pulsed from within the building, occasionally broken by cheers of the patrons inside. We walked past these people to the head of the line where we were met by a security guard that held his hand out signaling to stop.

"I'm sorry, gentlemen, but you'll have to go to the end of the line, unless your names are on the list," the security guard stated.

"I understand sir, but please allow me to introduce myself. I'm Grayson Osborne, son of Robert Osborne, a member of the House of Commons. I serve as a Lieutenant in her majesty's Royal Army and as a matter of security and safety would like to speak with the owner of this establishment," I responded showing him my military identification card.

"Sir, I appreciate your position, but I have explicit instructions to make sure that those who enter stay in balance with those who leave, unless your name is on this list," the security guard chided as he held his clipboard up in the air. "If you would like to speak to the owner, please schedule a time to meet with him at a more appropriate hour. Now sir, would you please move to the back of the line?"

I moved a step closer to the large man, with my back turned towards the line of people so they could not see what I was doing. Slowly, I pulled the lapel of my coat back to reveal the Glock holstered under my left arm. Kap followed suit. In a lower, more serious tone I said, "You don't fully understand the gravity of the situation. We really need to speak with the owner, now."

The man's eyes fixated on my weapon for a moment then moved to the weapon Kap was displaying under his coat too. Before he could respond, another security guard walked out from the entrance of the club. He was the same build as the first security guard and was dressed in the same attire. This man spoke into a headset before addressing us, "The owner of the establishment is unavailable at the moment," he stated, obviously aware of the situation. Perhaps he was able to see and hear what was going on from the small security camera that was mounted above the doorway. "Can either of you gentlemen produce paperwork that can demonstrate proper cause to enter? Otherwise, we'll not be able to allow you to enter with your weapons and may be forced to call the authorities."

Before I could respond to the man, the music from inside suddenly cut off and was followed by a crash and several screams from people inside. The second security guard placed his hand over his ear to hear something on his headset, before turning and running back into the club. Both Kap and I looked at each other and we each pulled a pistol from under our coats. The first security guard backed away from us quickly with his hands held up in the air signaling that he did not want to stop us from entering.

Taking full advantage of this disturbance, we moved past the guard outside and ran down a long, darkened hallway lit by red lights. A strangely dressed girl was standing behind a caged pay station, but she was not looking in our direction. She was instead turned towards her left staring out from behind a window that overlooked a dance floor. Neither Kap nor I stopped to ask the girl any questions, but instead pushed our way through the black curtain that hung to our right.

Another scream resonated above the rest. This was a scream of fear and extreme pain. I knew this agonizing cry all too well, having seen several men in combat loose limbs from IEDs while doing routine patrols. The wails of pain persisted as we closed in on its location within the club, fighting hard to push past the people desperately trying to escape. We finally made our way to a wide stairwell that led towards the main dance floor. About a hundred feet away from us we saw a clearing in the people and a brown-haired woman, dressed in black, standing in the center. A man was crumbled on the ground, wailing at her feet, holding his right arm that was dangling at the elbow.

"Holy shit! It's her!" I yelled as I continued to push beyond the waves of people trying to leave.

What I saw next froze me in my tracks. I watched in horror as the woman standing in the clearing fell forward and her skin broke forth with fur. Her arms and legs grew in size as her clothing ripped from her body. Her face was no longer recognizable as that of a human. A snout pushed forward from her mouth and oversized canine teeth protruded from either side. Pointy ears projected out from atop her head and her eyes glowed bright green against the red lighting of the club. The monster stood on its hind legs, towering over the man at its feet. It shook its head from side to side before letting out a snarling howl that sent shivers down my back along with flashbacks of the night Laryn was killed. The thing turned its head with a snap to the right and focused on a man trapped behind a small bar. The werewolf took two steps before leaping into the air and landing on top of the smooth wooden surface. I could hear it crack under the weight of the beast. It appeared to be staring down at the man.

I rushed towards the beast, knowing I had to get closer before I could fire. I stopped and took aim at the beast!

Pop!

I let the first bullet fly. It connected with its right shoulder, spraying blood onto the broken mirror behind the bar. It howled in pain falling from the bar top. It swung around with sinister speed to face me. It held its arms out to the side and let out another vicious snarling howl!

Pop! Pop!

I let the second and third bullets fly. The second one missed the beast altogether as I watched the wood of the bar splinter beside the werewolf. The third, however, punched a hole in the upper thigh of the monster. It howled in pain again as blood spilled down onto the floor. I quickly realized that I was not as precise as I needed to be to get a killing shot, perhaps because the bullets were silver the accuracy at that distance was worse than I had anticipated.

I began to move closer to the beast squeezing the trigger two more times. It lunged to the left to avoid the shots. It then turned and leapt down another darkened hallway. Most of the people in the club had already fled, so I let another few shots go in the direction of the beast. Kap quickly joined in with sending a barrage of bullets at the werewolf. A shot caught it square in the back as it howled and crashed to the floor in the hallway. Silhouetted against the red lighting, I saw the beast once again rise from the floor. It continued down the hall which turned to the right at the end. As it rounded the corner, seconds later we heard a collision and the bending of metal. I pulled the second gun from my holster, knowing it was fully loaded. I positioned the other gun back into its place under my left arm. Kap had both guns pulled now and aimed straight ahead down the hallway. Both of us were ready for the thing to spring forth and attack. Cautiously, we approached the corner, "I'm going to swing around first and aim high! You follow and aim low!" I quickly explained to Kap. He gave a nod but said nothing.

Both of us swung around the corner only to find an empty hallway. The double security doors at the end of the hall were dislodged from their hinges and the frame that held it in place was bent and twisted. Two other doors were on the left, one labeled MEN and the other labeled WOMEN. Both seemed to still be intact. With our guns drawn we made our way towards the smashed door. It led into a back alley, which was apparently used for delivering liquor to the club. Kap exited first moving to the left and I followed moving to the right. Both of us stayed close to the doorway and looked around for any sign of the werewolf. There was none. The alley was easily accessible from Greek Street to the right. To the left, it looked as though it led on to a tight, intricate network of other alleys. Pools of blood indicated that this was the way the thing went; however, in Afghanistan, many of the towns or cities had similar alleyways and I knew it was too dangerous to follow an enemy through them. Ambush was too prevalent. In the distance we could hear the sirens of the police.

"We've got to get out of here!" I spoke. "This isn't something we want to explain to the authorities!"

Both of us holstered our guns and walked quickly towards the main road, pretending to be just as dumbfounded as everyone else. Several police cars were parked outside the club. An ambulance was also there. Casually we walked back to the van, careful not to attract attention. We were both shaken by what we had witnessed but made great haste back to our van. Kap opened the back door; his hands shook as he fumbled with the keys. "Fuck'n hell! We hit it at least three times and that thing just kept gettin' up! Ya chaps weren't talkin' shite at all!" His breaths were heavy.

"Afraid not! I don't think the bullets were as accurate as they needed to be," I spurted out still trying to collect myself.

"Sorry. I had to make them relatively fast. They weren't the standard 15 Grain jacketed rounds, and the rifling was probably pissed on given the nature of the silver." He was still trying to collect his speech.

"It's all right, we're still alive. Get on the line with Snake," I said as we climbed into the back of the van, closing the doors behind us. "Tell him what happened and that we're on our way there. Tell him to be cautious! She may be heading back towards them."

Part IV

CHAPTER #24

Change of Heart
Marcus
Saturday, December 5, 2009
8:40 p.m.

I had another hour before I boarded flight 476 nonstop from London to Sydney, Australia. Heathrow airport was just like any other airport. It had a wide, open hallway with specialty vendors and food joints along with an occasional novelty store that sold everything from candy to replicas of the London Bridge to the mass-market paperback novels. There I sat in one of the many rows of uncomfortable chairs watching people mingle in and out of the storefronts. Most minded their own affairs with intermittent conversations of travel plans or business dealings. All around people seemed full of life, full of happiness, completely unaware of the dark scenes I had witnessed over the past month and a half. I could not keep my mind off Mya. I was absolutely terrified of her and of what she was, but also afraid that I had made a mistake by opting to leave.

Anxiety bubbled inside of me. It was hard to concentrate on anything. I was edgy. Everywhere I looked mental pictures of Mya and the terrible beast that she was assaulted my conscious mind. People passing by, reflections in the windows and mirrors all seemed to capture her image, but also the image of the beast. For a short time, I feared that I was beginning to lose my sanity and that these were more than just normal hallucinations. I rubbed my forehead. *It was the same after you were attacked by the dingoes in Australia* I thought. *You had the same fears and images about them as you do about Mya.* My nose was still sore from where Mya had backhanded me. Rubbing my forehead only prompted pain to pulse through my entire face.

When I woke after the incident, blood covered the front of my shirt and had drained considerably down the back of my throat. It made me sick, and I threw up shortly after only to realize my nose was pointing in a different direction than straight ahead. Having broken it before when I fell down a hillside in the Outback, I knew the best thing was to suck it up and reposition my nose as fast as possible. With a quick yank and a snap, I had pushed it back into place. It bled for nearly an hour after, but I could at least breathe again. This was the moment I decided that my efforts to help Mya were futile and had resolved to see a doctor when I had returned to Australia.

Desperate for some relief from the pain in my nose, I stood and walked towards a novelty store. All I had with me was my carry-on bag that contained personal items, a shirt, and the journals that I had been keeping through this entire experience. The rest of my belongings and my equipment were locked in protective cases and checked at the registry. The store was small. It had a flat-screen television mounted in the far-right corner that was broadcasting world news. Several newspapers were displayed on a miniature metal waterfall stand just outside the entrance. In front of me was another display that had caps, t-shirts, and sweaters that all had the insignia of London written across them. Personal toiletries hung on the wall such as hand wipes as well as travel size capsules of motion sickness pills and pain pills. There was not much of a selection, but I grabbed a couple packs of pain pills.

The world was still at war and airport security would not allow anything that could be interpreted as a weapon onto the planes. They took the bottle of pain medicine that I had purchased before coming to the airport. It mattered very little. I was more or less going to be sleeping on the plane. To my right was a shelf that covered the entire wall and contained numerous books. Behind a small counter to my left, a clerk looked up from a stack of papers she was viewing. I caught her flinch as she looked at the black and blue marks under my eyes.

Trying to make light of the situation I said, "Don't worry, it's not as bad as it looks."

This comment snapped her back into reality. She quickly switched into service mode, "Sorry, sir. Is there anything that I can help you locate?"

"No ma'am, I'm just really trying to kill some time before my flight," I replied kindly.

She simply nodded and went back to pouring over her stack of papers. Not wanting to prolong the uncomfortable moment, I made my way over to the magazine stand and began browsing. It was always the same magazines, some involving business, others involving stuff that famous people do. However, this stand had a few American publications. One in particular caught my attention. Across the cover was a fairly large white wolf with the title *Arctic Terror*! I stared down at the magazine for several moments before I picked it up. *Arctic Terror, these are more like pups rather than beasts.* It was terrible how the world had construed what was terrifying. The wolf had a look on its face that was *not* of ferocity, but more of fear. Perhaps the person taking the photograph had spooked the animal or accidentally ran up on its offspring. Its posture, barring of the teeth and the way it lifted its front paw all indicated a defensive position not one of aggression. Nonetheless, it was something I was used to reading about and would serve as a good transition back into the work that I had left a month and a half earlier.

I placed the magazine on the counter, along with the pain pills. The clerk immediately began to ring it up. "Is there anything else that you would like, sir?" Her tone was soft and polite.

"No, that'll be all." Again, I was reminded of Mya in the way that the clerk spoke and her youthful appearance.

"Very well then, it'll be £4 please."

I reached into my pocket to pull some of the loose change, but instead of pulling money out I drew something else.

Dangling from a chain in my hand was the golden charm of the Archangel Michael. It shimmered in the overhead lights as it swung back and forth. In the chaos of the events the night in the forest and the days thereafter, I had forgotten to give it back to Mya and I had neglected to notice it when I went through security. I looked down at the magazine with the arctic wolf on the cover and then back to the charm. Breath barely escaped my lips as I realized that there was no going back. No going back to the life and work I once had. No going back to a sense of normalcy. Demons were real and if they were real than God and the devil could very well be real too. I had seen the darkness and would be forever changed.

My trance was broken when the young girl behind the counter stated, "Sir, that'll be £4 please." For a moment I didn't know how to respond. I stood there staring back at the girl, dumbfounded. Blood rushed into my face as my nose pulsed with pain. "Sir, are you all right?" she asked.

"Ergh, yeah…I don't think I'm going to need these." I slid the magazine and pills towards her. I thought it was the best choice to leave the estate when I did, but what I did not know at the time was that I never really had a choice. I could not leave London knowing what I knew and simply return to my old life. I could not abandon a person whose posture was that of fear rather than aggression. Ever since the first night in the cellar, when I saw her change into that monstrous beast, I was locked into a tale of wicked ends whether I wanted it or not. Slowly I backed out of the store. A look of confusion spread across the girl's face as she watched me leave. I had to get back to Mya!

As I moved through the airport, I thought about the charm that I had put back in my pocket. The image of the Archangel Michael standing over the devil resonated deep within me. I felt that my role in all this madness wasn't yet through. I found my way back to the registry, where a middle-aged man was working.

"Excuse me, mate!" I said as the man looked up from the computer. "I must say that I have come under a bit of an emergency, and I won't be able to take my flight. However, I feel that my luggage may already be waiting to be loaded onto the plane."

"Sir, I can help you with that, but you do understand that there will be some fees associated with unloading your baggage?"

"Yes, I'm aware. It doesn't matter though. I cannot make my flight and I'm going to need my luggage," I replied slightly exasperated.

"Very well, sir. What flight were you on?"

"I was booked on flight 476 nonstop from London to Sydney, Australia."

He typed fast on the keyboard, and it was a few moments before he spoke, "Okay sir, what is your name?"

"Marcus Holland." My voice was frantic.

Without looking at me or saying anything else, the man simply typed quickly on his keyboard only stopping to click the mouse of his computer a couple of times. "Sir, I have located your baggage and have put in a request to have it removed from the loading area. It should take a couple of hours before the personnel can bring it here. Unfortunately, it must go through several security checks before it can be released. If you would like to wait for it, we have a sitting area just over there." The man pointed to several rows of benches.

My heart sank deeper and the anxiety inside increased. "Is there any way that I can get my luggage faster?"

"I'm afraid not sir, but we can have it shipped to an address if you need to be some place and can afford to be without your luggage for a day or so." He had clued into my urgency for his reply was empathetic.

I took a deep breath realizing that this was my only option. Reluctantly, I agreed to have the baggage shipped to the estate. I was not worried about any of the costs involved. Instead, I was more worried that the computer I had been using to track Mya's whereabouts was *not* going to reach me for another twenty-four hours. It was the one device I had that allowed me to know whether she was nearby as well as whether she had somehow changed into her demonic alter ego. I fumbled around in my carry-on bag for the journals I had been keeping. At one point, I folded the original letter that Mya had sent me and placed it inside the front cover of the book. Alas, I pulled it from the journal. I had placed it back into its original envelope. The address was listed in the top left corner. I showed the man behind the counter. "Can you have my items shipped to this address?"

"Certainly, sir. Would you like to place the charge on the credit card you used to pay for your ticket?"

"Yeah, that's fine mate."

"Very good sir, we'll have all of your belongings to you within twenty-four hours, pending that everything passes through security."

I thanked the man before turning to head out the main doors of the airport. Outside the weather was dreary. The air was cold and brisk against my face. It made the pain in my nose subside slightly. Cars were buzzing here and there picking people up and dropping them off. The transportation service that brought me to the airport was no longer available and required a scheduled appointment for their services. I was reduced to catching a taxi, which again did not bother me all that much. The fare was probably going to be high, but I had more than enough from Mya's payment to cover the cost.

I hailed a black cab that was parked in a designated area outside of Heathrow Airport. As I approached the man standing outside of the cab he immediately stated, "There is a minimum charge of £2.20 and a maximum duration of one hour."

"Can you take me to this address?" I asked showing him the address on the envelope. I also held out a wad of money,

"I'm willing to pay you £100.00 extra if it takes longer than it should."

Without any further questions the man motioned for me to get inside the car. Moments later we were pulling away from the airport. The cab driver tried to make simple conversations, but I was too consumed with my present thoughts to even hear the man. I did not know what to expect when I arrived back at the estate. I did not even know if Mya had returned and if she had her current state of being may pose an immediate threat. All I did know was that I left the tranquilizer gun resting atop a stand in the foyer. My hope was that it was still there along with the six darts that could be quickly loaded into the magazine.

I watched the darkened landscape pass by as the man drove along the road. We passed a small rural town that I had not noticed the other time I was brought to the estate. It was quite possible that I had not gone this way in the past. Lights from the local taverns and cafés shown through the windows and brightly illuminated the night sky. People could be seen laughing and casually talking to one another from within the walls. Other people were walking carrying bags of groceries and gifts, no doubt for the upcoming holiday. Dampness and puddles had built up along the sides of the road. Not enough to pose a concern, but enough that reflected the streetlamps' glow. *The scene is peaceful*, I thought. *This must've been painful for Mya to witness year after year with no one to share fond memories with or to love. What she has become is truly a curse.* This notion only strengthened my resolve to continue to help her until she was rid of her wicked nature.

Darkness filled the estate as we pulled up to the end of the drive. I noticed immediately that the Land Rover was gone. I stepped out of the cab, paid the fare along with the extra money I had promised the man. There was no need to argue about whether it took more than an hour. We had left the airport at twenty minutes to ten o'clock and the time was now past eleven. The man thanked me for the tip and merely drove off back down the road.

The wind howled around the edge of the estate, but everything else was eerily silent. Clouds rolled overhead, covering the nighttime sky. The moon was partially concealed. Even if it was entirely visible it was too early in the month for the moon to be full. This limited the chances of running into the werewolf but given the facts I had collected and the experiences I had had, the threat of running into Mya in a dangerous state was still eminent. I approached the manor cautiously, making sure to take in all my surroundings. Glancing left to right, I stopped at the top of the stairs as I noticed one of the windows to the right of the main doorway was broken. Shards of glass collected just below the windowsill along the ground. My pulse quickened. I could hear every beat of my heart and my breathing became shallow and acute. I reached for the handle of the door, but before I could grab it a gust of wind caused the big door to open slightly with a creek. Gently, I pushed the door open enough to slip inside.

It took a moment for my eyes to adjust to the dark. Thin rays of muted moonlight snuck into the house through the windows. Down the long hallway I could see a dim light rolling into the hall from one of the dens. I tried to remember if I had left a light on before leaving the estate but could not confirm it. Quickly, I felt around for the stand where I left the tranquilizer gun, but when I found it, the gun was gone along with the darts. Panic was beginning to set in on me. Someone had been in the manor and may still be here. Having no weapon my only thought was of defense. *I could make a sprint down the hallway to the doorway that leads down to the lower level,* I thought. *If I make it down the stairwell, I could possibly make it to the cage that held Mya.* It would be the only way I could survive if she had indeed returned and was in the state of the werewolf.

Slowly, I lowered myself to a sprinting position, but before I could move, I heard the fast-moving steps of something. I turned to my left just in time to see a large silhouette rushing towards me! *CRACK!* The blow to my head caused my vision to blur and my ears to ring. I hit the floor with a tremendous impact and noticed immediately that I was bleeding from the side of my head. My consciousness faded fast as pain screamed down the side of my head. The last image I saw as I looked up through blurred vision was the large silhouette towering over me. Then all was dark.

Chapter #25

Man or Beast
Marcus
Sunday, December 6, 2009
2:35 a.m.

I was running through the woods...my heart pounded, and my breath echoed in my mind...my feet stumbled...the ground was hot and hard...several low growls...the ferocity, then the teeth and the pain in my arms and legs. Dingoes surrounded me...then only one. It twisted and turned its head...snarling and thrashing...it grew larger the more it thrashed...it eyes turned green and glowed against the darkness of the night. It let me loose and towered over me, howling, never once releasing me from its malevolent glare. It charged again...mouth open, blood dripping...

Air passed over my lips as I took a quick breath and my head jolted up. I could feel my heart pounding. Both of my hands were bound behind me as I sat on a wooden chair. Pain spread across the side of head and down into my neck. Sounds were muffled, especially from my left ear. I moved my head to straighten my neck. As I did, I could hear my neck crack and pop. Instantly, I felt the blood rush to the areas that were constricted. It was an unpleasant side-effect from having been in this position for an extended period of time. There were several different noises that surrounded me. Voices, footsteps, and the occasional crash from something in another room were all I could hear. My left ear felt as though it was full of water, quite different from that of my right ear; however, nothing was clear. All the noises were coming from the left side of me, which meant my right ear was turned away from what was happening. I tried to open my eyes but only managed to open my right one. *I'm blind...no I can't be...I have no pain and I can still move it under my eyelid...why can't I open my eye?* I thought.

I moved my eye back and forth under the eyelid. Something was covering my eye, preventing me from opening it.

After several moments, I turned my head to the left to catch a glimpse from my right eye as to what was happening around me. This caused too much pain in my neck, and I let out a light groan of pain when I abandoned the effort. I heard footsteps moving closer to me. They were heavy on the wood floor, but they were at least human sounding.

"Boss, he's waking up," said a gruff voice. Several more sets of footsteps approached.

"Who the hell are you and what the hell are you doing here?" said a different voice. This one was more sophisticated sounding, less harsh than the other one. There was more than one person standing in front of me. Even though I could see a bit from my right eye, I still could not make out any faces.

I coughed a bit before I spoke, "Crikey mate, I could ask you the same question. Why can't I see out of my left eye?"

"Get a cloth to wipe his face," I heard the man say. A minute or so passed before I felt a wet cloth thrown onto my face before falling to my lap. The man that was asking questions knelt in front of me, grabbed the cloth and wiped my left eye without any care of comfort. I blinked a few more times and realized that I was able to see again. The man stood in front of me and threw the cloth back onto my lap. I looked down at it and noticed it was covered in blood. My left eye had been sealed shut from blood. Everything started to make sense. *Someone must have struck me across the left side of my head, rendering me unconscious, while the blood streamed down my face covering my eye. This also explained why my left ear feels as though it is full of water. It isn't water, it's blood.* I glanced back up at the man who wiped my face. He was middle aged, with silvering hair, and a round stomach. By the looks of it he may have been my age or a few years older. He was surrounded by several large men all of which were wearing black leather coats, except one. This man was only in a black t-shirt but had tattoos that stretched from his wrists to the end of his forearms, where new ones began but disappeared under the sleeves of his t-shirt. He stood with arms folded as though he was drawing attention to the tattoos on his arms. The middle-aged man broke my gaze when he moved in front of me. "Now, who are you and how do you know Dr. Bishop?"

I was not going to fight this request. I was in no position to demand anything. "My name is Marcus Holland, mate. Dr. Bishop hired me to help her with some research. I'm from Australia." I tried to keep my voice calm and clear so as to not provoke any unwarranted advances.

"Good, now we're getting somewhere." His voice remained authoritative. "What kind of research were you helping her with?"

"Animal research, I'm a specialist. Who are you people?" I asked as calm as I could.

The big man with tattoos on his arms uncrossed his arms and walked menacingly towards me. "I don't think ya should be asking any of the fuck'n questions!"

"Jinx! Let me handle this. I don't think it will hurt us if he knows who I am. Besides, he's not a threat at the moment. He's no more than a man just like you or I," the middle-aged man commanded. "My name is Robert Osborne. We're looking for Dr. Mya Bishop." He paused for a moment before continuing: "Now, since you're an animal researcher, I'm not going to pretend that you don't know what she is."

I knew as soon as he said his name that he was the father of the young girl that Mya had attacked. I made a mental note to be even more cautious of what I said and how I said it. This man had a sinister tone and with a good bet the intentions to match. I still did not know how things might play out. "What are you referring to?" I responded cautiously.

"A werewolf, you ass! Don't act dim-witted with me, sir. I've several men here that would be happy to extract the information we want in other ways, ways that aren't quite as civilized as our little dialogue we have going here. They'll start with breaking your damn legs!"

"What do you want from me, mate?" My contemptuous tenor matched Robert's.

"We want to know where Dr. Bishop has gone!" Robert said as he moved his face close to mine, seething as he spoke.

"I don't know where she is. The last time I saw her was yesterday evening."

"Where was she going?" Robert yelled in my face.

"She said she was going to do some research," I lied. I assume these were the same men that Mya had encountered at the library and if I could throw them off their own timeframe of the events that had occurred the better off Mya and I were going to be. I wanted them to think I truly did not know anything.

Another man emerged from behind the others. He tapped Robert on the shoulder, "Dad, let me talk to him," he said. Robert reluctantly moved away from me out of my line of vision, but still within close proximity. I could hear his heavy footsteps around me. This other man knelt in front of me. His demeanor was confident and secure. He spoke calmly but direct, "Sir…you said that you saw her yesterday evening about what time?"

"Around six o'clock," I responded, again trying not to give too much information. "I believe she was going to the library."

The man cocked his head as though he just discovered something that I didn't know. "Really," he said. "I don't know why she would go back to the library after she already trashed the place. I know I was there. Now where was she really going?"

"If she wasn't going to the library, then she must have lied to me," I lied again. I knew where she was going, and I had the suspicion that this man did too.

The man stared directly at me. I could tell that he was studying me. Studying my facial expressions and body language. I could also tell this was not the first time he had questioned someone. "No sir, I think you're the one that is lying," he finally said. "We had been here for nearly two hours before you came home. Where were you?"

"I had some errands to run."

"Yet you come here with nothing but a small bag. We found a plane ticket, one that was set to take flight at 9:45 p.m. Why did you skip your flight?" the man said as he stood upright. He didn't wait for my response. "Now we need to know how you were helping Dr. Bishop. We need to find her."

"I can't tell you anything, mate," I said, knowing full well that this was the wrong answer and that eventually these men were going to be able to find out whatever they wanted to know. I resolved at that moment that I could at least give Mya a fighting chance by being difficult with my answers; stalling, so-to-speak.

The man that was talking to me stepped away from me and motioned for the other man with the tattoos named Jinx to take over. He walked briskly towards me, reared back his arm, and swung with great force, connecting with my nose and mouth. Instantly my head whipped backwards, jarring the already-strained neck muscles. Blood poured from my nose and mouth down the front of my shirt. I spit out the blood that was draining down the back of my throat. This man had dislodged my nose again and split my upper lip. Swelling was inevitable. All I could do was close my eyes and try to endure the screaming pain in my face. Spitting out more blood I breathed heavily, trying to focus my mental energy on enduring the hurt.

The large man backed away from me as the other more controlled man stepped back in front of me. "We know she went to a club in London. We know because again we were there. We know she was looking for a man named Corbin Paige. She barely escaped our gunfire this evening. Now, we need your help to find out where she is." The demeanor of this man remained controlled yet imposing. My heart sank at the words he spoke. These men already knew the information I was trying to conceal, I could tell them no more than this. The cat-and-mouse game that I was taking part in was pointless.

"I don't know where she might be. She could be anywhere," I said, defeated through labored breaths.

The man with the tattoos I had discerned was named Jinx raised his hand up again and slapped my face hard from the right side causing my head to whip to the left. Blood streamed off my face onto my shirt and into my lap. Having suffered a tremendous blow to the head a few hours earlier, I felt the tunnel vision coming back. I figured I had a concussion, so I did not try to fight it when everything slipped into darkness for the second time that night.

I was awakened by water dripping onto my face. I took a deep breath and released it quickly. Standing in front of me was the same man that was questioning me before I lost consciousness. More light surrounded me, and I noticed that he was holding a wet cloth in his hand. I could only assume that it was close to dawn, perhaps six o'clock or so. "May I?" he asked gesturing to wipe my face. He did not wait for my response before he wiped the side of my face and the front of my mouth. He stopped once to dip the cloth into a basin of water. The cloth was cool and refreshing but did nothing for the pain. I was not able to get a good look at this man during the night; it was simply too dark. With more natural light from some windows above, I could see that he looked like the middle-aged man that first spoke to me. Except this man did not have the silvering hair and carried a much younger, stronger build. Behind his dark eyes, I could see anger, but also sadness. Satisfied with his task, he threw the blood-soaked cloth into the basin and lifted a glass of water to my mouth. "Drink," he said.

I drank greedily. The water washed away the coppery metallic taste from my lips and tongue. With my hands still bound, I had trouble controlling the amount of water that entered my mouth. Some of it spilled down the front of me. What went down my throat became a welcomed relief to the dry, coarse feeling I had. "My name is Grayson."

"I can't say that I'm pleased to meet you mate." My voice was raspy. I noticed that I was being held in the library where I was conducting all my research. Sitting behind this man Grayson at one of the smaller tables in the library was another man that had a snake tattoo that gave the appearance of the snake swallowing his head. He was not paying any attention to either of us; instead, he typed on his laptop computer. Several cords were extending from his computer and attached to another smaller device. It took a moment, but I realized that the smaller device was mine. All of my luggage must have arrived while I was unconscious. I assumed the man with the snake tattoo was trying to extract the data I had collected. "It's password encrypted."

The man did not even look up. "We know," Grayson stated. "It doesn't matter though. He'll be able to get around your encryptions in a matter of time. You might as well tell us the password to save us the trouble."

"Why should I?" I spat back at him.

Remaining calm, the man simply nodded his head. "I understand your commitment to Dr. Bishop. I'm a Lieutenant in her majesty's Royal Army and I've been carrying out special opts for the past two years in Afghanistan. I've led some of the noblest chaps I've ever known. But I was forced to leave them when my sister was killed. Killed by a horrifying creature. I've come to understand that there are greater evils in this world than what I was fighting. I had to take up a new mission. It nearly killed me to abandon my men and I understand that you don't want to abandon your mission, but I need to know what kind of beast we're up against. I saw her change in the nightclub. I saw her change from an innocent-looking woman to a monstrous thing. How could this happen? Everything I've come to know about werewolves suggests that the full moon is required for them to change from human to werewolf, at least in theory. Yet I'm at a loss when it comes to Dr. Bishop."

"You're right, mate. I don't want to abandon the person I was trying to help." At this point, I was not going to argue with this man about the statements that he made. His reasoning was clear and appropriate given his circumstances. The only way I could help Mya was to try and convince this man that there was more to this evil than what he knew. "She's cursed, mate. It was the curse that killed your sister, not Dr. Bishop. She cannot help what she does when she changes. Dr. Bishop sought my expertise with animals, specifically with that of the canine species, when she had reached her own wit's end." Grayson motioned for me to go on. "You saw her change because something excited her behavior. Something caused the chemicals to increase in her body, which probably increased the overall energy inside her," I explained, stopping to cough out some coagulated blood from the back of my throat.

"The moon wasn't full last night, and we were inside a building. I thought the full moon was the only thing that could cause a werewolf to change?" he asked, going back to his original point but now deeply interested in what I was saying.

"The full moon will always cause a change, but we discovered that anything that causes an extreme chemical change such as an adrenaline rush may also cause her to change. Until last night this was only a theory. I'm not pleased to be proven right. She was probably afraid or pissed off."

"How did she become a werewolf? I mean, she probably wasn't born like this," Grayson inquired.

"I had decided to leave before I could fully answer this question. My work with her had grown too dangerous and I didn't want to be another victim. But these were selfish means. I skipped my flight and came back to help knowing that she was bitten mate. She didn't choose to be like this…and if your sister would've survived the attack, I'm afraid she would probably also carry the curse. That's the best I can offer." He stood up straight at the mention of his sister. It was apparent that this carried deep emotion. I said this to him not to be combative but more so to further convey that the curse was no discriminator of persons and that behind the beast was the remnants of a human. The remnants of a life that was stolen, just like his sister's.

"How do we kill her?" he asked, blunt and to the point.

"We're dealing with forces that are unknown to all of us. We're dealing with darkness. Darkness that has been around for hundreds of years, maybe longer. I've exhausted all of my scientific methods trying to answer questions surrounding this evil. You would have better luck asking a priest how he deals with the devil."

Grayson stood in front of me, just staring as though he had come to a realization that had previously escaped him. "Got it!" the man with the snake tattoo exclaimed.

Grayson turned and walked towards the man. He stood behind him looking over his shoulder. He patted him on the back. "Well done Snake, well done," he uttered.

I knew that my password to access the files was broken and that all the information I had stored from charts and graphs to my personal log and recordings may be exposed. Several moments passed as they explored my files. Robert Osborne, the middle-aged man, came into the room followed by other men including the large man with the tattoos. I could hear them discussing something, but my attention was diverted away from what they were saying by weariness and pain. More mental pain than physical as I thought; *I'm sorry Mya, I failed.* I snapped back to the immediate situation when the man sitting at the computer stated, "Now that's just the dog's bollocks! This is a tracking device!"

Chapter 26

Father Preston Mathew's Log

Sunday, December 6, 2009,

I received a very peculiar voice message yesterday evening. The gentleman introduced himself as the son of a member of the House of Commons. It was unfortunate that I was unable to talk with man, for he mentioned that he was seeking information about Dr. Mya Bishop. After the talk with Dean William Garris and my visit to her home, I had all but given up on trying to locate her whereabouts and had resolved to let God care for his servant, only to use me again when needed. I tried to contact this young man but was unable to get through. Even though he left a return phone number, it was apparent that simply calling a member of the House of Commons is not as easy as dialing the number. I ran into an answering service, only to leave a message for the young man to call and stressed the urgency of the matter.

I waited eagerly for the call to come back but was again met with disappointment. During this time, I resolved to read the news in the hopes that something would be mentioned about Dr. Bishop. It is with great displeasure that I check the obituaries first. It has become a bit of a morbid habit. Nonetheless, much like the other times I have checked it was of relief to know that the listings did not include Dr. Bishop. I continued to read the world news, sifting through titled reports of the war in Iraq and Afghanistan, and the dealings in the foreign markets. It was not until I cast aside the world news for the local reports that I realized my search was not in vain. It appeared that the University of Cambridge had experienced an unpleasant event yesterday that involved a shooting and a chase. It turns out that Dr. Bishop was not only involved in this event but was the person being pursued. Though the report did not go into great detail due to lack of information, another shooting also took place at a nightclub in downtown London. Several were injured and the report spoke of a strange being, a wolf-like creature, inside the club. I fear that these two shootings are connected and that the young man trying to contact me may also be involved. Once again, I find myself locked in deep prayer for this servant of God. I fear what lurks in the dark places of the world and hope that Dr. Bishop has not been seduced by such darkness. Only God can save his servant.

- Rev. Preston Mathew S.J.

CHAPTER #27

Corbin Paige
Mya
Sunday, December 6th, 2009

It was difficult to tell what reality was and what was false. Mental pictures flooded my thoughts of inside the club, screaming, shots fired and pain, pain not like normal pain. This hurt was debilitating and relentless. My whole body was still consumed by it. Coldness filled my lungs from the outside air. Several muffled voices surrounded me, but I could not open my eyes. I was too weak. Too weak to do anything more than breathe. Something inside me, an eerie sense, suggested that I was in danger. *You must get up! They have found you! You must free yourself!* It was no use and within moments I felt myself being lifted off the ground and carried. The destination was unknown.

Flashes of light caused my eyes to blink. My surroundings remained blurry and every time I tried to move the pain returned with sinister vigor. It was as though parts of my body were in complete revolt against my conscious mind. The only thing I could make out were large silhouettes that hovered above me to my right and my left. "Don't try to struggle. It will only make the pain worse," a gruff, deep voice finally spoke. I needed to escape this situation, but the weariness in my body was too strong. It was not long before I felt myself sliding back into an abyss of shadows.

I do not know how much time had passed, but when I came to, I found myself lying atop of a metal table. A strap extended across my chest, but my arms were free. Other straps, one across my hips and several smaller ones around my legs, fully secured me to the table. I tried to pull against them but was met with immediate resistance. "No, stay still! You'll only cause yourself unnecessary agony and I still have to remove the bullet from your upper thigh!" a man said as he placed his hand upon my left shoulder. The deep voice was the same as before.

Fluorescent lighting above was blinding. The man turned from me and rummaged around at another nearby metal table to my left. He had his back towards me, but I could tell that he had placed several small devices in a row. They looked like surgical equipment. Being strapped down prevented me from seeing any further than this. From what I could tell, I was wearing a gown of some sort. *At least I'm not naked,* I considered. I reached my right shoulder with my left hand. Gauze and medical tape were strategically placed on the upper portion of the muscle. As I touched the spot a thought penetrated my mind. Instantly, I remembered staring down at a terrified man behind a bar and without warning a piercing pain shot into my shoulder. I remembered turning to face a man with a gun. *It must've been the same men from the library, but how did they find me so fast?*

The images from the night before were clearer than any other thoughts that I had had while in the form of a werewolf. Much of what happened in the club was clear. I remembered entering the club, avoiding security, breaking a man's arm, even the moment I changed. It was as though none of my thoughts were interrupted. No blackouts or gaps where long periods of time elapsed. The only time my thoughts were disrupted was when I had collapsed in the alley. Despite injuring the men who had tried to restrain me, a sense of relief came from knowing that no one was actually killed. Before I could inquire as to what was happening and where I was, the man turned back towards me. "I was hoping to have the bullets out before you were awake. I was able to remove the one from your shoulder as well as the one from your back," he said as he held up what looked like a pair of needle-nose clamps. "I'm sorry in advance if I cause you any further pain than what you're already experiencing."

He motioned to me that he was about to finish his work. I gave a small head nod and braced myself for the onset of more pain. The man was large with bulging muscles. From what I could judge, he stood close to six feet tall, maybe more. He reached across my lower body, placing his hand upon my thigh and lowered his face closer to get a better look at the wound. His hand was warm against my skin, a stark contrast to the coolness in the air. I tried to focus on this small sensation as he dug the tips of the clamps deep into the hole in my thigh.

"Owwwwe!" I cried.

"Hold still, hold still, I almost got it!" The metal clamps felt like teeth as it sent painful pulses up and down my right leg. I could not move it. All I could do was endure. I could feel the warm blood running from the opening as the man twisted and turned against the tautness of my flesh. Then, with a quick yank, the man pulled the clamps from my leg with a smashed silver bullet caught at the tip. He placed the clamps off to the side, quickly wiped my leg clean and placed a fresh piece of gauze over the opening. He held his hand over the wound for several minutes. The moment he finished I was able to move my right foot slightly and the painful burning sensation was gone. "Sorry about the straps. I didn't want you to be able to move much while I was removing the bullets. It would've made getting them out more difficult," the man said politely, yet stern.

He unbuckled the straps on my legs, followed by the one over my hips and finally the one across my chest. Dizzy from the pain as well as the hellish events of the club, I struggled but managed to sit up on the table and swung my legs over the side. I winced as I realized this probably was not the best position for my leg to rest. He was a black man that was dressed casually in tan slacks and a short sleeve, collared shirt that was deep red in color. Over this, he wore a white apron that hung around his oversized neck and extended the full length of his body. I assumed that he was no formal doctor or at least I was *not* in a hospital. No other person was present. Several other metal tables filled the area. The room was long and narrow with the fluorescent lighting that stretched in two rows the entire distance. There were no windows, yet I could feel a cool draft coming from the far end. "Where am I? How long have I been here?" Weakness filled my voice.

"You're safe," he responded sharply. Seeming to ignore my second question, the man handed me a cup of tea. I took it greedily but sipped it slowly. The hot liquid was soothing on my dry throat. Within a moment I could feel the warmth spreading throughout my body. I looked down at my right leg; slowly, I raised and lowered it as more feeling returned. The man took off the apron he was wearing and placed it on a vacant table. He then picked up the clamps and examined the bullet that he still held clasped at the tip. He dipped it into a small pan of water, shook it a bit, and then continued to examine it. "No need to stitch your wounds, they should heal now that this is out," he stated, still examining the bullet. "Crudely made, yet still harmful to us."

My head snapped upwards to look at the man. Despite my weariness, the words he spoke fell from the sky like a meteor. "Who are you? What do you mean…to us?"

"To our kind…werewolves. I know who you are Dr. Bishop. We have followed your writings for quite some time now. My name is Corbin Paige and it's a pleasure to finally make your acquaintance," he said with a slight bow of the head. I simply stared at the man. For nearly two hundred years I had searched for some clue, some shred of evidence that could lead me to the answers I needed. Finally, standing before me was another being that shared my same fate. "We never made contact with you for we too need to remain secret. We needed to know for sure that you were indeed a werewolf and not just someone who was well versed in our culture. We had placed the book by Father Bentini in the book depository at Cambridge in the hopes that you would find it, so that you could seek us out. However, once we learned about the incident at the library, we knew that eventually we would have to make contact and that we couldn't wait for you to discover us."

He stopped there not continuing to explain what he meant. "It was you that day at the library, wasn't it?"

"Yes, it was."

"And on the corner, across from the Arts and Humanities building?"

"Yes. We've been to all of your lectures Dr. Bishop."

"You keep referring to *We*. Are there more than just you?" I inquired. Despite feeling a bit on the hungry side, my body was already starting to feel stronger as I stood upright.

"Yes, there are many of us." Corbin handed me a pair of medical scrub pants and a top. He leaned against the table opposite me and folded his arms across his massive chest. "We are scattered throughout the world, but secret we remain."

Not questioning the choice of clothes, I placed the cup of tea next to me as I slid the pants on under my gown and turned away from Corbin as I pulled it off. The wound on my side was gone. I gently rubbed my hand over the spot it used to be before slipping on the top he gave me. They were a lavender color, which offset greatly with the metallic tables and the fair tinted walls. Turning back towards him I asked, "How? I mean I've been alive for over two hundred years and the only werewolf I've come across was the one that bit me!"

"Many are like you," he stated as he handed me a pair of sandals. "They hide in plain sight, but flee to different regions when the moon comes 'round again. A few have banded together here and there, but none have been able to establish what we have. Many have been hunted down over the years and destroyed."

"Why have I not heard of these events? I've constantly searched…"

"Those that have killed our kind aren't people that are a part of mainstream society," Corbin stated, interrupting me. His tone became more serious. "Typically, they travel as societal outcastes, hunting in the rural areas. When a kill is made, it isn't something that is broadcast on the news. Most of the time the remains are burned, leaving nothing to document. Their best weapon, like us, is secrecy. If we knew who they were, they would become the hunted."

I cringed at the thought of actually hunting a human. Too much death lingered in my past to even bear the idea. Not wanting to press the issue and being very aware of his grim manner, I changed the subject. "How long have I been here?"

"We found you early this morning just before sunrise, quite a bit down the alleyway. Lucky, I might say, your pursuers called off the hunt, you left a very clear path of destruction, and you were easy to locate. You've been here for less than a day."

"Where is here?" I asked, glancing around the narrow room.

"You're beneath the club," Corbin pronounced. "Not to worry though, it isn't easily accessible. There are a series of tunnels, mostly sewers that lead throughout the city that we've turned into a safe place for us. Some of the tunnels lead into crypts and larger tombs. It's the catacombs of the city. We've blocked off several portions of the passageways to give us a free reign when we change into…our better selves. We don't have to worry about others spying on who we are and what we're doing. Nonetheless, this particular space only has one entrance that is secret to the rest of the world."

I glanced around again taking in what he said. I had so many questions. So many answers that needed to be found, but I only managed to conjure up one more. One that was more pressing at that moment than all the others. "Are you the start of it all? I mean, are you…the original werewolf?" I felt silly, clumsy even, asking such an elementary question.

"No, I was made the same way you were. I was bitten. There's no other way to become what we are," he replied calm, yet direct. He looked away from me for a moment and sighed as though he was trying to remember something from long ago. "I was a slave to men. Stolen from my homeland in West Africa, the Ghana region, and forced to serve white masters that carried malevolent spirits. I was a priest among my culture and a medicine man. In fact, my original name Kabona was Swahili in origin but means priest. I had no love of violence, but they had heavy whips."

I could tell that his past bore mental scars that were as imprinted on his entire being much as mine were. I was about to inquire again about how he had become a werewolf, but he continued, "…After our village was destroyed by the 'White Demons', most of my African brothers and sisters were taken to the colonies across the sea to work on rice, tobacco, or cotton plantations. However, I was among the select few that were taken back to Northern Germany and The Netherlands before ending at British Isles to work on the estates of large merchant dealers. I started learning the English language. Quite often I would be forced to go on raids to collect other Africans to be sold as slaves. I would act as an interpreter and guide; if I refused, like I often did, I received the whip. Occasionally, I was beaten so bad that I would lose consciousness only to wake up in the servant quarters of the estate where I was forced to work. Other African servants would tend to my wounds and nurse me back to health. The worst episodes were when I would wake up at a completely different estate because the master had grown so angry with my insolence that he sold me before I had a chance to wake up. This is where I learned to tend to my own wounds and scrounge for food to regain some of my strength. Food usually consisted of rats that would run in and out of the slave quarters or scraps that were left over from other slave meals. During these times, no other slaves were willing to help me recover. Probably out of fear of the master's whip or from a general distrust of an unknown person being dumped into their lives. I would cook the rats I had captured over the remains of their fires they burned throughout the day. Every estate that I was transferred to was the same though. I had to earn my place among the other slaves."

Something in his voice was suggestive. I leaned against the metal table and listened intently as I continued to sip the tea that he had given to me. It was a blend, White Ayurvedic Chai and some other herbs I could not quite place. Nonetheless, I could feel my body regaining its warmth. "The last estate that I was on sat back away from the docking ports about a kilometer. The land was nice, with several green pastures lined with trees of all sorts. I later came to learn that it was located close to Portsmouth. I would've welcomed death if it had come to me; however, I had all but resolved to stop fighting with my white masters and accept that there was nothing I could do to improve my lot in life when the attack came. It was late in the trade season; the days grew shorter and the air colder. This restricted the merchants from sailing as often, which meant fewer trips to West Africa and less of need for my interpreting abilities. I hadn't been at the estate very long, maybe a month or so, when one of the overseers came rushing into my quarters hollering for me to rise and follow him. He stated that there was an emergency on the grounds and ordered me to assist. If I didn't, I knew that I would receive another flogging, maybe even death given the circumstances. Reluctantly, I followed. I remember making note of how full and bright the moon was that night. It was a trick I had learned to divert my mind from whippings or other horrible and cruel events that I witnessed while enslaved. Nothing could prepare me for what I was about to see."

Blood pulsed through my leg. I could feel the pressure in the bullet wound. Gently, I moved my foot around in circles to keep the blood circulating throughout my leg and to stave off cramps in the muscle. I sipped the tea again and continued listening to Corbin. "As we approached the main quarters of the master, we could hear screaming and yelling coming from around the side. Rounding the corner, we found what looked to be an oversized wolf devouring a member of the household. There was no chance at saving the individual. I had never seen anything like it, and I had encountered many types of wild animals in Africa. The wolf was the size of a lion and when the overseer yelled in horror and cracked his whip, it turned to face us immediately, standing on its hind legs. It leapt at the overseer, completely ignoring the snap of his whip. With one swipe of its front arm-like appendage the overseer's head rolled back off his shoulders as the rest of his body crumpled to the ground. Blood coated the earth as the wolf-like creature took large bites from the torso."

I shivered as thoughts of the night that I had attacked the young girl poured into my mind. Silent I sat, listening to every word Corbin uttered. "For a moment, I thought the beast didn't see me as it feasted upon its prey. Slowly, I began to back away not taking my eyes off it. I must have let out my breath too hard, for the giant wolf turned its head with a snap, baring its blood-covered teeth. Its eyes were pale white and glowed bright. Strong and fierce looking in the moonlight, it stared directly at me as though it could see into my very soul. Not but a moment later did it leap for me too. Having no weapon of any kind as well as being exposed to dangerous animals on the African plains, my first reaction was to dodge. It worked. The beast took a swipe at me and missed, but it was too fast, and the second attempt was successful. The monster sunk its teeth deep into my shoulder. The sheer weight of the thing caused me to collapse to the ground, where it took its second bite out of my stomach. I felt death overcoming me as I began to lose consciousness from the pain and shock of this ordeal."

Corbin rolled back the collar on his shirt to show me the first bite mark then rolled up the bottom of his shirt to show me the second. Seeing the wounds caused me to place my hand over the scar across my right thigh just below my new bullet wound. His scars had not gone away either. Bits of grey littered the top of his dark hair, similar to my own. "How did you survive?" I asked as Corbin let his shirt fall back over the scars on his stomach.

"Just before I lost consciousness, I heard several echoing reports from nearby pistols. Apparently, some of the other members of the estate had tried to shoot the beast. The gun shots provided enough of a distraction that it stopped attacking me and pursued them. I later woke to the sound of voices all around me. Several people were placing their hands on me, trying to cover my wounds with bandages. I heard one person mention that I probably wouldn't last throughout the night." Corbin closed his eyes and paused for a moment. "Perhaps it was all the beatings and whippings I had endured, but my body was strong enough to last through the night and into the next week. When I came to fully, I found myself in a prison cell. At that point I had no understanding as to why I was there. I figured it was because I was a slave and the general doctors in town wouldn't treat the likes of me, so I was placed in prison until I recovered or died. Every so often a person, perhaps a guard, would slide pieces of bread and water through a meal slot in the door. I couldn't move my left shoulder from the first bite, and I couldn't sit up well because of the second bite on my stomach. I managed to position myself close to the door slot to minimize movement when I ate the bread and drank the water. Fever raced through my body as sweat poured from my skin. I wasn't concerned as to where I relieved myself. Most of the time, I rolled painfully to my side to release the liquid I was consuming. My body gave no signs of the need to defecate, perhaps due to the lack of food I was being given or my lack of movement. Terrible nightmares of the wolf plagued my mind as I dozed in and out of sleep. Another couple of days had passed with no change in my condition. It wasn't until almost two weeks after the attack that I felt differently."

"What do you mean differently?" I was comparing his story to that of my own. I found it scary, yet fascinating how similar our symptoms were. I continued to move my foot and loosen my neck as we talked.

"Differently, as though new life had been breathed into me," Corbin replied. "Not only could I move my left shoulder and sit straight up without pain, my wounds looked to be almost healed. My skin had very little pigmentation, but the once gaping openings were now closed. I felt strong and healthy. I banged upon the door to my cell to gain the attention of the guard. I needed to inform him that I no longer needed a doctor and that I had recovered in the hopes that I would be released back to the estate from whence I came. Soon the guard came to see what all the banging was about. I informed him of my situation and all he did was laugh before calling me a Murderous Bastard. *You're going to burn for the murders you committed, we just figured you would die before this and we wouldn't have to waste the time on a slave,* he continued to say. He proceeded to laugh all the way down the corridor, ignoring my pleas of innocence and demands for an explanation. As I later came to find out, the werewolf had slaughtered most everyone at the estate, and I was one of the survivors."

"But why would they feed you bread and water if their intentions were to kill you?"

"Apparently, it was customary to sustain prisoners until they died or until the day their execution arrived, it would've been 'ungodly' to act otherwise. Accused are supposed to have a trial, but because I was a slave, I wasn't entitled to one. They felt me to be less than a human. Yet, they needed to look *just*. Perhaps just in the eyes of God. It was also easy to blame me for the murders rather than accept the truth that a werewolf did the killing. Perhaps they wanted me to live a bit longer so that they could justify other beliefs they had about me. They thought that I had committed the murders and wanted to accuse me of witchcraft but had no explanation as to how I had sustained my injuries."

Corbin turned to tend to things at the table behind him. The clamps and other instruments that he used to tend to me, he placed into a larger basin of water. It turned pink as the blood that was still on the equipment diluted with the water. Pain still resided in my wounds, but I was feeling better. "Did you ever come across the werewolf that attacked you at the estate?"

Corbin ignored my questions entirely. He turned to face me again. "Later in the week, I was fully accused of witchcraft when the local magistrate came to announce my charges and found me eating a rat. I had no means of cooking the vermin, so I was forced to eat the thing raw. At that moment, I felt an ache in my stomach like never before, one that couldn't be satisfied with just bread alone. The following days blended together; I lost all track of time. I do remember the night before I was to be executed being drawn to the only window in my cell. Though there were bars over it, the window gave me a good view of the night sky. I was fortunate that night the moon was full. I don't remember when I changed, and I only have vague images of the night. Images of me crashing through the door of my cell, attacking the night watchman and various other people to whom I had no personal connection, and running, running very fast for a long time. The next morning, I found myself lying in a woodland glade naked, covered in blood and physically sick. Images from the night before assaulted me; however, as I lay there amongst the trees and the sounds of the birds, a feeling of relief set in on me. I was away from my captors, and I had become something else entirely. The scars from the whips and beatings I had sustained while enslaved had vanished as though the events surrounding them had never occurred. All that remained were the two scars from where the werewolf had bitten me. That day I never ventured out from the cover of the forest and found refuge around a nearby brook. This is where they found me two days later."

"Who found you?" My voice was no longer weak. It was clear and soft again, mainly because of the tea.

"The others that you inquired about. These other werewolves that had heard of the events at the estate and were waiting to see if I would eventually change. When I did, they tracked me deep within the woods. I was nervous at first, much the way you are now Dr. Bishop. Except they offered me protection from those that would be hunting me. They offered me acceptance. There was one condition: I had to severe all human connections and go into hiding for many years. This was easy to do since I was a slave and most of my family was more than likely scattered around the world or dead. Over the years they have become my family."

"How is it then that you came to own a nightclub?" I was even more curious about him. Curious about how he managed to stay concealed for so long.

"The same way that you became a writer and a professor; through careful calculations of the possible consequences that might ensue; however, our necessities were simpler. We didn't need to search for any great truths and over the years we needed an establishment that would allow us to blend in with society. Since the nightclub was conveniently located above part of the catacombs, it seemed a logical choice. Besides, it was easy to run the electrical wires from the club to our space down here," Corbin clarified. His tone was still serious and his face expressionless as he spoke. "Come, let me show you."

I placed the empty teacup on the table. Gingerly, I walked close behind Corbin. My shoulder and back were still sore from the bullet wounds, but my leg having just been treated was much worse. It felt better and the hole had stopped bleeding, but I knew it was going take changing into a werewolf again before my leg was fully back to normal. With each step the muscle flexed, putting unwanted strain on the damaged area.

We walked through several corridors that were dark and musty smelling. The air was cool, with periodical gusts of a light breeze. No doubt from an opening that led to the surface. It reminded me of the lower level of my estate. Corbin took the time to point out several spots where the electrical wires had been installed to allow for lighting and the use of various other forms of equipment. We came to an area that was lit with softer lights than the fluorescent ones in the previous room. It looked as though it was some kind of hall, the sort used by noble kings that wanted to conduct a secret council. The walls were stone, and the ceiling was several feet higher than the corridors and the other room. An opening covered with glass at the top shown out to the surface. Sunlight poured through space illuminating a portion of the cement floor. I could tell that the opening resided between four separate buildings, perhaps in a courtyard. Several gothic, ornate chairs were built into the walls, all facing towards the center. Between each chair were separate corridors that stretched off in different directions. All were dark.

As we continued to walk through the hall, I could not help musing over how many werewolves, other than Corbin, shared this space. A twinge of frustration zipped through me with the thought that something like this existed and I was unable to uncover it throughout all my research.

After we moved through one of the darkened archways, we came to a smaller room that was dominated by an oversized fireplace. If I stood completely upright at the hearth, there would still be a half afoot of space before my head could touch the top. I was certain that several average-sized men could fit comfortably, side-by-side in the fireplace. Small piles of ash lay along the back wall and rustled a bit as we walked past. I paused for a moment just past the fireplace as I caught the scent of a different kind of odor. Not of burnt wood or coal, too acrid and pungent.

I did not have time to ponder the smell. Corbin had walked ahead and was standing at the foot of a stone staircase that spiraled upwards to the left. "This way Dr. Bishop."

I hurried across the room as fast as my leg would allow. At the foot of the stairs, I was met with another gust of wind and assumed this was one of the stairwells that lead to the surface. At the top of the stairs was another hallway that led outside. The daylight was intense, so much so that I was forced to cover my eyes. It was still cold, and the ground was still wet. As my eyes adjusted, I realized that I was in the courtyard between the four buildings. No other opening lead in or out of the courtyard. The ground was cement except for an opening in the center that was covered by a pane of glass. I walked to the edge of it and looked down into the darkness. Nothing that resided below could be seen. The glass was very thick, and I wondered why it was there.

Corbin stopped just beyond the glass and turned towards me again. "It allows the moonlight to shine through to the chamber below," he finally said. It was clear now. Changing into a werewolf in the catacombs below was smart and kept it secret from the rest of society. It was the same thing I had done in the basement of my estate. Only there I was contained. Here they were not.

Corbin walked to the middle of the wall directly in front of me. He placed his hands on two of the stones along the wall and pushed hard. He grunted slightly as the wall gave way. It swung open inwardly. Corbin motioned for me to follow him. I could see that it was a makeshift wall of sorts that was mounted upon hinges that would be concealed as the wall was put back into place. Past the wall was a small room with shelves on either side. They each contained basic bartending supplies and containers, nothing that was out of the ordinary. A couple of mops rested in the corner off to the right. Corbin allowed me to fully enter before he shoved the wall back into place. All was dark for a moment before he flipped the switch on the wall lighting the small room. As we exited, I glanced back at the wall noticing that it gave no indication of leading to the courtyard and to a normal onlooker this would appear to be a simple storage closet for bar supplies. The door to the small room bore a sign that read: *Employees Only*.

I stared out from the darkened area onto an empty dance floor, realizing that this was the VIP Lounge that I was trying to get into before being met by security. Flashbacks of the event filled my thoughts. The yelling and screaming, throwing the security guard, breaking the other security guard's arm, only to end in such a horrific and terrifying display. Corbin continued to walk ahead of me and ascended another set of steps to the left that led to the office of the establishment. Painfully I stumbled up the stairs. At the top, I immediately realized that this space was the glass office that overlooked the dance floor. No one else was up there except Corbin. I made my way over to the glass wall. The view allowed anyone in the office to see everything that was going on in the club at any given time. It was as though this club was a look-out post for the rest of the catacombs that rested secretly beneath. I turned to face Corbin. He stood in front of a flat-screen television, tampering with some of the equipment that resided just below.

"I want you to see this, Dr. Bishop." Corbin continued to adjust the dials on the devices. The television set came on with a blink and showed a rotating symbol with the word *LOADING* just below. Within moments the screen was alive with the video feed from the security cameras outside the entrance of the club and from the ones on the inside. It didn't take long to realize that this was the same video feed from the night that I arrived at the club. I recognized the repeated thumping from the bass immediately. Corbin continued to watch the screen with great interest, flipping back and forth from the one mounted just above the outside entrance to those mounted inside along the walls at various points. Corbin paused the video feed the moment I appeared at the outside entrance. He glanced at me briefly suggesting that I should pay close attention to the subsequent parts of the video.

I watched as I snuck into the club past the security outside as well as the girl that was accepting the cover payments from the patrons. I watched as I made my way through the crowd only to be stopped by some other security guard working by the VIP Lounge. I watched as I became angry by what the man was saying to me and the onset of the first security guard catching up to me. I watched as I threw him over the bar and broke the other man's arm when he tried to grab me from behind. I watched, with horror, as I turned into the werewolf. It was the first time I had seen myself change. People scattered in all directions, fleeing the monster that stood before them. Corbin paused the video at this moment and directed my attention to the view from another camera. He pointed to the men that were drawing their guns and advancing towards me. One of the men I did not recognize, but the other I recognized immediately. I had seen him the night I killed the young girl. I saw him standing next to his screaming father pointing a gun in my face. I remembered swinging my arm in his direction, knocking him back several feet. "Osborne." I finally let slip from under my breath.

Corbin turned to face me again, "We know." He let the video play out from that point. The entire video stole my breath. What could I say in return except something to try to explain my actions?

"I…I killed his sister," I finally said. Corbin stared intensely at me, urging me with his eyes to go on. "In an attempt to gather more information about what I am…she got in the way. An innocent child got in the way." Emotions were welling up inside of me and the onset of tears was likely.

"This is Grayson Osborne, a Lieutenant in the British Army and son of Robert Osborne, a member of The House of

Commons." I felt my insides turn at the presentation of this information. "Robert Osborne is a very powerful person. He'll be difficult to deal with."

All manner of thoughts and emotions raced through my mind. Sadness and regret mixed with fear and anger. Anger from not knowing, anger from trying to know more but only making matters worse. I lowered my head out of shame. "Corbin, I must know," I began. "How did I change into a werewolf without having a full moon?"

Without looking directly at me, he spoke, "You changed, Dr. Bishop, because you were scared." He said finally turning to face me. He grabbed a remote off a nearby wooden desk and pointed it at the television. It went dark. "Perhaps you were angry, or perhaps you were both. The moon will always have its sway over us, but it is those that have mastered the ability to change through their emotions that have been able to survive the onset of the passing years and, as you have found out, from those that hunt us."

"I know I just watched the video, but why are the images of last night so..."

"Clear?" Corbin finished. He leaned against the side of the desk in the office. "Dr. Bishop, the memories of last night are clear because nothing else besides your own emotions inside of you manipulated your change. You're the master of your own emotions."

I was awe stricken. Marcus was right. I thought. Perhaps Corbin knows the answer to the curse?

"Dr. Bishop, I have shown you this video so that you may come to understand that these men have to be removed. It's of no doubt that these men know where you live and were probably the same men that attacked you at the library," he explained as he placed a newspaper in front me displaying the report of the spoken incident as well as a separate article of the shooting here at the club. "If they were able to track you to the club, then it's a good bet that they know who I am as well."

"What are you going to do?"

"We'll deal with them in a manner that is most natural to us." Corbin's posture became more upright and his voice more malicious.

"Are you going to kill them?" I hoped that his implication was wrong and that there was something I was not privy to knowing.

"Yes, Dr. Bishop. All who know of our existence must be destroyed."

"You can't kill them!" I exclaimed. "I – I killed his sister, the daughter of Robert Osborne…"

"And do I deserve their vengeance?" Corbin snarled. His voice was deep with a growl that followed. "No, Dr. Bishop, I've suffered enough in one lifetime at the hands of mankind. I won't suffer for the pitfalls of another. We already have to close the club because your event which puts us in danger."

I recoiled a bit. "There has to be some other way? I read…I read in the library of the story of Johan Stich. He could be the source of this curse." I spoke quickly knowing this was a long shot.

"Curse? Hah! Dr. Bishop we've been given the greatest gift the world has ever seen!" I listened to his disturbing laugh and shuttered at the thought of calling what I was a gift. "And yes, I too have read that story. Supposedly, Mr. Stich is the father of us all. That it was through his deeds and his bite we are what we are. Yet, he was too weak to even survive the farmers that destroyed him."

"We discovered that he had offspring and that the devil could've cursed them to carry out these evil deeds…" my words fell off at the realization that I had used the word we. I saw that Corbin had also caught this slip of the tongue.

His voice was calm but remained sinister. "Dr. Bishop, who else knows of us besides these men?"

"He's no one, just a scientist. He's harmless, no threat to you at all." I was starting to panic.

"Not a threat. I've watched for many years as science and the people behind science have destroyed this world in which we live," Corbin stopped speaking for a moment and walked behind the desk. He pressed a button on the phone that sat on the corner. Anger seethed from every part of him, "Come up here! Dr. Bishop, I've no use for science especially when it was created by mankind and I've no reservations with eliminating those who seek to eliminate me. Mankind turned its back upon me long ago when it forced me into servitude. The only creatures on this planet that offered me acceptance without judgment and ridicule were those of this assembly. I care nothing for the creation of God. Should it be that Johan Stich is the source, damned by the devil or not, why would I want to end this great gift that was given to me? I'm offering you our protection and this one chance to be a part of us."

I drew backwards toward the staircase but was stopped by two larger men coming up the stairs. "There's no way that you'll be able to keep the death of a member of the House of Commons secret. He's too prominent of a person to just go missing. You'll be found out eventually."

"We have ways of disposing of the remains. The world cannot prove what it does not know exists."

My heartbeat quickened at the thought of the fireplace below the establishment. It was clear that the foul smell was that of human remains. They burned, deep below the city, whatever was left after a kill. I suddenly became very fearful for Marcus. No matter where he was in the world, he would be in danger by simply having known what I am. It would not take them long to figure out that I had worked with him. As much as I wanted to avoid Robert Osborne and his family, they deserved their vengeance. I could not be responsible for their deaths too. "You've strayed far from your priesthood. I can't do this the way you do. You sound too much like the devil. It's believed Satan's greatest trick was convincing mankind he didn't exist. I've too much blood on my hands already and I fear that I'll lose my soul entirely."

"That was the wrong answer, Dr. Bishop," Corbin claimed. With a sudden jolt the two men from the stairwell grabbed my arms and forced me to bend forward. Their grips were like steel, different from when the security guards had grabbed me. I knew instantly that they were also werewolves. I tried to pull away, but they simply pushed harder on the back of my shoulders with their free hands. The wound on my right shoulder burned and tingled under the pressure. Eventually my right leg, too weak to hold me, gave out and I collapsed to the floor. Corbin walked over to me and knelt on one knee. I could see that he was holding something in his hand. He grabbed me with force with one hand and jerked my head backwards, exposing my neck. "I'm afraid, Dr. Bishop, your soul is already lost."

Corbin lowered his right hand, still holding my head back with his left. I caught a glimpse of a syringe and a second later felt the prick on my neck. He released my head after he emptied the liquid from the needle into my body. I felt the world spinning around me as all the light quickly fell into darkness.

Chapter #28

Secret Revealed
Robert Osborne
Sunday, December 6th, 2009
5:25 p.m.

We kept Marcus secured to the chair in the library throughout Saturday night and into Sunday morning. Time passed slowly. He did not talk much. I could tell he was scared, but not of us. From what Grayson told me, Marcus was more frightened that we would find Dr. Bishop than what we could do to him by not helping us. *Bastard!* I thought. *It was clear that he himself wasn't a werewolf, but how could he protect this evil? How could he help Dr. Bishop knowing what she was and what she has done?*

Eventually the daylight faded again as the nighttime darkness slipped its shadowy fingers through the windows of the library. From Marcus' detailed notes that we were able to extract from his device, we knew it was used to track Dr. Bishop's whereabouts, yet we were still unable to utilize it to our advantage. Using the tracking component of the device required a separate ten-digit key code that only Marcus knew. Each time we tried to obtain the key code from Marcus he would just shut down on us or pass out for long periods of time from the harsh methods that Jinx and Rex were using. Grayson suggested that we unbind him, that he may be more compliant in a more comfortable state. Conversely, my patience had grown thin, and I had no sympathy for the man who had been helping the very thing we were trying to destroy. I had resolved to let Marcus stay bound to the chair until he made the decision to help us.

Snake continued to examine the files Marcus had on Dr. Bishop. All he was able to come up with were several process logs explaining what experiments he had performed on Dr. Bishop. Most were simply tests that involved blood work or measuring vital signs. Some consisted of cross-referencing these with a variety of canine species; however, nothing so far proved to be useful towards finding Dr. Bishop.

Kap spent most of his time developing more silver bullets. He claimed that the ones he and Grayson used at the club were not as accurate as they should have been and that it was a mistake that he was *not* going to repeat. Unfortunately, the bullets that he had been creating could only be fired from the handguns we have. Kap said that the more sophisticated bullets used in the semi-automatic assault rifles would take more time to craft and given the circumstances, time was working against us. Marcus had informed us that Dr. Bishop would probably go into hiding. No doubt to try and discourage us from trying to find her. We had learned that Dr. Bishop had done this on several other occasions in the past, changing her name and moving from place to place. Marcus' logs explained explicitly how she went about doing it for so long and that since she was supposedly over two hundred years old, "immortal" one could say. She could simply go into hiding with the intent to outlive us. Unfortunate for Marcus, this only heightened our sense of urgency.

I had to stay out of the library. The frustration I was experiencing was not helping the situation. I took to wandering around on the lower floors of the manor. The manor was huge, especially in comparison to that of my own. There were several dens and sitting areas along with an immensely lavish kitchen area that led into a private dining space. The hallways were all lined with ornate wood trim, with a rustic smell to match. Sconces were strategically placed at various points to supplement the light from the windows. Most of the natural light poured in through the high placed windows in the foyer during the day and even at night. It helped to illuminate the oversized marble spiral staircase that led to the second-floor spaces up and to the right. I could tell that this was the home of a wealthy family mainly due to the high ceilings in most of the rooms. A manor built in the 1700s would typically have such features, mainly to display their wealth. Other homes, smaller ones, usually had lower ceilings to trap the heat from the fireplaces. However, being of money a family could probably afford an abundant supply of wood or coal to burn, which may have been too costly for others of the time.

I was about to venture back into the kitchen in search of what little food was left by the men at the house when Jinx stopped me in the hallway, "Boss, I think ya need to come see this shit." Though Jinx was still vulgar, it was clear that someone, perhaps Kap, had convinced Jinx of the gravity of the situation. I followed him back to the library without question. "We found something on the twatter's device that may be of significance. Look."

I leaned over Snake's shoulder to look at the small screen. There was a green-colored grid with several land structures and topography. There was also a floor plan that resembled the layout of the manor. In the center of the house was a glowing dot that blinked repetitively. "Brilliant, you got it to work! What's the white dot?" I asked.

"We think that the white dot is Dr. Bishop…" Snake stated before I interrupted.

"What do you mean it is Dr. Bishop? That means she's here!" I felt the adrenaline rush through my body.

"No, no! Boss, this is just a recording. This was recorded nearly a month ago," Snake explained quickly. "See this grey dot…I assume this is the device. Apparently, this program can also record, and store files of the subject being tracked. Nothing detailed, just a grid with basic structures and topography. This is the first recording, probably when Marcus inserted a transmitter under her skin or something like that. It's a good way to monitor the vital signs of whatever may have the other part inserted into them. Here are all her vital signs. If I might say, this is a pretty advanced."

"Well, I'm glad you are so amused by all of this, but can we skip over all the rubbish? Is there anything recorded that can be of use to us?" I asked, sensing that my patience was once again being tested. I happened to glance over at Marcus and instead of sleeping or passed out, he was staring directly at us with a somewhat panicked look on his face. "Does this mean that we can use it to track Dr. Bishop?"

"No, we still need the key code. Every time I click activate it prompts me for the code. Most of the files are nothing more than the one we're currently viewing," Snake clarified.

"Then why did you call me in here!" I snapped at Snake. "I'm paying you to find things that are useful to us, not some damn…"

Snake held up his hand and pointed at the screen as if to suggest that I was missing something. "I said that most of the files are similar. These three that are stored were marked differently and for good reason. One file I recognized immediately. The dot represents Dr. Bishop inside a different structure. This different structure I think is the book depository where you all first encountered her. Her vital signs increase, and it also shows the dot, Dr. Bishop, moving at a very high speed out of the building. This is probably when she tossed this old boy here," Snake nudged Jinx and then pointed to the screen so that I could follow what he was saying. Jinx seemed a bit put out by this but remained quiet. "Another file was recorded nearly an hour before that put her here, inside the manor. This one is significant because it demonstrates the same spike in her vital signs, the same fast movement. Something happened here at the manor just before she encountered us."

I glanced back at Marcus, seething, knowing that he probably knew what had happened. He was still looking attentively at us and even more nervous than before. I returned my focus to what Snake was explaining, "Go on."

"This last file is the most peculiar. There are no structures, and I don't recognize the topography at all; however, Dr.

Bishop's vital signs are the highest during this recording and she is moving faster than the other times. I assume she's in the wilderness, the forest perhaps. Here I will let it play out entirely," Snake set it up to play as he continued to explain what he thought was happening. "It looks as though she was coming directly at this device but stops momentarily and doubles back on her own path, then shoots off in a straight line for several minutes. The date on this recording was November 27, 2009. It looks to be a Friday at 8:58 p.m. in the evening. I think there was a full moon that weekend, so this very well may be when she was in full werewolf form. The only thing in this recording that's a recognizable structure is…right there, that line. She comes to a fence line of some sort."

When Snake paused the recording and pointed to the screen, I felt as though the air around me had grown thick and the breath inside me was pulled from my chest. My knees began to wobble as I placed my right hand on the table next to Snake's equipment. I gripped my chest with my left as I realized what I was witnessing. This was the night Laryn was killed. Images of the ghastly scene poured into my head as I felt dizzy. I could still hear her screaming in pain. I could still see the beast consuming her and I could still see her remains. I remembered trying to hold her body close to me after the attack, but there was nothing to hold onto. Her blood soaked the ground. A tear streamed down my face.

"Boss, boss. Are ya all right?" I heard Snake ask. My reality came screeching back into focus. I did not answer Snake, but instead looked over at Marcus who knew exactly what I had just seen. Rage erupted inside of me. With a quick jerk of my body, I began walking briskly towards him.

"You son of bitch!" I yelled as I reared back my right arm, fist clenched. I connected with Marcus' stomach, and I felt the wind expelled from inside as he let out a deep groan of pain. His frame crumpled what little it could. I stood in front of him as I struck him a second time across the face with my left. The jolt from the blow caused his nose to start bleeding again. "You were there that night! You could've stopped her! My daughter could still be alive!"

I struck Marcus a third time across the face with my right fist. I could see his face swelling on either side. "Please, please, stop! I did everything in my power to stop her that night!" Marcus spoke through heavy breaths and intermitting spitting of blood.

"That sounds like a sack of rancid shit to me!" I screamed only inches from his face. The other men were caught completely off guard by this outburst but did nothing to stop me from engaging Marcus. "Now! What's the key code?"

"This is madness!" Marcus uttered.

I slapped his face hard with my right hand, "I grow tired of this game! What's the *fucking* key code?" Blood trickled from his nose and down the front of his shirt, but he remained silent. "Answer me! What's the code?"

"This won't bring your daughter back," he finally stated.

I backed away from him and walked over to the fireplace just off to the right. I grabbed the iron poker from its rack and without taking more than three steps towards him I shuffled and swung the poker at Marcus. It connected with his shin as the metal rang in my hand. He let out a wail of pain. "This is only a fraction of the pain I feel! What's the key code?" I roared. Marcus had begun to cry. I swung the poker again, aiming for the same spot. When it connected the second time, I felt his shin bone crack as he let out another wail of pain! "What's the key code?" I howled in anger again.

Marcus whimpered and sobbed uncontrollably. I brought the poker back for a third strike, but something stopped it and I felt a great force collide with the left side of my jaw. The blow was strong and caused the room to spin as I collapsed to the wooden floor. It was several moments before everything came back into focus. Standing over me holding the poker was Grayson.

"Enough of this!" Grayson yelled. Everyone in the room was staring at him, including me. "This is mad and torturous. Rex, unbind him and take him to one of the rooms. Help him get his face cleaned up. Kap go with him."

Both men did what he asked without question. They unbound Marcus and hoisted him out of the room. I could hear the moans of pain as they went down the hall. I was stunned by Grayson. "What are you doing? That bastard could've stopped the werewolf and he didn't!" I screamed, still lying on the floor staring up at Grayson.

He threw the poker on the floor across the room and looked down at me, "You've lost control of yourself," he stated before turning away from me.

I stumbled but managed to get to my feet. Both Snake and Jinx stood across the room from us watching to see how this was going to play out. "You senseless ass! That man has a recording of the night Laryn was killed, and you don't seem to be bothered by this. He could've prevented this from happening!"

"Nothing could've saved Laryn that night!" he spat back at me. "I know…I saw the thing that killed her. I watched as the Rigby rounds from Codie's gun passed right through it. We then tracked it to a nightclub and even after shooting the bloody thing three times with silver bullets, it still didn't die! What was this man going to do? Torturing him is not going to bring Laryn back, she's gone! If you kill him, then his blood's on our hands!"

"I don't think you get it! That man has a key code that we need to track down this monster and kill it!" If I had known at the time the impact my words would have upon Grayson, I wouldn't have said them at all, but my fury still fumed inside of me. "I'm also starting to think you don't want to find this werewolf anymore. As a matter of fact, I'm starting to doubt your resolve. Sending you to Sandhurst was a waste of time and money, it's no wonder it was so easy for you to abandon your men. You were afraid to do what was necessary for them just as you're afraid to do what's necessary for me right now!"

Grayson turned away from me again. "Snake, is there anything you can do to crack this code without Marcus?" he asked.

Snake hesitated before answering, still bewildered by what had just happened, "Well, I've had the device connected to this computer for the past six hours or so, running a series of possible number combinations that could make up the key code. That's the best that I can do for the moment. It'll eventually work, I just can't say when. Could be an hour, could be a day, it's really hard to predict when it's going to find the right set of numbers. These devices are some of the toughest to crack, mainly because much of the functions are…"

"I don't need a computer lesson, just stay on it. Also, see if you can hack into the cameras at the nightclub." Grayson interrupted.

"Both are going to take some time," Snake mumbled.

Grayson finally turned back to face me. He stood in front of me with fierceness in his eyes, "No one in this room has abandoned anything, except you. You have abandoned reason for anger! It has consumed you! You've let it cloud everything you understand to be noble. What I just witnessed was no better than what the werewolf did to Laryn, and she would expect better from you."

His words were heavy on me, but my anger was still too fresh. As he walked away from me, I yelled with as much venom as I could muster, "Where are you going now?"

He ignored me and yelled for Kap to come back into the room. Kap appeared at the archway moments later. He had blood on the front of his shirt, no doubt from Marcus. I listened closely as Grayson spoke to him. "How is he?"

"He'll live. We got him a bit cleaned up, still looks like a bucket of snots if you ask me. Also, we had a look at his leg. It's bloody mess!" Kap replied.

"How are those silver bullets coming?" Grayson inquired, tactfully changing the subject.

"Much better than the last time! I got several magazines filled with better calibrated rounds as well as an etching that perfectly matches the rifling inside the barrel of the pistols. Should be a bit more accurate than the ones we used at the club," Kap asserted.

"Nice work. Bring me what you have and tell Rex to come in here." Kap turned from the archway and disappeared around the corner. Grayson looked at me with an equal amount of distaste that I currently had towards him, "We're going to go question this club owner, Corbin Paige. At the moment it's the only thing we can do."

Both Kap and Rex appeared in the archway. Kap walked past Grayson and placed four separate pistols on the table in the library. Next to them he placed the corresponding magazines, all filled with silver bullets. Grayson addressed Kap first, "Excellent. I don't know how long it's going to take before Snake can crack the encryption, but in the meantime make as many bullets as you can. Rex, you're coming with me this time. I know where the club is as well as the layout, but I'm afraid I may be recognized on the security cameras, but you won't. This may be the only advantage we have. Besides I'm going to have you scope it first before we enter. After last night, they should be closed."

Kap turned and left again, while Rex, without asking any questions, began loading the pistols and placing the extra magazines in small spaces on the inside of his coat. Jinx approached the table and asked, "So while ya glory fucks are having a go with things, what the fuck am I supposed to do?"

"I want you to stay here and help Snake and Kap. Also to make sure that Marcus recovers. No more injuries!" Grayson said.

"Well, isn't this just a piece of bloody shit!" Jinx replied, however, he did not argue with Grayson.

"No worry mate, he is sedated pretty heavily. I don't think he will toss ya like the little lady did!" Rex said with a laugh. Jinx gave a two-fingered salute before walking out of the library.

Grayson put on his leather coat over the two-holstered pistols. He handed Snake a two-way radio before he and Rex also left the library. Not another word was exchanged between us. I moved across the room and leaned against the wall. Outside I could hear one of the vans starting up and this is when Grayson's words started to take effect. A deep pain from within filled my being. Thoughts of Laryn, Grayson, Codie and even Daphne, my ex-wife, swirled around inside of me. I was glad that Codie stayed behind. I do not know how he would have reacted to my display of anger. *How did I come to this moment? How did I destroy everything I had in my life? What have I done?*

Rex and Grayson had been gone for nearly half an hour when Snake stood quickly at the table. "Blow me balls, I've got it!"

I rushed over to his workstation and sure enough, a ten-digit set of numbers was blinking on the screen. "Quick, punch in the numbers!" I said, somewhat frantic. If we could get a lock on Dr. Bishop, Grayson and Rex wouldn't have to operate blindly. Snake dialed the numbers into the device and within a moment a green grid appeared and began searching.

"This is going to take a second. It's gotta find the subject host," Snake stated. "Come on, come on…got her!"

A bright white light began blinking on the screen. "Where is she? Where is she at?" I asked.

"It looks like she's not even an hour away. She's in some kind of structure. Hang on, let me punch these coordinates into my computer," Snake stated. His fingers moved like lightning over the keyboard. "It looks like she's in Cambridge at St. Teresa's Cathedral!"

"She's at a church?" I inquired, confused.

"Unless I'm wrong, which I rarely am, that's where Dr. Bishop is!"

"Bring up the address and get on the line to Grayson and Rex. Tell them that we'll meet them there! And tell them to be careful!"

Jinx appeared at the archway of the library, "What are ya two ladies squawking about?"

"We got her," I responded directly.

"Well it's 'bout fuck'n time! I owe this little bitch one!" Jinx hooted.

"Snake I need you to stay behind to watch Marcus and to keep us informed as to any changes," I ordered.

"You got it boss!" Snake replied.

We loaded the second van quickly. The air outside was cold and the sky was cloudy. It began to rain again, cold and icy. It was still too early in the month for a full moon. However, based on what Marcus had written in his logs, the moon being full did not really matter much. As we drove down the long private drive and the darkness encircled the van, I whispered for the first time in a long time, "God be with us!"

Chapter #29

The Beast Within
Mya
Sunday, December 6th, 2009
6:30 p.m.

No dreams came from the blackness. Damp air moistened my skin and filled my lungs as I continued to slowly breathe deep through my nostrils. I felt weak and my body was secured to a hard surface. The wounds I had sustained were still sore. Light was scarce and only came from two small torches that were mounted to the wall beside a stone stairwell that ascended into more darkness. This made it difficult for my eyes to focus. Behind me, I could feel a light breeze suggesting there was another opening that was not within view. I had no idea how long I had been in this state, but it reminded me of the time when Marcus had shot me with the tranquilizer gun in the lower level of my estate.

At the thought of Marcus, a sudden realization sprung to mind. *I'm in danger!* Memories of talking with Corbin and his anger caused me to gasp as a sinking feeling tumbled deep into the pits of my being. I forced my eyes to blink quickly to gain a better focus of my surroundings. Both of my arms were pinned tight to my sides with several straps that prevented them from moving. My legs were also secured, pushed together, and held tightly with more straps. I could not move. All I could do was stare at the stone ceiling above me. I pulled hard with my arms and legs but was unable to break free. Panic spread throughout my body. It was then that I heard a seething voice that struck me still with terror. "It's useless to struggle. You won't be able to break your bindings. The sedative that I have given you doesn't allow one's strength to return so quickly. By the time it does you shall be no more than a distant memory."

"Corbin, what are you doing?" My voice cracked from fear.

He did not answer at first, but instead walked from behind me so that I could see him fully. His dark skin blended with the shadows of the space. I could only make out his outline, but his eyes cut through the blackness with sinister clarity. "I'm doing what's necessary!" he growled, lowering his face closer to mine. "You've brought us no other choice."

His voice was low, but clear with intent. Two other silhouettes formed beside Corbin's as he stood more upright. It must have been the two men that had originally grabbed me in his office. They stood equal in stature to Corbin. Both were of European descent except one had pale looking skin while the other took on a more olive color. It was difficult to make out anything else since my eyes were still adjusting in the low lighting. The pale one placed a bag of objects next me on the table. It made a metal clank as it struck the stone block from which I was secured. "Why are you doing this?" Desperate, I tried to reason with Corbin, "The story of Johan Stich may be able to offer us a piece to this puzzle. If we work together, we can find an end to this evil. I know that mankind has been unkind to you, but the world has changed. It's better. You can still have a chance at a normal life. Please! Don't do this! God will forgive your sins..."

"Enough!" Corbin roared. "You've lost your opportunity to be a part of us. Do not speak to me of normal or even better when for two hundred and fifty years I watched God's beloved creation tear each other apart. Better is what I am!"

"God only delivers punishment to the wicked," I stated through short shallow breaths. Corbin let out a baleful laugh.

"You can keep your precious God. I have no need of him now. God punished me for no cause, but now I'll deliver the punishment to his servants. I've become more than the priest I once was," Corbin fumed. He turned the bag of objects upside down and its contents spilled onto my chest. The objects pressed down upon me. I could tell by the smell that the items were made of silver. It always gave off a metallic scent that was most often too subtle for humans to detect but was very distinct for a werewolf.

"God shall not be mocked," I whimpered in fear.

"I'll mock him as I please!" Corbin interrupted. All I could do was stare back at him, astonished by his hatred towards God. "The rest of the world has forgotten what you've done, but we know everything about you. We know your sins…your sins against us."

I could feel my body tense up and my senses became very acute. I was painfully aware that even though I spent a great deal of my life staying in the shadows of society I was not a secret to them. I feared what they knew about me and how that would lead to the pain of others. I felt my heart begin to pound inside my chest and the blood race through my body as Corbin began to recount the most clandestine details of my life that only I knew, and that Marcus had just recently come to know.

"We know how you've covered up your sins from the rest of the world. We even know about your friend, Marcus Holland. You were foolish to pay for his travel arrangements from the airport to your estate and he was foolish enough to use the same company to take him back to the airport. He has purchased a ticket to Australia; we'll visit him soon. The knowledge that he possesses is too much of a threat to us and you left too much of a trail. We also know that you've spent your life denying the thing that you are, regretting the loss of your family by your own hands."

The words fell like daggers upon my heart. At the mention of my family my fear began to turn to sadness and pain. Tears streamed down my face. "You were easy to follow through history. You don't embrace the gift that has been given. Instead, you try to rid yourself of it and hide it from the world. You aim to destroy others who have it too. That is why your body will lay rotting and stinking here, as a mockery to your God!"

Corbin paced in front of me as if he anticipated something in the next moment. "Do you know where you are Dr. Bishop? The crypt below St. Teresa's Cathedral. Few know about the sewer tunnel that spills into the river. We brought you here when we learned this was your church. We found it to be a fitting place for the end of your miserable, weak life!"

Corbin moved to the right side of me. He wrenched my right arm free of the straps and pulled it out straight before he pinned it to the stone slab with both of his hands. The olive-skinned man grabbed one of the objects that lay across my chest, held it tight in his left fist, a hammer in his right. The item was a silver stake. He positioned the tip of it on my forearm just above my wrist. He raised his right hand high into the air and brought the hammer down upon the top of the stake with an incredible force. The stake pierced my skin and continued through my forearm into the stone slab beneath. I let out a howl as a shockwave of pain ripped into my body. Blood poured from the newly formed wound. My arm shook from the pain before it went limp.

"Cry out for God, Dr. Bishop! Cry out for him! You're in His house! You're in your church! Let's see if he comes to your aid!" Corbin yelled mockingly. "Tell me Dr. Bishop, how do you think Marcus will die, crying like you?"

The pain was tremendous. Another wave of panic filled me. I realized that I did not have the charm of Saint Michael around my neck, and that Marcus still had it from when I gave it to him the night in the woods. Everything was so chaotic after that night I forgot to get it back from him. There was nothing I could do. I could hear death's footsteps approaching.

Corbin walked around to the left side of me. The olive-skinned man clutched another stake in his hand. Corbin pried my left arm from the straps the same way he did my right and pinned it to the stone slab. Again, I felt my body tensing; the sedative must have been wearing off, but Corbin was right, it was too late. The olive-skinned man positioned the point of the second stake in the middle of my forearm with his left hand. He drew the hammer back with his right arm and brought down another crushing blow to the top of the stake. The silver again pierced my flesh and muscle continuing through until it was imbedded into the stone beneath me. Pain again ripped through my body as my left arm shook the same as my right before going limp.

I turned my head to look at the stake. I saw and smelled a small whiff of smoke. The device that Marcus had inserted into my arm was destroyed. More tears streamed down the side of my face. There was no way Marcus would ever be able to track me again. I thought about the fear Marcus would have not knowing where I was or if I was still alive. I thought about how he would forever walk in fear of the shadows and that I caused this fear to exist in him. I felt my end was near. The only thing I could do was welcome death in the manner I knew, "Our father, who art in heaven…" I began.

Corbin swung his arm from across his chest, striking the side of my mouth with the back of his hand. My head whipped to the right from the force of the blow. "There's no place for those words within you. You are as much of a demon as the ones your God threw out of his kingdom. He does not hear you anymore!" Corbin snarled. "Remember, it was you that killed your family. We followed all the reports that appeared thereafter in the newspapers. We watched as a young girl named Martha went crazy in the asylum and later died. We thought that maybe she would turn, but she never did. Instead, she died of starvation. When you finally emerged, it was easy to follow your path through history to link you to those events."

Anger began to pour into my body. I felt it begin in the pit of my stomach. I began to whisper, "Saint Michael the Archangel, defend us in battle; be our protection against the wickedness and snares of the devil. May God rebuke him, we humbly pray…"

Corbin drew back his arm again and struck the side of my face, "I said there's *NO* place for those words within you! You killed your family! You're a murderous demon in the eyes of God and his angels. God does not love you! You slaughtered your parents and your other sister, Anna. We also know that you were to be married, but that never happened! Your fiancé didn't live long enough for it to happen. You killed him too. His name was Brayden Murphy, wasn't it?" Corbin let out a sinister laugh.

Brayden's name struck me like a spear as the anger turned to rage. The pain in my arms started to lessen. I felt blood speeding through my veins and the muscles in my body beginning to grow. The straps grew even tighter around me, and I heard them begin to tear. I closed my eyes as I continued to pray, only louder, "…And do thou, O Prince of the heavenly host, by the power of God, thrust into hell Satan and all the evil spirits who prowl about the world seeking the ruin of souls! Amen!"

"Kill her," I heard Corbin say as I finished the prayer. The olive-skinned man walked towards me holding another stake. He was going to drive into my chest cavity, piercing the vital organs.

I let out a snarling howl as I wrenched as hard as I could with my right shoulder against the stake. Blood poured from my arm as it pulled away from the stone and my forearm slid up the metal. My arm scorched with pain as the flesh tore away from the stake that held it to the stone. With a jerk my arm was free. Instantly, the limp vice that held my arm hostage released. I opened my eyes, and the darkness no longer impeded my vision. I felt my jaw breaking forward as the canine teeth pushed through to form a snout. The straps that held me in place tore even more. I heard Corbin yell, "Kill her! Kill her!"

The olive-skinned man tried to move quickly, but it was too late. I was faster than he was. I reached across my body and grabbed the stake that held my left arm down. I yanked hard, freeing my left arm. The olive-skinned man tried to pin my arm down again. Still holding the silver stake in my right hand, I jammed it hard into the man's rib cage. His ribs on his left side cracked several times as the silver plunged deep into his lung and heart. He howled with pain and his eyes flashed a bluish white against the dimness of the crypt. Fur erupted from my hand and spread down my arm in a wave. I released my grip on the stake and watched as the man's body crumpled and fell to the floor. Both the paler-skinned man and Corbin recoiled back a few steps.

The straps across my chest snapped completely as my torso grew. The same happened to the ones holding my legs. I rolled from the table landing on my hands and knees. I felt no pain as I let the darkness fill my body and changed from a human to the monstrous beast I had dreaded for so many years. Fear no longer held me hostage for the only feeling I had was rage. Free from the table, a sinister strength forced me to stand and face my captors. My thoughts were clear and full of fury. Fury like nothing I had ever felt before. Though standing before me were not fearful men searching for an escape, but two other beasts just like me. As I changed, so did they, one grey and one black. Their white glowing eyes stared back at me with hatred. I too, shared in this enraged abhorrence and sprung towards the black werewolf, the one I knew to be Corbin.

Chapter #30

Rex and I received a call from my dad about twenty minutes after leaving Dr. Bishop's estate stating that she was located at *St. Teresa's Cathedral.* Fortunately, we were not too far off from the church, and it was relatively easy to find with the GPS. Snake informed us that my dad, Jinx and Kap were en route to join us and were going to keep us abreast as to whether Dr. Bishop was moving. I figured they were probably a half-hour or so behind us. I had no intention of waiting for them to show. My dad had been quickly losing himself since the death of Laryn. I had seen the same thing happen many times in Afghanistan. As some of our comrades fell in the heat of battle, friends and other comrades would lose their sense of control. Often, they would do something ridiculously crazy and get themselves killed or simply shut down, unable to perform the duties they had been trained to do. The last thing we needed going into a dangerous scenario was a person that did not have control over their emotions. I loved my sister too, but I knew that losing control would not bring her back and would only hinder my ability to hunt down the thing that caused her death.

Outside the sky was cloudy with periods of icy rain showers. Combined with the cold temperature and the wind, it was simply wet and unpleasant. The church was tall and gothic. We could only make out the front face of the building from the lampposts along the street. The rest of the structure was concealed by the evening shroud of darkness. Rich mahogany wood doors contrasted well against the stone archway and pillars that stretched upwards to the heavens. We positioned ourselves across from the church a fair distance away and remained inside the van so Rex could scope the area with some protection in case we ran into anything unpleasant. "See anything?" I asked.

"No, nothing." He was using a spotting scope with infrared and night vision capabilities, the same ones we used to carry out night missions in Afghanistan. How Rex had come across one was beyond me, but I was thankful for it. "No one has come in or out of the church for the past twenty minutes we've been here. I suspect that Mass ended nearly two hours ago at 5:00 p.m. So, I don't think…Wait! I see someone!"

The door to the church opened and a priest exited, only to stop and lock it behind him. He adjusted his long overcoat and placed a cap on top of his head. He was a short man, but that was all we could really tell before he turned away from the door and walked down the street turning at the corner. "Snake!" I spoke into a two-way radio. "Snake, you there?"

"Yah, go ahead!" a voice stated from the radio.

"Do you still have a signal on Dr. Bishop?" I inquired.

"Yes, it's still strong and it hasn't moved, she's still at the church," he stated.

"Snake, I want you to find out the names of the priests that are a part of this parish. Talk to Codie. I know he was supposed to contact Father Preston Mathew but there may also be others that know of and may be helping Dr. Bishop. We just saw one leave the building," I explained before I clasped the two-way radio to my belt. Turning back to Rex, "Do you see anything else?"

"No, not really. I'm getting a heat signature from behind the walls, but the stone has got it muffled," Rex spoke as he continued to look through the scope. "It might be from a heating vent or something else in the church. I can't be sure until we get in there."

I checked the magazine of one of the pistols and made sure that a round was ready in the chamber. I placed it back into the holster space just below my left arm and did the same with the second gun. Rex moved away from the scope for a moment to tend to his pistols. He glanced back into the scope one last time, before I asked, "Ready?"

"Ready," he replied.

Wind swirled around the inside of the van as we slid the side door open and jumped out. Neither of us had a weapon drawn as we cautiously approached the church. Upon reaching the steps that led up to the doors, Snake chimed in on the two-way radio, *"Grayson!"*

I held up my hand to signal to Rex to wait a moment, "Yah, go ahead!" I whispered.

"Dr. Bishop's signal is gone!" he stated somewhat frantic.

"What do you mean gone? Is she leaving the church?"

"No, I mean the signal just went dead! One moment I had it and the next it just blipped off!"

I motioned to Rex to move towards the door. Without question he moved up the stairs and knelt in front of the door, "Alright, we're going to take a look inside."

"Grayson, the vital signs just before I lost the signal were starting to increase. Heart rate, blood pressure, temperature, everything, were starting to register on the screen. She might have changed into a werewolf," Snake voiced.

Rex placed his ear to the door, "I don't hear a thing," he stated. "I'm going to have to pick the lock."

"Be quiet about it, I don't want to draw any more attention to ourselves than we have to." Rex gave me a look of agreement and then focused on the latch in front of him. Within a moment the latch clicked, and he slowly pulled open the door. Quickly, we both entered the church.

Everything was dark inside except for the prayer candles that were lit and placed upon the cascading tables for display purposes. The light was enough to illuminate the side aisles that extended perpendicular to several rows of wooden pews. Another doorway to the left of the main entrance led off to another part of the church. I motioned to Rex to move down the center aisle first as I walked the right-side aisle, both of us drew a sidearm from our holsters. The flames of the candles flickered and spurted light between the seating that spilled into the center aisle. It was not a lot of light, but it was enough that Rex could see.

At the end of the center aisle, an altar was built atop a set of two stairs. The only light behind it came from a few small red lights along the floor that marked where the priest would exit from his chambers before Mass. The smell of incense was heavy on the air and not a sound could be heard. As we converged on the altar, I grabbed the two-way radio in my left hand and turned the volume down. "Snake, all is quiet in here. Are you sure we have the right place?" I whispered into the radio.

"I'm sure of it. I checked and double checked! The signal was coming from within the church. Look over the floor that yer on; there may be a door to a sublevel that didn't appear on the tracking device."

A sudden howl caused me to drop the radio and hold my gun up with two hands. Rex looked from the center aisle in my direction as if to say I heard it too. My neck hairs stood on-end as we both heard a second howl. I motioned that the howl came from below us. Rex nodded, also holding his gun with two hands. Slowly, I started to make my way back towards the front doorway where the other door was located. Rex did the same.

Just as we reached the end of the aisles, something slammed with great force into the door off to the left of the main entrance. We both heard it crack and splinter followed immediately with the sound of vicious snarling and biting. Rex stood twenty feet in front of me with his gun pointed at the door. I began to make my way towards him when the door gave way, breaking into shards of wood as two very large werewolves, one a deep brown in color and the other black as pitch, rolled into the main foyer of the church. Both beasts were biting and clawing at each other unaware of Rex and me. Without hesitation, Rex opened fire.

POP! POP! POP! POP!

The reports of the pistol echoed into the high ceiling of the church as the bullets whirled towards their target. Two of the bullets plunged into the black werewolf causing it to stop fighting with the other werewolf and howl in pain. The other two bullets disappeared into the blackness of the smashed doorway.

The black werewolf leapt down the far-left aisle and the brown werewolf still paying us no attention leapt after it! Rex moved forward, turning down the left aisle and continued to fire.

POP! POP!

Both shots imbedded into the back of the brown werewolf causing it to fall forward, crashing into the pews. I moved quickly to join him, but before I could a third, grey werewolf emerged from the darkness of the doorway. I fired twice but missed. The beast sprung upon Rex from behind forcing him to the ground before it sunk its teeth deep into the side of his neck and shoulder. The werewolf yanked upwards silhouetting a spray of blood against the candlelight. I took aim again and opened fire! One bullet bore into the back of the beast. It stood on its hind legs and turned to face me. I let two more bullets fly both piercing the chest cavity of the monster. It howled and fell backwards! I quickly made my way towards it, pointed my gun directly at it and fired three more times at close range. Blood poured from the grey werewolf as it breathed its last.

Rex lay face down in the middle of the aisle in front of the dead werewolf. I rolled him over onto his back and placed my hand over the wound on his neck. It was too late. Dark pools of blood covered the floor beneath him. Rex's eyes were blank in the darkness; he was gone. I had seen death too many times on the battlefield to know that this was not any different. I stood quickly to the sound of a deep, snarling growl. Standing at the end of the aisle was a werewolf. Its massive body silhouetted by the candlelight, with its eyes that glowed like green lanterns in the dimness of the church. I knew who was standing before me. I knew those eyes like no other. I knew it to be Dr. Bishop. Still holding my pistol in my left hand, I pointed it directly at the werewolf. I knew that I did not have many shots left so I began to reach for the second pistol holstered under my coat, but I heard another growl from behind me.

The black werewolf, with its piercing white eyes, advanced towards me from the other end of the aisle. I was trapped between the two monsters. I squeezed off the two remaining rounds towards the werewolf I knew to be Dr. Bishop. Neither bullet found their mark; the werewolf leapt sideways over the pews to avoid the shots. I turned quickly pulling the second gun from the holster only to be met by the other werewolf before I could shoot. The force of the blow took the breath out of me as we both crashed to the floor. The gun fell from my hands. Its claws dug into the shoulders of my leather coat as it pinned me to the ground. It reared its head back with its mouth open, ready to bite. A split second before the werewolf finished its attack, the brown werewolf crashed into it. My left arm wrenched backwards and broke under the weight of both beasts. They rolled down the aisle towards the back of the church biting and clawing at each other.

I could hardly breathe, but I forced myself to a sitting position. My left arm was completely limp. I stumbled but managed to stand. One of the pistols lay partway down one of the rows between two pews. Picking it up, I stumbled again towards the center aisle. Both brutes stood on their hind legs and faced off with each other in front of the altar. The black werewolf swiped at Dr. Bishop, catching her square across the face. Her head whipped to one side with a yelp, then turned back to face her adversary. They crashed into one another, but the black werewolf forced Dr. Bishop to fall backwards. It sunk its teeth into her shoulder. Howling in pain, she dug her claws into the back of the black werewolf and ripped downward exposing the muscles underneath. Blood poured from its back as it released its bite upon her.

I finally reached the center aisle just in time to the see the brown werewolf thrust off the other. Both came to their feet again. I took aim at the closest werewolf and opened fire. Four shots plunged into the back of the black werewolf. It arms splayed out to either side as its head lifted upwards in a howl. This was just enough of a distraction for Dr. Bishop. I stopped firing momentarily as I witnessed her bite down fiercely upon the black werewolf's neck. I heard bones break and flesh rip as the beast thrashed its head back and forth until the head of the black werewolf separated from the rest of its body. While it was distracted, I took aim again and pulled the trigger.

CLICK!

Nothing happened! The werewolf's head snapped upwards, and its glowing green eyes stared directly at me. It held its arms out to either side and gave a menacing growl. Blood dripped from the beast's mouth. Panicked, I took aim again.

CLICK!

The gun was empty! It must've been Rex's that had already fired six shots, not my other fully loaded gun.

It took only one leap for the werewolf to be on me. The creature sunk its claws into my shoulders and lifted me into the air, snarling, blood still dripping from its mouth. I forced my right arm across my chest and struck the werewolf across the face with the butt end of the pistol. This action proved to be futile, having no effect. There was nothing I could do. I stared back at the werewolf as it curled its lips up exposing its canine teeth, fully anticipating its attack. Instead, the werewolf turned and threw me down the center aisle, which caused me to roll head over feet several times. Dazed, I looked up to see the werewolf standing about twenty feet from me, watching me, but not advancing like the other had done. The massive beast stood on its hind legs, with its head poised upwards toward the ceiling and let out a deafening howl. It looked at me one last time before it turned, leapt twice, and crashed through the main doors of the church and disappeared into the cold night.

My heart pounded and my breath was labored as I sat up against the end of a pew. To my left, the body of a man, not a werewolf, lay dead, decapitated upon the ground in front of the altar. I suspected the other werewolf had also returned to human form. All was quiet except for the whip of the cold wind through the newly broken doorway. The only thought that resonated in my head was, *She didn't kill me!*

Chapter #31

Aftermath
Robert Osborne

Snake had informed us that he lost contact with Rex and Grayson. Anxiety filled my stomach at the thought of what I might encounter once we got to the church. The last words Grayson and I had spoken were in anger and I could not bear the thought of his loss too.

"Bloody Hell! Can ya drive any fuck'n faster?" Jinx blurted out to Kap.

"Piss off!" he retorted. "I don't want to just speed up to a bleam'n hornets' nest! I've seen this beast in its true form and it's nothing I'm going to just piss on!"

Jinx was the only one in the van that had not truly seen the werewolf and his mannerisms reflected this obvious fact, cocky and arrogant. As much as I wanted to get to the church, Kap was right. It was not something that we wanted to speed into. Having also seen the werewolf face-to-face, I was fully aware that it could easily handle all three of us. Besides, we did not know if there was anything else that posed a threat.

Rain fell from the sky intermittently in heavy gusts as we arrived at the church. The ground was wet and full of puddles, which reflected the flashing lights of the police vehicles that had already arrived on the scene. My heart moved into my throat and began to race as I saw two ambulances outside the church parked next to the police vehicles. Dryness overcame my mouth as I held each breath longer than normal. We pulled off to the side of the street a good distance away from the church. I left the weapon I had in the van, but informed Kap and Jinx to keep theirs and that if anyone asked, they were part of the security personnel that were assigned to the members of The House of Commons. Down the street a bit from us was the van that Rex and Grayson drove.

"Jinx, make sure that's our van."

"You got it boss." This was the first time Jinx obeyed without any question.

"Kap, stay close."

He did not respond but walked closely behind me as we approached the church. Loads of people swarmed the outside of the building. Both of us approached the church with a brisk walk as Jinx walked over to the other van. We were stopped by a young policeman that was assigned the duty of crowd control.

"I'm sorry sir, but I can't allow anyone into the church," the policeman stated, holding out his hand in a *'stop now'* posture.

"Let me past! My son was supposed to have a meeting with a priest at this church. I was talking to him on his cell phone when he stated that something was happening at the church; then I lost contact with him!" I lied. I was not about to tell this man the real reason we were there. "I tried to call him several times, but I wasn't able to get through. I need to know if he's okay!"

"Sir, I'm not allowed to disclose the events of the evening, nor let you pass. This church has become a crime scene," the policeman responded.

"Listen! My name is Robert Osborne, and I am a member of The House of Commons! I am authorized to pass along with my security personnel!" I yelled trying to use my authority. Before the man had time to respond, two men wheeled out a stretcher with a body bag on top zipped shut. I motioned to Kap to move past the policeman and inspect the body. Jinx caught up with us.

"The van is ours," Jinx whispered as he made his way towards Kap.

"Hey, wait a minute! I said you're not allowed..." the policeman started to say as I caught him by the arm.

"You'll allow my men as well as me to pass or I'll make sure that your pathetic existence as a law enforcement agent is short lived. Am I making myself abundantly clear?" I seethed, narrowing my gaze to the man's eyes. The young officer was clearly caught off guard and recoiled, no doubt to report this incident to his superiors. Seized by an opportunity, I made my way over to the body bag that Jinx and Kap were inspecting. Inside was a pale-skinned man I had never seen before. There were several bullet wounds in his chest.

"We don't know this bloke, but it looks like he has been shot with a 9mm pistol," Kap stated.

"How do you know?" I asked.

"I've been around it enough and I know what a bullet hole would look like if it struck a body," Kap explained. I did not need to know anything further about Kap. As keen as he was with his observation, I was resolved to trust him at his word, mindful not to probe any unwanted details. "This means that this fellow might've been a…well you know," he finished in a low voice. I just stared at Kap as the implication of his words set in on me.

We did not spend too much time examining the body. I was worried about Grayson, and I had to know if he was inside dead or alive. All three of us pushed through several other people streaming out of the church. The doorway leading into the building was smashed. Bits of wood covered the stairs and the remaining pieces of the door that were still attached were mangled as if something immense had crashed through it. My instant thought was of the library when we first encountered Dr. Bishop. The metal door that she collided into was virtually destroyed with the hinges bent and torn from their mounts the same as the ones displayed on the church.

"Bloody Hell!" Jinx whispered as we moved passed the door.

Inside the overhead lights were bright. The ornate columns stretched towards the ceiling in nothing less than an awe inspired spiral. It was easy to feel taken by a higher presence in a structure like this. However, a fiendish awareness of a horrid event hung amongst the gun smoke that still lingered on the air. Several men were standing around talking, while others were walking about trying to piece together what happened. Straight down the center aisle, a man of African descent lay dead in front of the altar with his head torn from the rest of his body. A pool of blood had collected on the marble flooring and splatters could be seen on the two steps leading up to the altar; the scene was grisly. Another man was taking pictures of the dead body. Two other men were taking more pictures of something off to the left. From what I could see blood was pooled there too and another body lay motionless. My heart immediately jumped at the sight of Grayson standing off to the right of the center aisle as a medical worker was looking over him. He was alive!

"Grayson!" I yelled and ran over to him. The medical associate glanced at me once and gave Grayson one last look over before walking away. I embraced Grayson with a heavy hug. "Thank God you're all right!"

"Ouch!" Grayson said pulling away. I noticed his arm was in a sling. Bloody gauze pads could be seen on both shoulders under the tears in his shirt. "My arm's broken and I'm going to have stitches."

"Well isn't this a fuck'n mess! Grayson, what the hell happened?" Kap asked.

Grayson did not answer. He seemed preoccupied with his thoughts. "Jinx!" he finally said as he motioned with his head towards the other men taking pictures. Without question, Jinx went over to inspect the scene. "We ran into three werewolves," Grayson finally stated in a low whisper only loud enough for Kap and me to hear.

"Fuck!" Kap responded. Kap pointed to the man in front of the altar, "Was this fucker one of them?"

Grayson nodded to confirm. "We buried six silver bullets into its back, before one of the werewolves tore his head off."

"Shit!" Kap said still looking at the man. "Grayson, you don't suppose that he's Corbin Paige?"

"I don't know, but we'll find out soon enough," Grayson replied.

Jinx returned a moment later, "There's another body over there. It's Rex and the whole side of his fuck'n neck has been torn out!" His breaths were labored.

Grayson simply nodded suggesting that he already knew. "What did you tell the police?" I asked.

"Nothing. I haven't said a word until now," Grayson replied.

"Good, I spoke to the policeman outside and made him believe that you were trying to get an appointment to talk with a priest. Codie was supposed to get in contact with a priest of this establishment. When we met with Dean William Garris, he had told us about a priest that had come to see him. It was the first thing I thought about when we were stopped outside," I said pausing as I remembered the last conversation with Grayson. "Grayson, I want… I want to…" I began.

"Save it, we'll discuss other matters later. The police are going to want a statement before I leave but I can't have these weapons on me," he paused to tap the back of his shirt with his right arm. Turning to Jinx and changing his tone to a lower whisper, "Jinx, under my shirt in the back are two guns with the remaining silver bullets tucked into my waistline. I picked them up before the police got here. Take them out, now."

Jinx quickly moved behind Grayson pretending to adjust the sling and pulled the two pistols from Grayson's waistline. He gave one to Kap and hastily placed the other in his back waistline. Grayson must've figured that I would use both Kap and Jinx as security, so the fact that they had a pistol wouldn't draw too many questions.

"Do ya got the keys to the van outside," Jinx asked as he walked from behind Grayson.

"No, Rex had them."

"Well fuck…I'll have to strip the van and wipe it down.

"Just hot wire it and get it out of here," Grayson said.

"What are you going to tell the police…about all this?" I pointed the carnage behind us.

"I'm going to stick with the story that you started outside," he responded very a-matter-of-factly.

"How did you know that I was going to say what I did outside?" I wasn't fully following the direction Grayson was going.

"I didn't. We're trained that if captured by enemy forces, not to say anything at all if interrogated. Mainly due to the fact that undercover informants in the field would often speak on our behalf and we would have to wait until we got a small piece of that information before we could run with the lie. They might say for our protection and theirs that we were coming to see them for religious purposes or to trade. Until they offered that piece of information, we were trained to say nothing. This situation here at the church is no different. I'm going to tell the police that I was troubled from my service in war and wanted to talk with a priest and confess my sins, but when I arrived, these men had trespassed to defile the church, hence the nakedness. Being of a military background, I'll say that I was trying to stop them. I'll blame the injuries to Rex on the gun fire and that the man by the altar was killed by Rex and the other man. They shot and then they decapitated him before I could help. I'll suggest it had something to do with race, since he's of color. Rex unfortunately will have to go unnamed. It's too dangerous for us to claim that we know him. The story's thin, but will buy us an innocence card to play. The police will want to take me to the hospital to get my arm and shoulders looked at properly. If I leave with you now, I look guilty. Follow us to the hospital, there you can tell the police the same story. We'll rely on your experts in the law thereafter."

I was impressed by Grayson's ability to cover his tracks. He was right though, the story was weak and the more the police inquired the more they would uncover; however, we had an advantage, the general public did not believe that werewolves existed. In fact, the very mention of their existence would be cause for someone to undergo psychiatric evaluations. The police would have a hard time determining where the damage came from if not from a human. Even though the wound on Rex's neck as described by Jinx resembles an animal attack, placing a large animal inside a church would be preposterous to even the most dimwitted of individuals. The best thing I could do would be to give the statement he mentioned and do exactly what he said.

Grayson had stated that they encountered three werewolves, but there were only three dead bodies, one of them being Rex who we knew not to be a werewolf. The third werewolf wasn't accounted for. "Dr. Bishop? Was she…?"

"Yes, she was here. She escaped," Grayson interrupted before I had time to finish the statement.

A slight twinge of frustration pierced my stomach. "How? I mean, both you and Rex had silver bullets, you're a trained professional!" I probed again, not fully understanding what had happened.

"I'll tell you the whole story later. For now, know that we were ambushed by three werewolves when there was only supposed to be one. Two are dead. The third…" again Grayson paused, but more so in disbelief as what he was about to divulge. "The third, who I believe to be Dr. Bishop, had the chance to kill me but didn't. She let me live instead."

"What do you mean?" Kap asked. Jinx stood close by listening. Any mention of Grayson's failures or slip-ups seemed to amuse Jinx more than anyone else.

"I mean what I say. The werewolf I thought to be Dr. Bishop had the opportunity to kill me, but chose not to," Grayson restated.

"That's impossible! These things are mindless beasts that need to be destroyed! You must have misinterpreted the situation," I threw out.

"You weren't here!" he spat back at me with a cold venomous growl. "I tell you she had the opportunity to kill me and stopped. She had more control than the other werewolves. She was the one who killed that one right there, not Rex or me. She tore off his head just after I put the remaining bullets into his back. Now I know my experience with werewolves is limited, but nothing about a werewolf killing another werewolf, then sparing my life, makes any sense at all." Grayson strongly stated as he pointed with his good arm towards the dead man by the altar.

"Grayson you have to understand your body and mind are in shock. You're probably reading the situation one way when it happened a completely different way," I tried to reason. Both Kap and Jinx listened without saying anything to disrupt the conversation.

"Well then, is that how it happened with Laryn? The werewolf stopped that night too, or has your anger blinded you to that fact as well. Dr. Bishop could've killed us that night but for whatever reason she didn't. There's truly more to these creatures than just a mindless beast,"

I could feel the frustration turn to anger in the pit of my stomach and start to bubble like an active volcano at the mention of Laryn. Her memory twisted and turned inside my thoughts all the time. She was an innocent girl that did not deserve her end. I wanted to yell out until I couldn't yell any more. Yet, for as much anger that was inside that needed to be let out, I was thankful for the interruption from the police inspector that had noticed Grayson was talking and seized the opportunity to collect his statement.

"Excuse me gentlemen, my name is Inspector Lawrence. Since you've come around to talking again…" he sarcastically stated looking directly at Grayson. "…we would like to get a handle on what happened tonight. I'm going to need to take a statement from all of you. I would like to know your involvement, no matter how ghastly the details are. I'm going to start with you, sir. Right this way if you would please."

Grayson looked at me one last time with a seeming distaste for our conversation that the inspector had interrupted just moments before. He turned and walked with the inspector to where Rex's body lay. I knew the conversation was not over. "What now boss?" Kap asked quietly.

"I'm going to have to give a statement too. Then we'll follow Grayson to the hospital. Damn fool has lost his mind."

"Sir, if I might say. When we went into club and well, saw the werewolf change, it was Grayson that truly kept his wits about him. I merely followed what he was doing. If he wasn't there, I might've did something in my pants if ya know what I mean," Kap explained.

"Well ain't that sweet! The little fuck'n dolly pisses her pants when the big dog comes 'round!" Jinx insulted, clearly directed towards Kap's defense of Grayson.

"Hey *fuck* you! We'll see how well ya hold your piss when the huge fuck'n howling dog's in your face!" Kap snapped.

"Both of you, enough! You guys can continue this pissing battle when we get out of here. Right now, it would be wise not to draw too much attention to yourselves. Remember you're supposed to be a member of the security personnel that are assigned to members of The House of Commons," I scolded. I was not about to blow our cover as well as Grayson's because of personal grudges.

Leaning against one of the pews, I watched, from a distance, as Grayson recounted the fictional story of what happened inside the church and how he attempted to be courageous in stopping the defilement of the church. Kap and

Jinx stood quietly on either side of me. Not by choice, but more by my order. Fresh air filled the church. The smell of gun smoke from when we first arrived had cleared. A cold wind blew in from outside through the wrecked doorway of the church and gave me a chill. As I looked outside into the darkness, a mixture of sadness and anger cut like a knife into my conscious, knowing the thing that killed Laryn had escaped and that the likelihood of finding her again was slim.

CHAPTER 32

Deportation
One Week Later
Marcus Holland

I had been unconscious for several days before I woke. As it turned out, I was in a hospital. The room was not anything special. It had another bed to the left of me, but with no one in it. White walls, an overly sterile smell, and the frequent beep from the machine that monitored my vital signs completed the atmosphere. There was a small bathroom just to the right of the main door. On a built-in shelf across from my bed was a small flat-screen television. I lay on my bed recounting the events of late that had me bewildered.

A nurse indicated that I had taken a nasty fall. This is why my injuries were what they were. Though all my memories of my injuries were fuzzy, I did not recall falling down a set of steps. It was not until she informed me that I was brought into the hospital by several men claiming to have seen me fall, that I realized this was not the truth. Robert Osborne and his hired mercenaries had probably dropped me off here when they realized that my injuries were too extensive to address by themselves without proper medical supplies. My nose was obviously broken and sported a brace that kept my airways slightly open, despite the amount of swelling. I was more than likely facing a surgery to minimize the amount of permanent damage as well as functionality of my sinuses. One of the doctors had informed me to seek out my regular physician upon leaving the hospital and returning home to Australia. On the left side of my head was a set of stitches, thirteen to be exact, from where I was struck when I had arrived at the estate. A plastic air cast was placed around my left leg, extending from my ankle to just above my knee. It too was broken. I had a compound fracture of my tibia and until the wound healed on the outside, I would not be able to have a plaster cast that was sturdier. Infection was the biggest threat, since the bone had been set while I was unconscious, a fact I was thankful for.

Several times hospital personnel questioned me as to what happened. Being in no condition to discuss anything further than the story that had already been told, I resolved to simply continue the storyline by adding a few of my own embellishments to make it more believable. I was also concerned as to what Robert Osborne and his men were going to do with me from this point. *They blamed me for what happened to his daughter, but lied to the hospital staff as to how I was injured. I'm not going to test this motive any more than I have to, but I bet our dealings aren't over*, I thought.

Because of the nature of my broken leg, I was ordered to stay completely off it. A good portion of my stay at the hospital involved me lying flat on my back with my leg propped up with a few pillows on the bed to allow the blood to drain from the injury. One leg had a sock that extended to my mid-thigh that resembled women's nylons, whereas my broken leg the nylon extended only to mid-calf. Apparently, they were to prevent blood clotting. Crutches were prescribed to me for mobility, but it took a while before I felt I was ready to use them. In the meantime, I took advantage of the flat-screen television in my room. From what few channels I had, I was able to catch up on the results of some of the sporting events around London and that were popular around the world, mostly football. In between bouts of highlights and commentary, occasionally I switched to the local news station in hopes of catching something about the events I had been through. Of the many broadcasts, only one caught my attention. The reports recounted an event that happened at a church, St. Teresa's Cathedral.

"Murder at St. Teresa's Cathedral has left the Cambridge community in shock. Three people were found brutally killed in a manner that have people believing that these deaths are linked to

possible satanic practices aimed at defiling the church. I must warn that the following footage may be inappropriate for younger viewers..."

The video went on to show the front of the church with its massive wooden doors reduced to nothing more than shards and splinters of wood, while inside they portrayed a black man decapitated at the end of the center aisle. Fortunately, most of the image was blurry for censorship purposes and cut out quickly returning to the news anchor. I listened closely as she continued to divulge the information about the event.

"...Corbin Paige, owner of the popular night club, Club Red, in the Soho district was among the dead and the only name released by police. The other two bodies remain unidentified. Reports have indicated that there may have been others injured or even killed during the massacre. For now, police are still investigating the incident and have no leads other than possible occultic practices that may have been racially motivated. However, a hero did emerge from this grisly scene. Grayson Osborne, military Lieutenant, and son of prominent member of The House of Commons, Robert Osborne, was apparently coming to the church to seek a meeting with one of the priests when he encountered the men. Though we were unable to get a statement from Grayson, the police reported that he fought with the men and helped to put a stop to their practices. Grayson was treated and released at a nearby hospital for a broken arm that he sustained during the fight. We will have more on this story as it develops."

I turned the television off after the broadcast and did not turn it back on for the remainder of my stay at the hospital. Even though there was a slim chance, I did not want anyone among the hospital staff to associate me with these events, even though I was indirectly involved. My thoughts returned to Mya. *Was she there that night? Did she cause the deaths? Marcus, you'll go mad if you try to answer these questions.*

Crutches took some time to get used to, however it proved to be easy enough to manage. Another day had passed, and I had made some significant gains. I was on one of my many attempts to move around my room with my crutches when I encountered my captors again. Robert and his entourage walked sternly into the room, forming a perimeter around me. I shrunk back at their presence. I had nowhere to go and even if I did my injuries would certainly play a hindrance.

"What do you want with me?" I spat immediately. "You've already gotten from me all that I can offer."

The look on Robert's face was cold and menacing. The other men, who were the same as before, stood poised, ready to seize hold of me if I tried anything that did not fit their liking. One of the men bore a sling and had a *grim* look upon his face. I recognized him from the description on the news broadcast as the son of Robert, Grayson, and the one who first tended to my face when I was initially captured. He carried a black bag with his good arm and placed it upon the floor next to the only chair in the room.

"Mr. Holland, your involvement with Dr. Bishop cannot go unaddressed," Robert responded calm, yet with a brooding tone. "Seeing that you're fit enough to move around, I think you had better come with us."

"To what end?" I asked nervous, but direct.

"To whatever end we desire. My daughter came to her end unjustly and I plan on seeing that you spend the rest of your life rotting in a cell to atone for it!" he fumed.

"Your daughter's death wasn't my fault…" I began.

Robert moved so close to me that our faces were only inches from one another. "How dare you speak as though you're innocent, you were there that night! You helped plan the affair and did nothing when it went sour!"

Our eyes locked like two fighters before a boxing bout. His gaze was broken when his son intervened, "There's hospital staff within ear shot and you don't need any more attention drawn to you since you are facing an inquiry at work, which is led by Hugh Bennett."

Robert's head snapped around to face his son. His face changed from ominous to utter shock. Clearly, Robert did not want me to know this fact. "Grayson! What are you doing?"

"What we've done is also punishable by jail," Grayson stated calmly, looking squarely at me fully intending for me to follow what he was saying.

"You seek to betray me?" Robert asked, his anger returning.

"I saw on the news what happened at the church and apparently, *torture* isn't something that a member of The House of Commons frequently does and wouldn't bode well since those events are being deemed as occultic and satanic practices," I spoke, understanding what Grayson was aiming at. Why was still unclear.

"Shut up!" Robert yelled drawing his arm back positioned to strike me with the back of his hand. Before he could strike Grayson pinned it to his chest with his good arm.

"His ability to speak out about what has happened can completely sabotage our mission. If Mr. Bennett gets a hold of any of this information, your career is through. Might I advocate for a different course of action? Deportation. Send him back to Australia. This way both of you can avoid any unwanted ramifications for the recent events. News such as this would cause you to lose your seat in Parliament without the need for any inquiry. People may believe that you've gone mad," Grayson suggested.

"Why, Grayson? Why are you doing this?" Robert questioned vehemently. "You've betrayed your sister and now me!"

Grayson's face went to stone. He didn't respond. Robert yanked his arm free and again Grayson did nothing in response. The other men in the room stood watching with bewildered looks strewn across their faces. Their gazes transferred from me to Robert to Grayson and back to me repeatedly.

Robert finally turned his attention back to me. Reluctantly, he pointed his finger at me and said, "You've two days to leave this country and if you step foot on this land again, you'll never see the light of day. All of your work will be tarnished and discredited!" Robert turned back to Grayson, "We're not through!"

Robert then turned and walked from the room. The other men followed except Grayson. I looked at Grayson, baffled by what he just did.

Wearily I leaned against the hospital bed to stabilize myself. I could feel my heart pounding heavily. My nose throbbed as the blood sped to my head. A headache pierced my temples as I slowly rubbed them. When I looked up again Grayson was still standing in the room. "Crikey mate, why?" I could not help but ask.

"You deserve to go home. My father is filled with rage from the loss of his daughter, my sister, Laryn. He doesn't realize it yet, but he needs help. What was done to you was equal to the loss of my sister and what happened at the church requires time to blow over," he explained grimly. He reached down to grab the bag that he had placed by the chair and slung it onto the hospital bed. "Inside are your journals, your device and a few other items I threw in that may be helpful. Also, here's your plane ticket. I took the liberty of purchasing you one ahead of time. You'll be flying coach. It leaves tomorrow afternoon. Your belongings have already been shipped to your address in Australia. I'll talk to the hospital staff to see if they can expedite your release papers. No doubt my father is probably already doing this." Grayson turned to walk out of the room.

"Why are you really doing this, mate?" I asked sensing there were other reasons that motivated him behind what was already disclosed. He stopped at the doorway placing the hand of his good arm on the door jam and looked upwards as though a complicated thought just leapt into his mind.

"She was at the church," he stated still not fully looking at me. Finally, he turned to face me again. "She was at the church, with two other werewolves. There was no full moon, so this means that there are not only more werewolves besides Dr. Bishop, but they can also change without the full moon being out. My father won't understand the seriousness of this situation, but from your journals I feel that you would."

I swallowed hard before I spoke. "Were you bitten?"

Grayson hesitated at my question, but still answered. "No. I know what you're getting at. My brother was also attacked by Dr. Bishop the night Laryn died, but not bitten. He has shown no signs of becoming anything like her. I suspect the same applies to me."

"No fevers? Nothing?"

"Nothing." He paused for a few moments before he continued. "One more thing, Dr. Bishop had the chance to kill me, but she didn't. She stopped. In fact, I think there was a moment amongst the chaos of that night where she may have saved my life. This is something I cannot explain."

"There are forces at work here that go beyond science and explanation." Grayson nodded his head. He started to turn again when I blurted out, "Once you've stepped into the darkness, there's no going back, mate."

Grayson glanced up again, considering for a moment this notion, then looked directly at me with an expression of great seriousness. "I know..." he answered before disappearing from the doorway.

Later that evening a doctor came into my room, gave me a look over and allowed me to sign my release papers. He stated that the papers allowed me to leave in the morning seeing that I don't run into any complications throughout the night. The doctor also prescribed an antibiotic to ward off infection and a heavy dose of pain medicine that he claimed would be beneficial during my flight tomorrow. I couldn't help but think about whether it was Grayson or his father that orchestrated my release from the hospital. Nonetheless, I was happy to be leaving given the circumstances.

The night passed slowly. Pain in my leg as well as headaches and the ever-throbbing soreness in my nose kept me awake. I watched as shadows danced across the walls of my room each time a person walked past the doorway disrupting the light from the hallway. When I did fall asleep, nightmares invaded my subconscious mind. At first, they were of Robert Osborne and the man with the tattoos on his forearms. The dreams would begin with these men screaming at me, threatening me with violence; telling me that I must pay for the loss of his daughter. When I would plead for mercy, they would laugh with the utmost of sinister laughs. Their laughter would change to snarling growls as their heads would snap forward and their skin would split to reveal the beast within. Each dream followed this same pattern, with one thing that remained constant; it was always the same werewolf with piercing green, lamp-like eyes, huge canine teeth and an insatiable appetite for flesh.

Waking from the dreams left me in disarray. I would sip on some water to combat the dryness in my throat and to calm my body from these night terrors. Drainage from my broken nose would give me a bad taste. Sometimes I would choke and be forced to spit out bloody mucus into a nearby tissue. Dawn eventually broke through the curtains on the window from the other side of the room. Drowsy, yet awake, I forced myself to eat my last meal at the hospital and laboriously dressed myself in the pants and long sleeve shirt that Grayson had placed into the black duffle bag. While searching through the bag for my passport, I noticed another book that was placed inside. It was not one of my journals, but instead was an old, leather-bound diary. With a slight gasp I realized that it was Mya's diary. Sticking out from between a few of the pages was a handwritten note. It read:

Marcus,

    I found and read this diary. I now understand why you were helping Dr. Bishop. The information within these pages is probably best served in your hands.

Grayson

    Just as I had finished reading the note, one of the nurses walked into the room. I closed the diary quickly with the note contained therein. On a small tray were several small packets of pain medicine and a stack of papers with instructions on when to take the medicine. She also gave me two prescription papers to be filled upon my earliest convenience. Soon thereafter, another worker brought in a medium sized plastic bag that contained my shoes, the coat that I had been wearing and a few other items that were inside the pockets of my pants that they had to cut off my body. I dumped the contents of the bag onto the hospital bed. My coat had been cleaned of all the blood that had dripped onto it from my head wound. I put one shoe on first and placed the other one into the duffle bag. There was no point in trying to get the other one onto my foot with the broken leg. Besides, I was not going to let it touch the ground and having a sock over it was enough to protect it from the cold. The time was nearly at hand for me to leave and the hospital had arranged for a taxi to pick me up. I slipped my coat on and stood next to my bed leaning on my crutches with my leg aloft waiting for a staff member to come back to my room with a wheelchair.

    Atop of the bed covers was some loose change that was in the plastic bag. I leaned forward a bit to grab it, careful not to fall over. As I scooped up the coins, I noticed something else tangled amongst them. It was the charm of the Archangel

Michael that belonged to Mya. I stared at it for a long moment in awe. *Maybe this was the reason I was going home instead of jail,* I thought. The sight of it caused an ache deep within the pit of my stomach. Clutching it tightly in my fist, I held it close to my chest and thought of all the evil I had witnessed, *Robert was no different than Mya. They were fighting against the same beast within.*

I stuffed the charm into the inside pocket of my coat as the hospital worker returned with a wheelchair. It did not take long to wheel me down to the ground level. An eerie feeling poured over me as the bright light from outside met my eyes. I felt that I was being watched, closely monitored as my bag was loaded into the taxi. The feeling stayed with me even as I waited in the airport. It was not until I was safely airborne, above the clouds, that I started to feel at ease. The seat next to me on my right was empty, which allowed me to stretch my broken leg out into the aisle but still look out the window. All the airplane stewardesses made a point to keep me as comfortable as possible. With a brace on my nose and an air cast on my leg, I thought that I must've looked fairly pathetic. Periodically, they would check on me to see if I needed a pillow or anything to drink. Estimated length of the trip was about thirteen hours or so. With that I watched the light from the day fade and the brilliance of the nighttime darkness overtake the sky. The moon pushed into the sky, casting a hypnotic glow across the clouds. It was full and bright against the dark background. I reached for my coat that was now lying on the seat next to me and pulled from the inside pocket the charm. Dangling from the chain in my hand, the gold caught the moonlight and sparkled. I thought of the night in the woods when Mya first gave it to me and recalled the words she spoke before leaving. Godspeed Marcus, she had said. I was going home, but nothing would ever be the same knowing that somewhere down below the moon, evil was rising all over again. "Godspeed Mya," I whispered.

CHAPTER #33

One Year Later
Father Preston Mathew's Log

Friday, December 24, 2010,

This Christmas Eve I write with an ill feeling in my soul. I have nothing to say bad about this evening's Mass. In fact, people were caught up in the spirit of the season and only spoke merriment to one another. To most this would look like a pleasant picture of worship of our Lord, quite the contrast from the horrible scene of last year's death and defilement.

I did not notice it at first. It was not until I made my way down the center aisle singing the hymns of praise and worship to match the service that this feeling caught me up and left me for a moment breathless. It was so strong. My thoughts initially were of our Lord. I thought there was a message to be heard, but I quickly realized that this feeling was more wicked, malevolent in nature. I proceeded with the service as usual, but the feeling never left. All through the readings, I found myself glancing through the crowd in hopes of pinpointing the source of this feeling. Hundreds of people had come to this evening's Mass, but nothing stood out. All that was before me as I read the Gospel was a sea of faces, yet something evil beckoned to me. Prayer was my refuge, my link to God. I prayed over the gifts from the Lord. Before the Eucharist, I squeezed my eyes shut, tightly as I prayed over the offering, searching and listening for something from God. Something to reassure me, to calm my spirit that was experiencing unrest. As I turned to face the crowd and welcomed God's children to the feast, there was one that broke the norm. A woman sat at the very back of church in the last pew. She wore a burgundy, vintage cloak with the hood drawn up and her head hung low. I could not see her face, but she remained still as everyone around her came to receive the body of Christ as well as to drink from the cup that contained his blood. As we stood to pray and lift our hands to the Lord, she remained seated. I was sure that this was the source of my unrest. This servant of God was in great pain, and I longed to help alleviate at least some of it. I watched her closely from behind the altar. Panic set in as the final hymn was being sung and the procession began. She finally stood but turned and walked away without even raising her head. I quickened my own pace down the center aisle in hopes that I could catch up to her. Though her back was turned from me, I was haunted by a memory. The memory of a young woman that was deeply wounded in her spirit and had cried out for help to me on many occasions.

As she passed under the archways that led into the main foyer of the church, I called out to her. I called out the only name that came to mind. Dr. Bishop! I yelled. She did not stop walking. Fearing that she did not hear me because the final hymn was still being sung, I yelled out her name again. Only this time I yelled, Mya! The woman in the burgundy cloak stopped at this call and slowly turned to face me. I continued to walk closer to her, relieved that I had finally found her, but stopped abruptly as the iridescent green of the one eye that was not covered by the cloak met mine. My breath left me as I felt my heart move into my throat. Expressionless, it was as though the young woman that I once knew was no more and staring back at me was a dark, menacing force. I pray once again for her tonight, for as the final hymn had come to an end, the people in the congregation spilled into the foyer. In an instant, she was gone. Disappeared amongst the crowd. I tried to push past the people, but it was folly. By the time I reached the steps outside the church she was nowhere to be seen. The fiendish feeling inside of me was also gone, but I felt empty as the cold wind blew and carried whips of light snow that pelted the ground. May God be with you in the places I cannot reach, my dear Mya.

- Rev. Preston Mathew S.J.

END OF BOOK #1

Acknowledgements

I would first like to thank God for giving me the desire and patience to write what was inside of me. Though some days have been dark, never once did He leave my side.

Thank you to my family for always encouraging me to chase after my dream of writing and for talking me down off the ledge on multiple occasions.

Many thanks to the amazing publishing team at Reader2writer Press for helping to make this book a reality. Thank you to my awesome editors Bart Bishop and Kayla Hardin for your wonderful insights and enthusiasm.

A special thanks goes to Lindsey Knight for taking the time to be a reader of my manuscript and for offering your critiques. They helped to shape the story into what it is today. Thank you to Karen Majoris-Garrison for your mentorship and encouragement.

This list would not be complete if I didn't include some of the faculty members of the creative writing department at Northern Kentucky University. Thanks to Ms. Kelly Moffett for showing me the art of compression. Thank you to Mr. Stephen Leigh and Mr. P. Andrew Miller for helping me to comb the knots and tangles out of the world I created.

Thank you all.

About the Author

After 15 years of experience (...and counting) teaching Middle School English and Language Arts in urban districts, two master's degrees, and a massive amount of black coffee, Brian came to realize the dire need for creativity and imagination in a classroom setting. Taught at The Ohio State University in his graduate program to design lessons and curriculum from scratch, yielded very minimal opportunities to indulge his profound love of writing. Ultimately this led him to Northern Kentucky University, where he acquired his second master's degree in English/Creative Writing. Since then, he has produced multiple lesson plans, materials, short stories for adolescents, and several other manuscripts for both adolescents and adults.

ALSO BY

"Dark Steps", A demonic tale of torment, torture, and retribution!

Watch your step...

"Life Like", A story of two girls that learn a very valuable lesson about stealing!

Available Wherever Books are Sold!